QUICK CURTAIN

When famous producer Douglas B. Douglas launches his new musical extravaganza, *Blue Music*, he expects the packed theatre will be dazzled by the performance. What he isn't expecting is for his star Brandon Baker to be killed on-stage. While the shooting was in the script, the use of a real bullet certainly wasn't! Then the actor who fired the gun is discovered hanging in his dressing-room. It seems a relatively straightforward case of murder followed by suicide. But audience member Inspector Wilson of Scotland Yard is now investigating — together with Derek, his journalist son — and he believes otherwise . . .

Books by Alan Melville
Published by Ulverscroft:

DEATH OF ANTON

ALAN MELVILLE
With an Introduction by
MARTIN EDWARDS

QUICK
CURTAIN

Complete and Unabridged

PUBLISHER SELECTION
Leicester

First published in Great Britain in 1934 by
Skeffington
London

First Ulverscroft Edition
published 2019
by arrangement with
The British Library

A catalogue record for this book is available
from the British Library.

ISBN 978–1–4448–3865–7

Published by
F. A. Thorpe (Publishing)
Anstey, Leicestershire

Set by Words & Graphics Ltd.
Anstey, Leicestershire
Printed and bound in Great Britain by
T. J. International Ltd., Padstow, Cornwall

This book is printed on acid-free paper

Contents

Introduction

Quick Curtain is a witty detective story, originally published in 1934. It is one among many
books that enjoyed brief popularity during the
'Golden Age of murder' between the two world
wars but subsequently fell out of sight. The author,
Alan Melville, was a successful playwright and
man of the theatre, and he uses his knowledge of
backstage life to good effect in this breezy whodunit.

Reviewing this novel for the *Sunday Times*,
the eminent crime writer Dorothy L. Sayers noted
that Melville 'gets great enjoyment out of scarify-
ing all the leading lights of the profession, from
producer to dramatic critic': She was troubled
that Melville 'blows the solemn structure of the
detective novel sky-high' — but his aim was to
have fun with the genre. He supplies a storyline
with a twist at the end, but the real pleasure of
the book comes from his satiric darts.

Blue Music is a 'musical comedy operetta':
written by Ivor Watcyns, starring Brandon Baker
and Gwen Astle, and produced by that master of
publicity Douglas B. Douglas. The slender plot
revolves around the shooting of the leading man,
but when the show opens at the Grosvenor
Theatre to a packed house, Brandon Baker is
killed by a real bullet. When another member of
the company is found dead, initial appearances

suggest a straightforward case of murder followed by suicide. But there is, of course, more to it than that.

The audience includes Inspector Wilson of Scotland Yard and his son, an enthusiastic young reporter. They make an amusing variant on the Holmes-Watson pairing of sleuth and sidekick, although it has to be said that Wilson's detective work is scarcely as brilliant as Sherlock's. Melville enjoyed playing fast and loose with conventions of the genre as much as he relished teasing theatre folk. Sayers noted that his satire included 'several thinly veiled personal attacks', but for a modern reader, the amusement lies not in personalised specifics, but in his guying of types. An excellent example is the drama critic who — relying on the predictability of so many shows — hardly bothers to watch the musical comedies he reviews.

Sayers took reviewing seriously, and she chose to assess this book in the context of an analysis of the way different crime writers treated police procedure. This may explain her reservations about a detective story that she regarded as a 'leg-pull . . . This happy policeman . . . never turns in a report, acknowledges no official superiors, bounces into country police stations and bullies the constables without reference to the local authorities, and does all his detecting from his private house with the sole aid of his journalist son. Light entertainment is Mr. Melville's aim, and a fig for procedure!'

Melville was not, of course, aiming for realism in his presentation of police work, and in any event, humorous detective novels are not to every taste. Sayers said, with a hint of disapproval, that Melville regarded 'all this detective business as a huge joke': but the real challenge for anyone who attempts to write a witty whodunit is: how to sustain the joke? Even the great P.G. Wodehouse, who loved detective fiction, concentrated on writing short stories with a mystery element rather than full-length novels, when dabbling in the genre from time to time. In fact, Melville's humour has worn better over the past eighty years than many would have expected. Admirers of this book include the eminent American scholar of the genre, Allen J. Hubin, who described it a few years ago as 'amusing and satirical and worth tracking down . . . it all fits together so neatly, even if rather messily for another member of the cast . . .'

Alan Melville was the pseudonym of William Melville Caverhill (1910-1983), whose varied CV included a stint as a BBC radio producer, scriptwriting (he adapted some of A.P. Herbert's *Misleading Cases*), and countless appearances on television in the 1950s and 60s, sometimes as a an actor, but more often as a presenter or celebrity guest. His first boss at the BBC was Eric Maschwitz, who — under the pen-name Holt Marvell — collaborated with another BBC insider, John Gielgud's brother Val, on a successful whodunit, *Death at Broadcasting House*, which was subsequently filmed. In that novel, a radio actor is strangled while recording a play, and Melville borrows the idea of 'murdering in public' for his novel, written shortly afterwards.

Melville's love of the theatre came to the fore with innuendo-laden lyrics for Ivor Novella's final musical *Gays the Word*; recently revived, the show was described by the *Guardian* as 'a camp curiosity that makes *Salad Days* look positively astringent'. Melville's other successes on stage included *Dear Charles*, a comedy adapted from a French play, which was a hit in the 1950s with Tallulah Bankhead in the lead role; a twenty-first-century revival featured Joan Collins. *Simon and Laura* was an early stage satire targeting soap operas; it helped to establish Ian Carmichael's reputation as an exponent oflight comedy, and was later filmed.

Satire tends to be ephemeral, and so was much of Melville's work, for all its popularity. Yet his detective novels, written in a short burst of energy when he was in his twenties, do not deserve the total neglect into which they have fallen. They are dated, yes, but they possess a certain charm. The British Library's revival of this book, and *Death of Anton*, offers a new generation a chance to appreciate the work of a writer with a genuine talent to amuse.

Martin Edwards
www.martinedwardsbooks.com

GROSVENOR THEATRE

Tuesday, June 18th, at 8.30 p.m. prompt
Subsequently at 8.45 p.m.
Matinées Wednesdays & Saturdays at 2.30 p.m.

DOUGLAS B. DOUGLAS
PRESENTS

BLUE MUSIC
A Musical Comedy Operetta

WORDS AND MUSIC BY IVOR WATCYNS
ADDITIONAL NUMBERS BY CARL CARLSSON

Cast:

Mimi	JOSEPHINE CRAIG
Prime Minister	EDWARD WILLIAMS
Serge	JOHN RIDDELL-WHITE
Otto	ARTHUR DANELIGH
Proprieter of the 'Blue Music' Café	GEORGE GIANELLI
Count von Arankel	C. FISHER THOMSON
Suzette	CONSTANCE OWENS
Marie, her maid	PHYLLIS DE LA MARE
Madame du Cregne	MILLICENT DAVIS
Abdul Achmallah	DOUGLAS MARTIN
Phillipo, a rebel leader	J. HILLARY FOSTER
Hiram P. Whittaker	GEORGE FULLER
Coletta, a native dancer	EVE TURNER

AND

Kay	GWEN ASTLE
Jack	BRANDON BAKER

MR. DOUGLAS'S 110 LADIES AND GENTLEMEN OF THE CHORUS.
THE TWENTY-FOUR BALLET WHOS.
AUGMENTED ORCHESTRA

The entire production under the personal supervision of
DOUGLAS B. DOUGLAS

CHAPTER ONE

M. René Gasnier's bald pate loomed suddenly over the rail of the orchestra pit. M. Gasnier smiled to a few complete strangers in the stalls, opened his score, pulled down his cuffs, tapped on his desk with the tip of his baton, reminded his first violins that the double pianissimo sign called for some slight restraint in their playing, and launched his orchestra out on the overture and introduction to Act One.

Blue Music, as a glance at the programme will have told you, was a Douglas B. Douglas production. Not that it was at all necessary to pay sixpence for a programme to learn that bit of news. London, and, indeed, the whole country, knew it pretty well off by heart by this time. Mr. Douglas was a master of publicity.

Not the loud, blatant kind of publicity that hits you in the eye, yells at you, knocks you over, and ruins green fields that once were beautiful. The other kind, the softer, subtler variety. The kind that had London rumouring, long before *Blue Music* was ever written, that D.B.D.'s latest show was a hundred-per-cent knockout. The kind of publicity that got people really interested. That made them talk about Mr. Douglas's show, write to their cousins in Canada about Mr. Douglas's show, discuss Mr. Douglas's show at company annual general meetings and Dorcas Society

1

outings. The kind, in fact, that made everyone become publicity agents themselves for and on behalf of Mr. Douglas without actually knowing it.

Mr. Douglas always believed in a preliminary canter at Manchester. A very good idea, that. Not only did it provide an added dollop of publicity (for most of the London papers sent down their critics to Manchester for a provincial skirmish), but it saved a lot of money.

Mr. Douglas thought a man several varieties of idiots if he went to all the trouble and expense of having endless rehearsals in an empty theatre if the good people of Manchester could be persuaded to come and witness those rehearsals at eight shillings and sixpence a stall. And, afraid of being thought unappreciative of something that was obviously going to be a success in London, Manchester paid its eight-and-sixpence like a man and applauded vigorously.

And London, equally afraid of being thought behind a place like Manchester in the way of appreciating a good thing, paid its two-pounds-ten on the opening night in town and applauded rather more vigorously. Everyone was pleased. Manchester was pleased at getting its rehearsal before anyone else – although, of course, it was billed not as a rehearsal but as a 'world première'. London was pleased at getting a Douglas B. Douglas production that had been licked into shape and had the few blemishes removed in its little sojourn in the provinces.

And Mr. Douglas B. Douglas was very pleased indeed. The only fly in a very satisfying brand of ointment was that he had to turn away two thousand and fifty-eight applications for first-night seats at two-pounds-ten. That was unfortunate. But Mr. Douglas bore up wonderfully well over it, and kept his stall prices for the opening fortnight of the show up to thirty shillings – and that for a seat which any normal-minded person would have recognized immediately as the third or fourth row in the pit.

Tuesday, June 18th, you will have noticed, was the great day. On Sunday, June 16th, when most of the *Blue Music* company were still in Manchester and finding out the truth of all those jests about the provincial Sabbath, seven grim females parked seven rickety camp-stools outside the gallery entrance of the Grosvenor Theatre.

They were joined a little later in the evening by four more females and a lone male. They unpacked sandwiches and munched. They uncorked thermos flasks and drank hot coffee out of the aluminium tops of the flasks. They discussed with one another Mr. Douglas, Miss Astle, Mr. Baker, Mr. Douglas's past successes, Miss Astle's last divorce, Mr. Baker's profile – both the port and the starboard view. They half slept. They suffered endless agonies on their stupid, unreliable camp-stools; they each contracted stiff necks and shooting pains in the lower reaches of the spine; they were photographed for their pains by a man in a dirty waterproof and appeared on the back page of the *Daily Post* under the title 'Gallery Enthusiasts' Three-Day Wait for New Douglas Show'. They were still there on Tuesday morning, proudly in the van of a fair-sized queue. The lone

3

man who had arrived late on the Sunday night felt his chin and decided to go and have a shave, leaving his precious site guarded by a street entertainer for the sum of threepence.

At seven-thirty, when the gallery early doors were opened by a massive royal-blue and yellow-braided commissionaire, they staggered inside the theatre, past the box-office, up the Everest of stairs, and flopped wearily on to the unsympathetic seats of the Grosvenor gods. Bleary, dirty, sore, and ill-tempered. Nitwits, you say. And you are perfectly right. But you forget that this was a Douglas B. Douglas production.

What is there, you wonder, about a Douglas B. Douglas show that makes normally intelligent and sober individuals behave in this extraordinary way – some of them paying a working-man's weekly wage for a bad seat in row M to witness the first night, and others – if they cannot afford this – leaving their homes and husbands and children for three days so that they may end up in the front, instead of the second front, row of the gallery?

Well, first there is the fact that nobody is quite sane on a first night. The players themselves alternately shower one another with passionate kisses and then instigate libel proceedings against one another. The audience, on their side of the heavy red curtain, are equally affected. Their sense of what is a long period of time, or of what is a large sum of money, is, as we have seen, warped and twisted by the importance of the occasion. So is their sense of what is good and what is rotten.

The god of the gods, the hero of the show, opens

4

with a wrong entrance and is wildly cheered for five minutes. The leading lady sings her big number on a key quite unconnected with that in which the orchestra is playing the accompaniment, and the house rises to demand seven encores. The low comedian, realizing that his material is definitely on the thin side, introduces most of the old gags he put over when he made his first big success at the Gaiety in 1909, and the audience collapses under its seats, helpless with mirth.

So it is that very often those wise men, the dramatic critics, end their notices the following morning with the remark, 'It is only fair to add that, in spite of the above remarks, the entertainment appeared to meet with the approval of the first-night audience.'

There is that, then, about a Douglas B. Douglas first night – or about any first night, for that matter. There is also Mr. Douglas B. Douglas himself. They say that nothing succeeds like success, and certainly nothing succeeded like Mr. Douglas's successes. Even his failures – he had had quite a few – were brilliant failures. Mr. Douglas was a short, squat man with a total absence of hair and a flair for picking legs, spotting personality, and persuading the public that something merely mediocre was something simply sensational.

In his day he had been most things. Bell-boy at nine, porter in a railway station at fifteen, steward on an Atlantic liner at twenty. At twenty-one Mr. Douglas had found his true vocation, joining the Henry Phillips West End Repertory Players when that company were on their beam-ends in the not exactly cheering town of Gateshead. Mr. Douglas had made a notable success of his first part on the following Monday, Tuesday and Wednesday, serving the sherry as the butler in *Interference* as if he had been on the boards for years instead of hours. On the Thursday, Friday and Saturday of the same week (Gateshead demanding a bi-weekly change of repertoire) Mr. Douglas had scored an even greater success as a monk in *The Rosary*. On the Sunday after *The Rosary* Mr. Douglas had drawn the company around him, explained in a few well-chosen phrases exactly what was wrong with them, had offered his services as producer and general manager at a salary of three pounds ten per week, and had launched the West End Repertory Players out on their first stretch of calm water. From that date, Mr. Douglas had rarely looked back. When he did, it was always with a pleasing sense of satisfaction.

There was also Mr. Brandon Baker. Brandon Baker was an idol of the gods, a household god of the orchestra stalls. He had been so now for nearly thirty years, but no one bothered to think that kind of thing out, for Mr. Baker kept himself very Juvenile Leadish with the aid of massage, mud-packs, Turkish baths, and a resetting of his permanent wave at least twice a month. It was his profile that did the trick. It used to be the profile and the waist combined, but now – massage or no massage – it was the profile alone. There was no getting away from the fact that Mr. Baker's was an uncommonly good profile. Particularly the west side, which Mr. Baker was always very careful to place towards the footlights. (There had been quite a number of occasions in his career when Brandon Baker had thrown up an otherwise good part because some inconsiderate fool of a producer had demanded that the east side be shown to the audience all through a long love-scene.)

If you had bothered to take a census of those seven determined females who parked their camp-stools outside the gallery entrance on the Sunday night, it is almost a certainty that you would find all of them to be members of the Brandon Baker Gallery Club. Membership – slightly over two hundred thousand, scattered all over the world. Mr. Baker employed three secretaries to sign the autograph books of the two hundred thousand. They met – the two hundred thousand, not the secretaries – at various festivals in the year, such as Mr. Baker's birthday or the anniversary of Mr. Baker's first success or the night of Mr. Baker's five hundredth performance in *Hotter Than Hell*, and went through quite a complicated system of devotional rites. A valuable asset, a profile.

And then there was Miss Gwen Astle. Another curious sidelight on the psychology of the theatre. If any other young woman had behaved as Miss Astle behaved – had married six times, twice into the peerage, had been divorced six times, twice out of the peerage and much to the relief of the dowager countesses concerned – the world would merely have screwed up its nose in an end-of-a-drain sort of way, and expressed its feelings by spitting out the word 'Bisom!' sharply and spitefully.

But then, you see, Miss Astle was On The Stage,

7

and you had to make allowances. Also she was really rather a dear. And so the more Miss Astle Carried On, and the harder it was rumoured that last week-end at the Savoy ... or that the reason why the Rumanian Ambassador had been recalled so suddenly was that ... the more that sort of thing went on, the higher Miss Astle soared in the public's affections. Respectable middle-aged spinsters, reading their *Morning Posts* in the shadow of Bournemouth aspidistras, dropped a silent tear at the dreadful things Miss Astle was made to confess in the witness-box, and muttered sympathetically, 'The poor lamb!' as though they themselves had been through it all and knew all about it. Spectacled school-ma'ams, learning that Miss Astle had announced her engagement to young Mr. Johnson P. Lambert, son of the well-known American multi-millionaire, of Lambert's Self-Supporting Brassieres and Corselets fame, on the same day as her decree from Lord Keverne became absolute, thrilled at the thought and said, 'How romantic!' Hard-boiled business men, hearing over the wireless that Miss Astle's jewels and famous pearl necklace had been stolen from her Park Lane hotel by her publicity agent for the third time in four weeks, picked their teeth and said, 'Poor kid! Damned shame, isn't it? Nice bit of stuff, too.' Miss Astle, you see, for all that people said, was Rather a Dear. Mr. Douglas, in a moment of inspiration, had billed her in *Blue Music* as The Girl Mae West Came Up and Saw.

Douglas B. Douglas, Brandon Baker, and Gwen Astle, then. As cast-iron a recipe for a success as ever landed in the West End, even without Manchester's preliminary okay. Not that that was all about *Blue Music*. There was Ivor Watcyns (book and music), and Carl Carlsson (lyrics and additional numbers). Mr. Watcyns was another of the public's darlings. He was young, naughty, witty, spicy, terribly, terribly brilliant. And he had hair almost as wavy as Mr. Baker's, which of course clinched the matter. Mr. Carlsson had, unfortunately, straight hair, but he had a most attractive foreign accent to make up for this regrettable omission. True, the accent went astray at times and had been described as more Cockney than Continental when Mr. Carlsson lost his temper, but the public knew none of that. There, then, you have the team.

Oh ... George Fuller (very low comedian) in the part of Hiram P. Whittaker, Miss Astle's millionaire poppa (there were going to be some rather *risqué* jests on the subject of Miss Astle's latest engagements) – and Mr. Douglas B. Douglas's One Hundred and Ten Ladies and Gentlemen of the Chorus. Revolving stage. Scenery designed by Karismajinsky. Dance Ensembles by Boy Batterly, specially imported from Hollywood for the occasion – the occasion being an all-British musical comedy. Gowns by Clair of Paris. Shoes by Phillipsons. Aeroplane in Act One, Scene Twelve, kindly supplied by International Aero-Routes, Ltd., Miss Astle's evening gown in Act Three, Scene Four, designed and executed by Norman du Parque. Augmented orchestra under the direction of René Gasnier. Entire Production under the Personal Supervision of Mr. Douglas B. Douglas. Right...

The seven grim females and the rest of the gallery queue revived in time to applaud each distinguished arrival in the stalls below. Many of the arrivals were a little surprised at being applauded, having, in their own opinion, no claim to such fame; on the other hand, several unemployed West End actresses who came in unrecognized were extremely put about, and flashed their teeth gallerywards in an effort to catch the eye of the public.

Most of the Cabinet was sprinkled over the stalls, there being nothing more important on at the House than a vote of censure on the Government's unemployment programme. Mr. James Amethyst, dramatic critic of the *Morning Herald,* filed his usual protest regarding the seat he was invited to occupy, and whiled away the time until the rise of the curtain by engaging a complete stranger on his left in a one-sided discussion on the Mentality of the Cinema-Going Public. Mr. Watcyns arrived in a stage box – alone as was his custom. He smiled sadly at the reception given to him, and patted the corrugation of his hair with his thumb and forefinger. Mr. Douglas B. Douglas ushered in a distinguished party to the box opposite – Mrs. Douglas, a younger member of the Royal Family, two well-known screen stars, and an American cabaret singer. Mr. Watcyns smiled weakly across at Mr. Douglas.

Mr. Douglas was to blow his nose loudly on a red silk handkerchief at the end of the show; that was to be the signal for Mr. Watcyns to go on the stage and say that this was the happiest, proudest moment of his life and thank you all terribly for your marvellously kind reception. The house lights dimmed at eight-fifty, exactly twenty minutes late. M. Gasnier brought his overture to a snappy close, and the curtain rolled up smoothly.

Just in case you didn't see *Blue Music,* perhaps a sentence reminding you of its plot – such as it was – might not be out of place. A sentence will do, because Mr. Watcyns had written the entire book between the grapefruit of one breakfast and the tomato juice of the lunch immediately following that breakfast. Even so, it had suffered a good deal of cutting and mauling and general mal-formation to bring it into line with Douglas B. Douglas's own requirements. The story of a string of pearls, then, belonging to the daughter of a wealthy American, stolen by a charming and quite impossible brigand, restolen by a rival and a very unpleasant gentleman named Phillipo Consuelo, recovered by the charming brigand (who wasn't a brigand really, of course) and returned in Act Three, Scene Eight, to the beautiful daughter to the tune of the big hit 'Say My Heart is in Your Hands'. Not strikingly original, and well below Mr. Watcyns' real capabilities.

But the important thing about it was that it was strung together so loosely and so elastically that it allowed Mr. Douglas, the scenic-artists, the One Hundred and Ten Ladies and Gentlemen of the Chorus, and the revolving stage all to have a real good night out. Mr. Douglas's recipe was, roughly, to stage the biggest spectacle possible, show it for approximately two minutes, draw along the tab curtains and send out the second comedian or the soubrette to fill up the necessary

11

minute or two while the scene was being changed, and then provide another spectacle that made the one that had gone before look like a rough, unfurnished interior in a Russian drama.

He did this to some effect in *Blue Music*. Act One, Scene One (The Swimming Pool of the Whittaker's Country House in Florida), made even the jaded Mr. Amethyst forget his bad seat at the end of row R, and was followed (after two minutes' back-chat in front of a drop-curtain representing A Street in Paris) by another colossal scene, this time The Ballroom of the Blue Music Café in Budapest ... a scene that made the seven grim females perched high in the gallery quite thankful for their stiff necks and spinal aches. And so on, through the Palm Beach Lounge of the Grand Hotel, London, to the Promenade Deck of the S.S. *Emperor of India*, via an Andalusian Cabaret, a Mosque in Algiers, and the Garden of Jack Waters' House at Maidenhead.

Musical comedy skips about the atlas in a de-lightfully easy manner, and *Blue Music* outskipped all its predecessors. At a quarter to ten it arrived at its finale to Act One (Abdul Achmallah's Palace at Algiers), the entire company massed itself and was duly revolved by the mechanics, Mr. Baker and Miss Astle obliged with a *reprise* of their number 'Two Eyes, Two Hearts, One Love', and the curtain fell triumphantly. To rise again several times, as it happened; for the Gallery Club were there in full force, determined to see as much of Mr. Baker as was possible for their two-and-fourpence.

Mr. Amethyst muttered, 'Excuse me,' all along

row R, and edged himself out of the auditorium and into the orchestra stalls bar. He had written his notice several weeks before, and was in two minds about going back to see the rest of the show. He had had a good deal of experience of Douglas B. Douglas productions, and he knew that this was very much the mixture as before, prescribed, perhaps, in slightly more lavish quantities.

'Good show, James,' said Mr. Duncan, a literary colleague of Mr. Amethyst, and the pen behind 'The Play's The Thing' column in the *Daily Observer*. 'Old man Douglas done it again, methinks.'

'It will please the masses,' said Mr. Amethyst. 'And as Douglas apparently exists for the masses, I've no doubt that it will please Douglas. Thank you, a large whisky-and-soda.'

'It's well put on, anyway,' said Mr. Duncan. 'You can't deny that. D.B.D. certainly knows how to stage a big show like this. Credit where credit is due, James.'

'My dear Duncan,' said Mr. Amethyst, 'one cannot, so far as I am aware, exist permanently on credit. Was that the bell? – summoning us to Heaven, or much more probably to Hell? Hear it not, Duncan. There's time for another one.'

Mr. Amethyst and the rest of the drinking males made their difficult way back to their seats. The long-suffering females of the audience garnered in their ermine wraps, opera glasses, chocolates, and programmes, and allowed their feet to be trodden on and their gowns to be crumpled in the return of the prodigals from the various bars. M. Gasnier's bald head appeared again, looking a

13

little less worried than at the beginning of Act One. Act One on a first night is always rather a trying experience for a conductor. M. Gasnier smiled again to a few more strangers in the stalls, pulled down his cuffs once more, and invoked his percussion. The house lights dimmed smoothly. The curtain rose again.

Act Two, Scene One, of *Blue Music* was described in the programme as The Rebel's Stronghold in the Moroccan Hills. You probably picture at that a sort of *Maid of the Mountains* scene, composed largely of bright magenta mountains and large canvas rocks. Again you're forgetting that this was a Douglas B. Douglas production. There were mountains, certainly, tier upon tier, stretching away for what seemed several miles until they met at last a sky backcloth of unbelievable blue. But there was also a great deal more, the full effect of which was not obtained by the audience until the stage had been rid of the presence of the One Hundred and Ten Ladies and Gentlemen of the Chorus, who opened the second act in a breezy fashion by singing and dancing the hot number 'Rough Riff Ruffian Rag' ... fifty-five of them clad sparingly as Harem Girls, and the other fifty-five as members of the Foreign Legion. (Mr. Amethyst in the end seat of row R wondered what so many of the Foreign Legion were doing inside a Rebel's Stronghold, and put it down as merely another little idiosyncrasy of the musical-comedy world.)

The last gyration of the 'Riff Ruffian Rag' over, the Ladies and Gentlemen of the Chorus exited smartly into the O.P. corner, and the full splendour of the scene dawned upon the audience. Mountains, yes; but also a massive stone turreted affair on one side of the stage, also a real live waterfall on the other, also a small forest of gently waving palms in the centre, also (a typical Douglas B. Douglas touch, this) a trio of real live camels sleeping and smelling contentedly in the prompt corner of the stage – borrowed specially from Whipsnade, to lend verisimilitude to the Rebel's Stronghold. And also, most important of all, Mr. Brandon Baker centre, enjoying a slight lapse from virtue with Coletta, the Native Dancer.

At this part of the play, Mr. Watcyns' original script went something like this,

COLETTA: And now, white man, we are alone, no?

JACK: Alone!... At last!...

COLETTA: You kees me, please, yes?

JACK: What would Phillipo, your lover, do if he found you in my arms like this?

COLETTA: Phillipo no my lover. Phillipo peegswine. But he keel, yes, if he find you kees me. So ... kees me...

JACK: To be killed for a kiss! There's no sting in a death like that, Coletta.

(They embrace passionately. Cue for Jack's song 'Say My Heart is in Your Hands'. At end of song, Jack and Coletta embrace again. Phillipo enters unseen by them at top of mountains extreme Right. He watches them for a moment, and then pulls out his revolver and aims at Jack.)

15

A fairly gripping situation, you see, especially for the opening scene of a second act, where nothing very much ever happens except a dance ensemble by the chorus or a song by the second lead. There were, of course, some slight deviations from the script as Mr. Watcyns wrote it, Phillipo had to enter on the extreme Left ridge of the mountains instead of the extreme Right, owing to something to do with the revolving stage. And Mr. Baker had to sing 'Tell Me Something with those Eyes' instead of 'Say My Heart is in Your Hands', because Miss Astle had a bout of temperament at the dress rehearsal and said that she wasn't going to have the best number of the show wasted on a walking-on part, and unless 'Say My Heart' was sung to her she was walking out of the whole lousy business and going on a Mediterranean cruise. But otherwise the scene was played pretty much as it was written. Mr. Baker and Miss Eve Turner (the young lady playing Coletta) embraced passionately, disentangled themselves neatly, and Mr. Baker took his cue smartly and launched himself out of verse one of 'Tell Me something with those Eyes'. M. Gasnier finished the number rather more than two beats ahead of Mr. Baker, owing to the latter's habit of hanging on to a good note when he found one. Phillipo, the Rebel Leader, entered along the mountain-top Left according to schedule. Unfortunately the Gallery Club demanded an encore from Mr. Baker, and the Rebel Leader had to retire once more into the wings. The encore was given, Mr. Baker and Coletta embraced rather more passionately than before, and Phillipo reappeared on the mountains and said tersely, 'So!... You make love to my woman, eh!' It was the only line of more than four words that he had to deliver in the entire show.

Mr. Amethyst sat up, interested. He could not bring himself to believe that Mr. Watcyns would have the courage to bump his hero off before the show was half over, especially when the hero happened to be played by Brandon Baker. There would certainly be hell to pay from the Gallery Club if he did. Mr. Amethyst turned to his neighbour in the adjoining stall and bet him ten shillings that if a shot was fired it would only result in a slight flesh wound, that Mr. Baker would appear in the next scene swathed in beautiful bandages, and would have recovered sufficiently to do a song-and-dance *reprise* of 'Say My Heart is in Your Hands' before the end of Act Two. The man in the next seat, being also an inveterate theatre-goer, refused Mr. Amethyst's bet politely.

Mr. Amethyst sighed and returned to the goings-on on the stage. He heard Mr. Baker's spirited rejoinder to the Rebel Leader, 'You say she is your woman, yet you treat her like a dog!' He saw the bold, bad Phillipo draw his revolver slowly from his belt. He heard Coletta's feverish, 'No, no, not that!' and saw her nobly attempt to put herself in the way of the bullet, and Mr. Baker equally nobly pushing her aside and behind his manly protective chest. He heard the lady in the seat in front of him squeak at the report of the revolver being fired, and smiled as she muttered, 'I wish they wouldn't do that. I was quite sick after *Journey's End.*' And he saw Mr.

17

Baker fall efficiently on the stage with two spot-lights marking the spot. Mr. Amethyst made an inward vow that if Phillipo had really done in the handsome hero, he would rewrite his notice for the *Morning Herald* and call the play 'an original and commendably unconventional musical production.'

Miss Turner (Coletta) shrieked. Mr. Douglas had had a lot of trouble with the girl about her shrieking. She put no feeling into it, no emotion. Just a sort of high-pitched dither, like some of the sopranos you heard on the wireless. But he had managed to lick her into shape during the three weeks' try-out at Manchester. That to-night had been a very good shriek. Very good indeed. Rather to Mr. Douglas's surprise, Miss Turner shrieked again.

There was something quite different about the second shriek. Mr. Douglas thought it not quite so genuine – a little too theatrical, if anything. Mr. Amethyst, on the other hand, thought it extremely well done, and decided to rewrite his notice in any case and give Miss Turner a special line all to herself.

This talented young actress can put over horror and genuine fright in a way which compares favourably with many of the famous tragediennes.

The expression on her face at this moment for instance, an admirable bit of acting.

Mr. Douglas B. Douglas was also rather interested in Miss Turner's acting at the moment. He didn't think the girl had it in her. Mr. Douglas

18

snatched his opera-glasses rudely from his wife's lap and focused them from her short-sighted eyes to his own long-sighted ones. He swept the two lenses of the glasses across the stretches of purple mountains until at last he found Miss Turner and the prostrate Mr. Baker in their twin spotlights. He did not like the look on Miss Turner's face at all. Nor did he like the peculiar dark mark on the stage, just where Mr. Baker had fallen. Mr. Douglas gave another twist to the swivel of his opera-glasses to bring them exactly into focus. He fixed them again on the dark mark. It was blood.

CHAPTER TWO

Look again for a moment at the programme. Any mention of the name Herbert on it? Of course not. Everyone (except Herbert) agrees that it is a crying shame, but there the matter rests. You will find a Herbert behind every big musical show. Toiling and sweating through the weeks of rehearsal and through each performance. Something awful would most certainly happen if Herbert got influenza or went home in the sulks, the leading lady would miss her cue, or the waterfall in Act Two, Scene One, would run dry or upwards instead of downwards, or the orchestra would play the opening music for Act Three before Mr. Baker was inside his boiled shirt.

Mercifully, Herbert never seems to suffer from

either influenza or the sulks, and so the show is a success. He left the theatre this afternoon at five-fifteen, after putting right the forty-seven things that Mr. Douglas B. Douglas saw wrong with the final dress rehearsal. He was back at six, to make everything ship-shape for the opening. Already he has lulled Miss Astle back to normal from a fit of temperament; already he has provided a flask from his hip-pocket to give Mr. Baker the necessary lightness for his tap-dance in Act One; already he has seen the chorus safely out of their beach pyjamas and safely into their brassieres and slips in the schedule time of fifty seconds.

Herbert will not appear at the end of the show any more than he appears on the programme or in the Press notices; no applause, no speeches, no bouquets for Herbert. He couldn't, anyway, wearing that greasy overall and with his shirt-sleeves up almost to his shoulders. Whereas Mr. Douglas, who has Personally Supervised the Entire Production (and Herbert doesn't even see anything funny in that) is immaculate in white shirt-front, tails, red carnation and maidenhair fern button-hole, and will be there in the spotlight to say that all the labour and work and worry he has put into the show has been indeed well worth while when it has resulted in this magnificent, terribly kind reception.

'Come along, girls' said Herbert, standing in the wings and holding back the front curtain to allow fifty-five of the chorus to disappear from the stage at the end of their opening number in Act Two, 'Get a move on, now. Only a minute and a half to get changed, you know.' The chorus bounced off to their dressing-rooms; Herbert kept a keen eye on the stage. The view of a stage from the wings is a far more interesting affair than that obtained from the stalls or the circle, you get only a slice, it is true, but it is a very discriminating slice, revealing the most important and leaving the rest mercifully screened behind canvas and curtains.

From where he was standing, Herbert was able to see the point where Mr. Baker's *toupet* joined his own hair. He noticed that Miss Turner's shoulder-strap had slipped with that last bit of passionate embracing, and hoped that things would be all right until the end of the scene. He could just see Mr. Foster, as Phillipo the Rebel Leader, climbing laboriously up the ladder and on to the little platform from where he would appear striding over the mountain-tops.

Mr. Foster was getting on; it was rather a shame to send a man with chronic rheumatism up a ladder like that. He could see, high in the opposite wings, the two men on the spotlights quietly arguing about Sheffield Wednesday, and immediately below them the front pair of the Twenty-four Ballet Whos flouncing out their ballet skirts and getting ready for the next scene. He saw, too, M. Gasnier's hand come forward to bring in Mr. Baker on the right bar of 'Tell Me Something with your Eyes' ... it was funny that a man who had been singing juvenile lead songs for the past twenty-nine years should still require to be brought in on the right note. Herbert also saw the dark blot of blood when Mr. Baker fell.

'What the – *curtain!*' said Herbert.

He ran along the stage with the curtain, holding

its two halves in position when they met in the centre of the stage. He heard the audience's applause. Rather more applause than Manchester had ever given for that scene.

'Bert, for God's sake!' said Miss Turner. 'He's shot.'

Stage directors of musical comedies are like pursers of ships. They get the brunt of things banged at them one after another, crises, hitches, sensations. And all the time the show or the ship must go ahead smoothly and uninterrupted, if possible without anyone being aware of the presence of a hitch. Herbert's first thought, being a good stage director, was not of Brandon Baker's body, nor of Miss Turner's near-hysterics, nor even of the figure of Mr. Foster, still standing on the mountains in his gay Rebel Leader costume. It was of the audience on the other side of the curtain. They might wait sixty seconds, but no longer. Sixty seconds was a long time for a change of scene in a Douglas B. Douglas production, and the audience in front was the kind that knew that. Herbert ran back to the wings and picked up the telephone connecting with M. Gasnier's desk in the orchestra pit.

'Play the introduction to Act Two again,' he said, 'and the Scene Two opening number right after that.'

'Why?' said M. Gasnier. 'Anything wrong?'

'Nothing. Do as you're told. John, pull your grey tabs along. Now, girls. Carry on, and for God's sake get an encore. And *smile*.'

The grey tabs trailed along. For an unpleasant half-minute Herbert thought that they were going to fall behind, instead of in front, of the dark smudge of Mr. Baker's blood. Mercifully they hid it – just. The pale-grey fringe at the bottom of the tabs swept over the dark mark and smeared it further along the stage.

'Get a cloth,' said Herbert.

'Oh, God!...' said Miss Turner. 'What's happened to him? What's happened? Is he ... is he dead?'

'I don't know. Off the stage, everyone. *Off the stage.* Phillipo – come down here. Boy! ... get Mr. Douglas on-stage at once. Box A. Sprint like hell. John – round to the box-office and see if there's a doctor left the number of his seat there. If there is, get hold of him and bring him here. Off the stage, everyone, will you?... Oh, there you are, sir.'

'Yes,' said Mr. Douglas. 'I saw it. Didn't like the look of it, either. Is he living? Have you sent for a doctor? What the hell happened, man?'

'I don't know, sir. I just saw him fall when I was standing over there in the wings. Didn't realize anything was wrong. Then I saw this blood ... there's the girls' number finishing now, sir. What d'you want put on? We can put Serge and Mimi on in front of the tabs until we get the–'

'Don't talk bunk!' said Mr. Douglas. 'You can't carry on with the show with a man dying on the stage. Drop the curtain. Tell René to play something. There's a doctor I know in the house – Armitage, Harley Street man – about six rows back in the stalls ... send out for him.'

'What about the police, sir?'

'I suppose so. Wait a minute ... that fellow Wilson's in the theatre as well. A little further back than Armitage. You'd better call for them both. No good trying to hush anything up.'

'We'd better move him, sir.'

'Yes. No ... if the police are coming in right away leave him where he is. Until the doctor sees him, anyway. Where's Phillipo?'

'Phillipo! ... boy – find Mr. Foster. Quick.'

'What's happened?' asked Miss Astle, appearing suddenly in négligé. 'What's the matter? Oh ... my God!'

'Better clear off the stage, Gwen. Go to your dressing-room. There's been an accident. I'll come and see you in a minute.'

'Brandon!... Is he – dead? Tell me – is he?'

'I think so.'

'Good God! Brandon ... oh, my God!'

Miss Astle started to laugh. Not a pleasant laugh. 'Shut up, for God's sake!' said Mr. Douglas. 'Don't let them hear you making a din like that. *Shut up!*' Miss Astle did not shut up. She laughed and laughed hysterically, madly ... flopping at last into Mr. Douglas's arms.

'Take her to her dressing-room. Give her some brandy. Don't let her on the stage until everything's cleared up.'

Miss Astle was led away limply.

'That's interesting,' said Mr. Douglas. 'Were they ... she and Baker, I mean...?'

'I've no idea,' said Herbert. 'Here's the doctor, sir, I think.'

Dr. Armitage had seen most first nights, but very few in their entirety. To-night he had come fully expecting to be summoned to the arrival of an heir to a peerage half-way through *Blue Music*.

24

When the attendant had called his name along row F of the stalls, Dr. Armitage had risen with an air of Christian martyrdom, and expressed the hope that it would be twins – and both of them girls – for taking him out of the theatre at such an interesting stage of the play. He had not expected to be summoned backstage. A tall, quiet Scot, Dr. Armitage, with a methodical, funereal way of setting about his duties that exasperated Mr. Douglas tremendously.

'There's been an accident here, doctor,' said Mr. Douglas. 'Mr. Baker... Will you see what's the matter?'

Dr. Armitage dusted the floorcloth on the stage carefully and knelt beside Mr. Baker's body. He unloosened his Arabesque costume and leaned over his chest. Mr. Douglas played a little tune on his teeth with a nail of his thumb – a habit of his when impatient. On the other side of the curtain the orchestra rallied for the finale of their overture. There would be silence in the theatre in a minute now.

'Well?' said Mr. Douglas.

'Far from it,' said Dr. Armitage. 'In fact, he's dead.'

'Dead?'

'Shot through the heart. Must have been instantaneous.'

News travels fast backstage. The call-boys spread it out of the wings and along the dressing-rooms corridors. The babble in the chorus dressing-rooms hushed suddenly. 'Brandon Baker's dead.' The man on duty at the stage door heard it within a minute. 'He's dead ... Brandon Baker's

25

dead.' Little groups of oddly clad members of the company spread on to the edge of the stage and stared fascinated at the figure lying still at Mr. Douglas's feet. The men on the spotlights craned down over their gallery to see it, casting huge shadows of themselves on to the stage. 'He's dead. Hilary Foster shot him. Brandon Baker's dead...' The orchestra finished their overture with a spirited attack on the percussion.

'Well...' said Mr. Douglas. 'I'll have to go out and say something, I suppose. Herbert, I leave you in charge. See that nothing's moved. If Wilson doesn't turn up in a minute or so send out for the first bobby you can lay your hands on. Get all this bunch off the stage. And get hold of Phillipo, for God's sake.'

Mr. Douglas parted the curtains and blinked at the sudden glare from the footlights.

'Ladies and gentlemen,' said Mr. Douglas, 'I ... I am very sorry to have to tell you that there has been an ... an unfortunate accident on the stage. It ... it is, I am afraid, impossible to continue the performance under the circumstances. Er ... Mr. Brandon Baker ... Mr. Baker has been shot. I would ask you to leave the theatre, please. I can only express my great regret that such an unfortunate ... I will arrange for the holders of reserved seats to have their money refunded or their tickets exchanged ... the ladies and gentlemen in the gallery will have the price of admission refunded to them as they leave at the gallery box-office ... I can only say how very sorry indeed...'

It was unfortunate for Mr. Douglas that eighteen months before he had produced the thriller *Persons Unknown*. In that play a fairly satisfactory murder was committed as the curtain to the first act. The shot, it was believed, had been fired from the auditorium by a revolver fitted with a silencer. Mr. Douglas staged the situation well. He made a speech from the stage himself. He introduced M. André Proinet, the celebrated French detective, who happened to be occupying a stage box. He refused to allow any of the audience to leave the theatre, even for a drink in the bars, and had each exit guarded by actors clad in the blue of the Metropolitan police.

Acts Two and Three were taken up with the solving of the crime, which turned out to have been committed by an elderly spinster in the front row of the dress circle. The show was a great success and ran for over a year, mainly because Mr. Douglas shifted his murderer at each performance and none of the audience could say definitely that the person sitting next to them had not fired the fatal shot. (Mr. Amethyst, in fact, was charged with doing the dirty deed by a middle-aged woman in a tiara who sat next to him during the show and accused him of behaving in a highly suspicious manner all through Act One.)

The annoying thing was that the public had not forgotten *Persons Unknown*. They listened to Mr. Douglas's announcement in a polite silence and then realized, of course, that this was another typical Douglas B. Douglas stunt. They laughed. And then they applauded. Mr. Douglas had never been quite so staggered in his life.

'Ladies and gentlemen...' said Mr. Douglas. 'Please ... *please!* ... I assure you this is no part of the performance … I wish it were… Please!…'

The audience enjoyed the situation. It was good, original. In another minute the detective would arrive, and the 'police' would come snooping down the gangways in the auditorium, searching for clues. Then somebody would be arrested, and there would be a court scene, probably. Very good fun. Quite a number of people in the stalls searched their programmes to find the name of the actor who was going to impersonate the detective and, failing to find it, decided that that was just another Douglas B. Douglas touch to keep up the air of mystery. They applauded rather more vigorously. On the stage, Mr. Douglas looked completely blank.

'Stop!' said Mr. Douglas. 'Silence, please.… Apparently, ladies and gentlemen, you refuse to believe that what I have said is not part of the play. There is, I am afraid, only one way to convince you of what has happened. Curtain, please.....'

The dress and upper circles and the gallery hushed at once. They could see the unpleasant, growing mark beside Brandon Baker's body. The stalls had to stand up to see it; in a minute the theatre was completely silent.

'Now, ladies and gentlemen, will you please leave the theatre as quickly as possible?... Er ... you will find a statement issued to the Press in time for to-morrow's papers... Thank you... Curtain!'

The audience trooped out of the theatre in a dazed fashion. High in the gods, a member of the Brandon Baker Gallery Club began to sob hysterically. The pressmen present sprinted round to the stage-door in a mob. The one and only taxi outside the Grosvenor main entrance received a surprise and bumper patronage an hour and a half before it had expected the theatre to empty.

Mr. Wilson from Scotland Yard had arrived on the stage while Mr. Douglas was making his announcement. You would never have suspected Mr. Wilson of being connected with anything so worldly as the Police Force, he was tall, grey-haired, immaculately dressed in full evening dress, and the possessor of that brand of features that goes down in novelettes as 'rugged'. A barrister, perhaps, or a specialist in the disorders of the stomach – but never a policeman.

'Mr. Douglas?' said Mr. Wilson in his quiet voice. 'How d'you do? Wilson, Scotland Yard. Oh, this is my son Derek. I'm afraid I shouldn't have brought him on the stage, but he would probably have come in any case in his own right. He's a reporter on the *Gazette*. A very unpleasant business, Mr. Douglas. This, I mean, not reporting.'

'Damned unpleasant,' said Mr. Douglas.

'Anything been moved?'

'Nothing, sir,' said Herbert. 'I saw to that.'

'Excellent,' said Mr. Wilson. 'Usually, after an affair of this sort, everybody seems to think it necessary to indulge in an orgy of spring-cleaning and general upheaval. You've had a doctor round, I suppose?'

'Yes,' said Mr. Douglas. 'Here he is. Dr. Armitage – Inspector Wilson of Scotland Yard.'

'How d'you do?' asked Mr. Wilson. 'Aren't you the fellow who's always killing rabbits and then

29

bringing them back to life with a funny sort of glandular injection thing?'

'Yes,' said Dr. Armitage. 'That hasn't anything to do with the present case, though, Inspector.'

'No, of course not,' said Mr. Wilson. 'Of course not. I wasn't suggesting for a minute that Mr. Baker was... Is he dead?'

'Yes. Shot through the heart. The bullet entered almost exactly in the centre of the heart and went right through the body.'

'Very unpleasant. Derek ... you might go out and get a couple of bobbies roped in, will you? I'm afraid we'll have to arrest Mr... What was his name? – the fellow who played the Rebel Leader?'

'Foster,' said Mr. Douglas. 'Hilary Foster. He's vanished.'

'Vanished?'

'I've had a couple of men looking for him ever since the curtain dropped. Not a sign.'

'Dear me,' said Mr. Wilson. 'Well ... would you ask all these ladies and gentlemen to leave the stage, please? Thank you. And I think we might take the body to somewhere a little less public. A dressing-room, or somewhere like that. Oh, just a minute, before we do that. Has anyone such a thing as a stick of chalk?'

'Chalk!' said Mr. Douglas. 'Chalk. Come on, somebody. Quick of – chick of – *stick of chalk*, quickly!'

'Here you are, sir,' said Herbert – the man who would have such a thing in his overall pocket. 'Chalk, sir.'

'Thank you,' said Mr. Wilson. 'Derek, you might just draw a line round Mr. Baker's body, will you? I know it's not a very nice job, but it's often rather helpful to know exactly where and how the body fell. I'd do it myself, only this waistcoat... Thanks, that's fine. Now we can take him away, I think. Oh, just a minute. This is one of those revolving stage things, isn't it? I mean, where Mr. Baker's lying just now – is that on part of the revolving bit?'

'Yes,' said Mr. Douglas. 'Just on the rim of it.'

'I see,' said Mr. Wilson. 'Draw a straight line out from Mr. Baker's head, will you, Derek? On to the other part of the stage – the fixed part, I mean. It's not much use marking the spot where the body fell if the whole stage behaves like the planetary system and spoils everything, is it? Right, that's about all, I think, thank you.'

'No need to lift him from there, sir,' said Herbert. 'Just a minute and I'll send the stage right round. Then we can carry him into his dressing-room.'

Mr. Wilson planted his feet firmly on the stage as it swung smoothly round from the glare of the footlights into the half-light up-stage.

'Very ingenious,' he said. 'Rather like the flying-boats at the fair, isn't it? Now I want to find Mr. Foster. How many exits are there from the stage to the street, Mr Douglas?'

'One,' said Mr. Douglas. 'The stage-door only. Unless he went through one of the two doors at each side of the proscenium. They lead to the staircase and corridors opening on to the boxes at each side of the stage. Once he was there he could get out by any of the main theatre entrances, of course.'

'Of course,' said Mr. Wilson. 'Then that's not much help, is it? Still, you might arrange for someone to ask the men at each exit if they've seen the gentleman, would you? The man at the stage-door too, of course. And I wonder if you could put rather more than two men on the search inside the theatre? Two men after a third man isn't really much good, you know. Thanks so much. I'm not putting you to too much trouble, am I?'

'Not at all,' said Mr. Douglas, wondering how many unsolved crimes Mr. Wilson had had to deal with. 'Smith – Jackson – Anderson – you, and you – and you two – search the whole damn' place, and don't come back until you've found Foster. You two – go round every exit and make sure he hasn't left the theatre. Go to the stage-door first and ask old Roberts. Get a move on.'

'Thank you,' said Mr. Wilson. 'So nice to have to work with people who are really helpful for a change. That notice about smoking – does it mean what it says, Mr. Douglas?'

'Have a cigar,' said Mr. Douglas in reply.

'No, thanks. I'll stick to my pipe, if you don't mind. I've been aching for a pipe all night, but I was sitting between a dowager duchess and a young man who looked as if he'd be sick if I brought out the thing. That's the worst of putting on a boiled shirt and sitting in the stalls. Now I'd rather like to find that bullet–'

Mr. Wilson lit a pipe slowly and carefully, using five matches in the process and scattering tobacco over most of Herbert's newly cleaned stage. He then walked back to the spot where Mr.

Baker had fallen.

'It's gone,' said Mr. Wilson.

'What's gone?' asked Mr. Douglas.

'The chalk outline we made of his body. Oh, of course ... we've revolved the stage, haven't we? Stupid of me ... I'm not used to these wonderful mechanical contraptions. Could we have it back where it was, please? Steady – steady!'

Mr. Wilson had unfortunately placed one of his large feet on the revolving stage and the other off it. He sat down abruptly and was carried off in an arc until he freed himself of the revolving part.

'Very funny,' said Mr. Wilson sadly, picking himself up and dusting the seat of his trousers. 'Very amusing indeed. I wonder you theatre people don't use the idea more in your shows. Now then ... a little further round, please. Woah. Back just an inch or so. There ... that's fine. That's the exact position occupied by Mr. Baker when he fell. Clever of me, wasn't it?'

'Extremely,' said Mr. Douglas.

'Now ... I want to know exactly where this fellow Foster would be standing when he fired the shot. Up there, wasn't it? Derek ... would you go up and represent the gentleman? I'd go, but this waistcoat – you know, not for mountains. Thank you.'

'A little to the right, sir,' said Herbert. 'Bit more still. There. That's as near as dammit, sir.'

'Splendid,' said Mr. Wilson. 'Now, then. He stood up there and he fired at Baker down here. Wasn't it a funny thing to do, by the way? Shooting a man in full view of about two thousand people, and with not the chance of a lump of margarine in hell of getting away with it.'

'But he *has* got away, blast you,' said Mr. Douglas, exasperated.

'Oh yes,' said Mr. Wilson. 'So he has. I'd forgotten that. Well ... he fired. Mr. Douglas, will you come and be Mr. Baker for a minute, please?'

'Me?' said Mr. Douglas.

'Yes. It's all right. Derek hasn't a revolver. Just stand there, please. That's right. Now, the bullet would go through there, wouldn't it?'

Mr. Wilson prodded Mr. Douglas's breast pocket with his forefinger. Mr. Douglas felt slightly sick.

'Right through you, and out the other side ... and on. You wouldn't like to collapse on the stage, Mr. Douglas, just as poor Mr. Baker did?'

'No,' said Mr. Douglas, 'I wouldn't.'

'No, of course not. It's a very dirty stage. The seat of my... Yes, right on in this line. It would hit the side wall of the proscenium, wouldn't it?'

'I don't know,' said Mr. Douglas. 'Would it?'

'Yes,' said Mr. Wilson. 'And it did. There it is, you see. There's the little black-guard. I'll get Anderson along tomorrow to dig it out and have a look at it.'

Mr. Wilson took a long, interested gaze at the little black mark where the bullet had entered the white plaster of the proscenium. Some of the plaster had broken off and lay on the stage.

'Has anyone got a footrule?' asked Mr. Wilson. 'Or a tape-measure, or anything like that?'

'Yes, sir,' said Herbert, producing footrule from the little pocket down the side of his dungaree trousers and tape-measure from around his neck.

34

'Here you are, sir.'

'Thank you,' said Mr. Wilson, taking the tape-measure. 'You seem to be a very remarkable man. Positive walking Woolworth's, aren't you? You haven't got such a thing as a double whisky on you, by any chance?'

'I had, sir,' said Herbert, perfectly seriously. 'But I gave it to the leading lady – Miss Astle, sir. She had a fit of the jim-jams, sir.'

'I see,' said Mr. Wilson, placing the tape measure up the wall of the proscenium. 'That's odd,' said Mr. Wilson. 'Very odd indeed.'

'What's odd?' demanded Mr. Douglas.

'Nothing. Nothing at all. Right, you can come down now, Derek. Thanks very much. You look quite attractive up there on the Alps. Quite like Garibaldi.'

'Mr. Douglas!'

'Well, what is it?'

One of the squadron detailed to hunt for Mr. Foster appeared on the stage.

'Mr. Foster's dressing-room door's locked, sir. We can't get an answer.'

'Force it open,' said Mr. Douglas tersely.

'Right, sir.'

'I'd like to come and see what's to be seen, if you don't mind,' said Mr. Wilson. 'Coming, Derek? This way, is it?'

It was, of course, Herbert who forced open the dressing-room door. No one else had a spanner on their person. A few deft attacks on the lock with the spanner, and a mighty heave from Herbert's left shoulder, and the trick was done. Herbert shot inside the room, followed rather

35

ceremoniously by Mr. Wilson and Mr. Douglas.

'Wouldn't you have thought you would have looked here *first?*' asked Mr. Wilson quietly. 'I mean, surely this was the natural place...'

Mr. Foster was in his dressing-room. Hanging by the neck.

CHAPTER THREE

It certainly made a lovely story.

Under the circumstances, Mr. Amethyst decided to rewrite his notice altogether. He did not waste the first effort, which had been a good one and full of slightly naughty puns, but used it on the following Friday for the new show at the Hippodrome. A few names had to be changed here and there, but otherwise it stood firm and seemed entirely suitable. For the unfortunate first night of *Blue Music* Mr. Amethyst wrote,

One is getting a little tired of hearing every theatrical writer in London say that Mr. Douglas B. Douglas has Done It Again. If Doing It Again means (as I take it to mean) that Mr. Douglas has concocted the same mixture from the same prescription and served it to the same patients in the same doses, then I suggest that it is not altogether a complimentary remark. My colleagues, however, are unable to say that Mr. Douglas has Done It again with regard to his latest production Blue Music, *which opened at the Grosvenor last night and closed the same evening. It is only fair to add that Mr. Douglas was stopped from (presumably) Doing It Again by a murder.*

I have very often felt a strong desire to put an end to Mr. Douglas's spectacular musical shows in a similar manner; fortunately for my readers, there had always been something or other to restrain me from carrying out this decidedly praiseworthy ideal; My machine-gun has been stupidly left at home in my flat, or I have been wedged in the centre of a row of seats, between a corpulent countess and a pot-bellied politician, where escape would have been difficult if not altogether impossible. However, the idea has been used by someone more fortunately situated, and while I hold no brief for killing in cold blood (even if it be the killing of an actor who has long warranted assassination), it is, I feel, one of those situations which make one support the people who are always crying out for the abolition of the death penalty.

Mr. Douglas's latest venture, before it came to its timely end, was another musical comedy in which both comedy and music were conspicuous by their absence. The only trace of commendable acting came from Miss Eve Turner as Coletta, but as this transpired to be not acting but actuality, it is perhaps over-generous to do more than mention the fact that Miss Turner can shriek. In the leading rôle, Miss Astle wore a succession of charming frocks and showed how simple it is for a musical-comedy heroine to take a high C if the brass in the orchestra are sufficiently intelligent to blow very hard at the right time.

A great deal could be said about Mr. Brandon Baker's performance as Jack, but since there is a particularly restricting proverb concerning speaking ill of the dead, I will merely mention that the last thing

37

Mr. Baker did was the best thing Mr. Baker did. The chorus were well-trained, over-worked, and under-dressed, and I have no doubt that after a decent length of time has been allowed to lapse Mr. Douglas will have the temerity to restage Blue Music *and that it will probably run for two years. Unfortunately, even in these stirring and unsettled times one cannot count on a murder at every first night...*

The *Morning Herald's* actual report of the crime was slightly less amusing in its own loud way:

FAMOUS MUSICAL-COMEDY STAR MURDERED BRANDON BAKER SHOT DURING FIRST NIGHT PERFORMANCE

WEST END THEATRE TRAGEDY

FELLOW ACTOR'S SUICIDE

By Our Special Correspondent

The gaiety and glamour of a typical Douglas B. Douglas first night came to a sudden and tragic end at the Grosvenor Theatre, London, last night, through the murder of Brandon Baker, the well-known musical-comedy star, before the eyes of a crowded and fashionable audience. The tragedy occurred at the commencement of the second act, when Mr. Baker was shot dead by J. Hilary Foster, another member of the company, who was also on the stage at the time. The amazed audience were astounded to see Mr. Baker fall suddenly in the front of the stage, and their supposition that what had happened was only part of the perform-

38

ance gave way to horror when they saw a thin stream of blood flow from the famous actor's body towards the footlights. The tragedy had a sensational sequel, Foster being found hanging dead in his dressing-room shortly after the curtain had been lowered. It is thought that in the confusion resulting from the fatal shot, Foster was able to escape unnoticed from the stage, lock himself in his dressing-room and there commit suicide.

Inspector Wilson of the C.I.D., who was in the theatre at the time of the outrage, was quickly on the stage, and has the matter in hand. Photographs of Brandon Baker in some of his most famous rôles appear in our back page today, and tomorrow we are presenting with every copy a special Brandon Baker Souvenir Supplement, artistically printed on art paper, and giving a profusely illustrated story of this famous actor's meteoric career – a souvenir that will be treasured by the countless thousands to whom Brandon Baker was a household word. The demand for to-morrow's issue is sure to be enormous – make sure of obtaining your copy by placing an order with your newsagent NOW...

Mr. Douglas B. Douglas, the famous theatrical impresario and producer of the show Blue Music, which had so tragic and short-lived a run, gave an exclusive interview to our special representative before leaving the theatre last night, 'It is a terrible shock to us all,' said Mr. Douglas. 'Mr. Baker was one of the most popular and capable artists I have ever had the honour of dealing with. I cannot imagine what possible motive Foster could have had for this dreadful crime. The show, of course, will be postponed for a little while, but you can tell your readers that I intend putting it on again at the Grosvenor in the very near

39

future, and that I hope to have a Continental actor of world-wide reputation in the late Mr. Baker's part. It is the biggest and most spectacular production I have ever been associated with, and I am certain that it will make a big hit with the London public.' ... Miss Gwen Astle, the leading lady of Blue Music, *was still suffering from the shock of the tragedy when our representative 'phoned her last night, but she was able to send a message to* Morning Herald *readers, 'It is simply terrible,' Miss Astle said in a voice still quivering with emotion. 'He was the nicest man I ever knew in my life. I can't imagine anyone making an enemy of him. He was a regular trouper. I feel I want to give up my association with* Blue Music *now that this has happened, but I have my duty to my public to consider first of all, and I shall resume my part when the play is put on again. It is a glorious part – quite the best I have ever had.' ... An article on 'Pagliacci Puppets – Former Tragedies of the Theatre World' appears to-day in page 12, and in Saturday's issue of the* Morning Herald *Miss Gwen Astle will commence a revealing series of articles entitled 'Brandon Baker as I Knew Him'. These intimate glimpses into the private and public life of Britain's favourite musical-comedy star are sure to arouse tremendous interest, and readers will be well advised to place a standing order with...*

Mr. Wilson read the *Morning Herald's* version of the business and smiled sadly. Mr. Wilson bought *The Times* for news, the *Morning Herald* for amusement's sake, and the *Daily Gazette* for gossip. Meet Mr. Wilson sitting in the morning-room of his flat in Gower Street. Not looking at all like a detective (but then Mr. Wilson never did that), and not

living in at all the sort of house one would asso-
ciate with a detective. No massive volumes of
criminals' biographies on the bookshelves; no
relics of the chase suspended over the mantelpiece; no set of magnifying-glasses neatly dangling
in a fretwork frame to the left of the fireplace. And
Mr. Wilson is wearing neither the beater's cap nor
the pipe with the Mae West curves that your true
detective ought to wear; he is, in fact, looking
extremely spruce for a man of over fifty in a
dressing-gown of pale-blue silk with a white fleck
running over it, and smoking a perfectly ordinary
Virginian cigarette. Disappointing, but true. Mr.
Wilson, then, sighed sadly at what the *Morning
Herald* had to say about the business, and turned
back to his coffeepot, against which a leather-
bound omnibus of William Shakespeare was
propped.

''Morning, dad,' said Mr. Wilson, junr., appearing suddenly in a slightly less tasteful dressing-
gown and making straight for the grapefruit.

'Our revels now are ended,' said Mr. Wilson,
senr., in reply. 'These our actors, as I foretold you,
were all spirits, and are melted into air, into thin
air ... and, like this insubstantial pageant faded,
leave not a rack behind. We are such stuff as
dreams are made of, and our little life is rounded
with a sleep. Good morning. Have some coffee?'

'Thanks,' said Derek. 'Why the Shakespeare at
this time of the morning? It was Shakespeare,
wasn't it?'

'I'd been reading three newspapers and I
needed soothing,' said Mr. Wilson. 'And I don't
believe it was Shakespeare. As a matter of fact, he

41

pinched it wholesale from a bloke called Stirling. But it's most appropriate, don't you think? To last night's business, I mean?'

'Most,' said Derek. 'Toast.'

'The manners of the modern generation,' said Mr. Wilson, passing the toast, 'are simply appalling. When I was your age and wanted the toast to be passed, I should have said, "Please, sir, would you mind passing the toast?" Only we never had toast for breakfast then–'

'There you are, then,' said Derek. 'Now pass the sugar and don't blether so much.'

'What time did you get in last night, Derek?' asked Mr. Wilson.

'Four. You don't know what work is, you policemen. Snooping round marking the spot where the body occurred with a bit of chalk, and then going home to your hot-water bottle. While we poor benighted reporters have to stay up all night concocting a juicy story for our nitwit readers.'

'Find anything?'

'Nope. I rang up Miss Astle, bless her. Unfortunately she'd been rung up earlier in the morning by the *Morning Herald*, the *Daily News*, the *Daily Observer*, the *Morning Courier*, and practically everyone else except the *Christian Herald* and the *Feathered World*. All she said was, "Oh, go to hell!" Just like that. Crisply and snappily. Not a bit lady-likely. Not even leading-lady-likely. But I made a half-column exclusive interview out of it, so it didn't really matter.'

'Funny business, isn't it?'

'Think so? You've a queer sense of humour, then. Pass the mustard.'

'Can't you reach for anything?' said Mr. Wilson peevishly. 'No, but I mean ... when a bloke kills another bloke he doesn't usually choose the centre of a floodlit stage, with two thousand people looking on, as the most suitable place for doing it.'

'Agreed. Usually he chooses the depths of Pine Tree Crook, or the deserted quarry down Badger's Lane, or the backside of the Battersea Power Station. In this case he didn't, though. I suppose nine out of every ten murderers are on the verge of insanity when they actually commit the dirty deed. And this fellow Foster was the tenth. He was completely loopy.'

'But why? Why did he do it at all?'

'Search me,' said the younger Wilson. 'Perhaps dear Brandon cut in on his best line in the show. He had only about three to say in the whole night, so far as I could see. Enough to make any-one murder anyone.'

'I was speaking to Douglas about him last night. It seems he's had parts in Douglas's show for a good many years back now, and D.B.D. ventured the opinion that Mr. Hilary Foster was one of the two sober, respectable, quiet-living men connected with the British Stage to-day.'

'Did he say who was the other?'

'No. He didn't. I gathered it was himself.'

'Joke over,' said Mr. Wilson, junr. 'That bacon's a bit obstinate, isn't it?'

'It's all wrong, you see, Derek. If Foster were a highly strung, temperamental sort of fellow, you could have understood him doing Brandon Baker in in that way. If he were the kind of man who

43

might have been one angle in an eternal triangle, another angle of which was the said Brandon – you could have understood it again. But he wasn't. A most respectable married man, with a wife and three children in Winchmore Hill. A man who went straight home from the theatre every night and had malted milk and biscuits in front of the fire. It's all wrong, I tell you.'

'I don't see what's biting you,' said Derek. 'The thing's as plain as your face–'

'May I remind you that a great many people, including your Aunt Susan, are of the opinion that you take after me in looks?'

'Hard words,' said Mr. Wilson, junr.

'I agree,' said Mr. Wilson, senr. 'Go on.'

'I don't see anything to worry about. A fires at B with a revolver. B dies gracefully in the glare of three spotlights and to the accompaniment of an augmented orchestra, under the direction of M. René Whoever-it-was. A very nice death, I'm sure. A then does a bunk and is found suspended from a suitable beam in his dressing-room. Deductions from the foregoing, one, murder of B by A. And two, suicide of A as a result of murdering B. I should have thought the whole thing was absolutely straightforward, even to a detective.'

'Thanks very much,' said Mr. Wilson.

'I suppose you're worrying about a motive?' asked Derek.

'No, I'm not. I think far too much fuss is made about motives. I once spent three months concocting a perfectly wonderful motive for a gentleman named Hepplewaite, who battered his wife more or less to pulp with a frying-pan in the

44

autumn of 1928. An absolutely cast-iron motive, I had, for the poor chap's carrying-ons. It turned out eventually that he was subject to violent epileptic seizures and hadn't the slightest idea what he was doing.'

'Too bad,' said Derek sympathetically. 'More coffee, please, dad. What is worrying you, then?'

'The bit of plaster where the bullet hit the proscenium wall,' said Mr. Wilson, pouring out simultaneous flows of black coffee and hot milk like an expert.

Mr. Wilson's son and heir wiped a few odds and ends of egg from around his mouth and looked interested.

'Well?' he asked.

'It was about four feet too high,' said Mr. Wilson. 'If you draw a little triangle–'

'Isosceles or eternal?' asked Derek, drawing several on the table-cloth with the prongs of his fork.

'Right-angled, as a matter of fact,' said Mr. Wilson. 'Put Mr. Foster at the top of one side with a revolver in his hand. And put Mr. Baker at the end of the other side opposite the right angle, with a half-naked dancer in his arms. Make Mr. Foster shoot a bullet bang at Mr. Baker, and what happens? Unless Mr. Baker has abnormally chromium-plated bones inside him, the bullet goes on *downwards* after passing through his innards. In this case it didn't. Apparently Mr. Baker's heart was so hard that it was deflected up again, and went on almost parallel with the level of the stage until its little journey was stopped by the proscenium. Do you get me?'

'Not exactly,' said Derek. 'You mean that the bullet ought to have been buried at the very bottom of the proscenium instead of about five feet up?'

'Quite. For a reporter you're very quick at picking up things. In fact, I'm not so sure that it would have ended up in the proscenium at all. More likely it would have hit the actual stage. Or gone on and put amen to the fellow who bangs the percussion in the orchestra. That's how any respectable bullet would have behaved under the circumstances. But, of course, this is all supposition. Mr. Baker may have the kind of heart that deflects bullets. I don't know. I've never had to deal with the murder of an actor before. There's one way we can find out, though.'

'And that is?'

'Go round to the theatre and reconstruct the crime. Have you finished eating?'

'I've finished what there is to eat, so I suppose so,' said Derek. 'Are you going now?'

'Yes,' said Mr. Wilson. 'Are you busy, or can you come along?'

'I'm covering the Baker murder case for the *Gazette*, as it happens,' said Mr. Wilson, junr.

'My God!' said Mr. Wilson, senr. 'All right. Go and get your collar and tie on.'

'Same conditions as usual, dad,' said Derek. 'You don't keep anything up your sleeve, and I don't give the paper anything without your permission. Okay?'

'Okay,' said Mr. Wilson. 'If you must use such a vulgar expression.'

There is nothing quite so depressing as an

46

empty theatre. In comparison, morgues are merry. The dust-sheets stretched sadly over row after row of red-plush seats, the dirty plaster ornaments on the walls looking filthier than ever in the half-light, the stage a drab and dismal affair robbed of its scenery and curtains and lighting. It is a funny thing that the wise housewife, if she wishes to conceal the fact that she missed dusting the top of the mantelpiece this morning, dims the lights in her sitting-room as much as possible; whereas the wise man of the theatre, in the same situation, switches on every ounce, therm, unit, or whatever it is of his candle-power and makes everything shining and dazzling in the glare.

Wilson *père et fils* arrived at the Grosvenor at half past ten, having called in at Mr. Douglas B. Douglas's office en route to obtain permission to look over the theatre and a large bunch of keys to help them in the job. Three buxom charladies were scouring the foyer entrance very thoroughly. They knew quite well that there would be no performance that night, but they had not yet received orders to down tools, and they were blessed if they were going to lose a full week's salary if they could help it.

'I wish people would be more careful where they're putting their feet,' said the most buxom of the three pointedly as Mr. Wilson and Derek stepped across the marble floor of the foyer.

'I'm so sorry,' said Derek. 'My father's a policeman, and you know what policemen's feet are. No restraint.'

'It's you I'm talking to,' said the charlady, wringing out a scouring-cloth in a vicious manner.

'Look at them marks there. Didn't you see the mat as you came in? Really, if a poor 'ard-working woman 'asn't enough to do without–'

'Ha!' said Mr. Wilson, senr.

'Come on, you,' said Mr. Wilson, junr.

The only other inhabitant of the theatre appeared to be an elderly man with a beery moustache who lived most of his life in a little glass case at the stage entrance, handling letters to the chorus from their boy friends, and keeping the boy friends themselves at a safe distance. ''Ere, 'ere, 'ere, 'ere!' said this gentlemen, on catching sight of the Wilson family. 'What d'you think you're a-doing of, you two, eh? 'Ere, 'ere, out of 'ere. *'Ere!'*

'Hear, hear,' said Derek.

'Shut up,' said Mr. Wilson. 'I'm sorry to trouble you. I'm Inspector Wilson from Scotland Yard. I have Mr. Douglas's permission to look over the theatre in connection with the murder of Mr. Baker last night.'

'Oh,' said the gentleman with the beerstained moustache, obviously impressed. 'Scotland Yard, eh? Arrr. Go right ahead, sir, in that cise. Sorry to ave cort you up sharp-like, but you've got to be careful-like, especially arfter larst night's to-do.'

'Quite so,' said Mr. Wilson. 'Is there anyone in the theatre? Any of the stage staff, I mean?'

''Erbert's 'ere,' said the moustache.

'Splendid' said Mr. Wilson, and went in search of Herbert.

Herbert was making a wonderfully successful attempt to dismantle Act Two, Scene One, of *Blue Music* (The Rebel's Stronghold in the

48

Moroccan Hills) alone and unaided, and pack it neatly away until further required. He had half of the Stronghold folded flat against the wings of the stage when the Wilsons appeared.

'Hi!' said Mr. Wilson.

''Morning, sir,' said Herbert.

'Don't take that bit down. I want it.'

'You're welcome to it,' said Herbert. 'Heaviest bit of ruddy scenery I've ever handled.'

'Dad's come to reconstruct the crime,' said Derek. 'You'll upset everything, moving about all the little clues like mountains, you know.'

'Sorry, sir,' said Herbert. 'Didn't think you'd be here again. I thought everything was more or less settled up now that poor Mr. Foster was found ... you know.'

'I know,' said Mr. Wilson. 'Just idle curiosity, that's all. Herbert, would you mind being Mr. Foster for the next few minutes?'

'Eh?' said Herbert, feeling his collar.

'On the mountain. Not in the dressing-room. Go and stand as near as possible to the spot where he stood, will you? Oh, and take one end of this bit of string with you. Go on, man, don't look so worried. It's string – not rope.'

'I don't know how you can say such things, sir,' said Herbert, and scaled what was left of the Stronghold.

'Now,' said Mr. Wilson, 'I'm going to be poor Mr. Baker this time. Where's that chalk-mark? Ah, yes... He'd stand about here, wouldn't he? Derek, get hold of that string and pull it tight towards me.'

'What is all this?' asked Derek. 'Knotty Tests for

49

Britain's Boy Scouts?'

'More or less,' said Mr. Wilson. 'Bring it over here. Keep it tight. Okay, as you would say in your disgusting slanguage. Put it on the pocket of my overcoat. Hold it there. Now I'm going to collapse gracefully on the stage, just as Mr. Baker did, poor chap. And I want you to carry on the string, keeping it perfectly tight, until something stops you.'

Mr. Wilson collapsed, but not gracefully. Mr. Wilson, junr., walked on with his bit of string, very nearly pulling Herbert off the Stronghold in obeying his father's remark about keeping it tight. The line of the bullet which ended Brandon Baker's brilliant career came to an end itself exactly where the stage and the proscenium met.

'You see?' said Mr. Wilson, getting up and dusting himself. 'Now that's a sensible sort of place for a bullet to land in the circumstances. Now let's try to find out why it didn't. What about a little more light on the subject? This place is about as well-lit as Erebus.'

'Where?' asked Derek.

'Erebus,' said Mr. Wilson. 'A village in Fife. The main street is lit by two oil-lamps. Go up that ladder, Derek, and pull a few switches.'

'Third from the left, top row, sir,' shouted Herbert from the heights. 'That's the house lights. And the one next to it is your battens.'

Derek pulled a few switches as ordered, but not, apparently, as advised. The first resulted in a green spotlight being centred on Mr. Wilson's bowler-hat.

'You do look nice, dad,' said Derek. 'Like that

50

time at Dover. You'd make a most attractive Demon King, really. "But stop, my fairy foe, and not so fast. My evil powers are not yet past."'

'Shut up!' said Mr. Wilson. 'And put on some lights.'

Mr. Wilson, junr., tried again. The house-lights went up and then down. A blue spot appeared on the back curtain. At the fourth attempt, the entire theatre was plunged in darkness. It was then that a door slammed and a pair of feet were heard running at a pretty pace up the side gangway of the auditorium.

'Who's that?' barked Mr. Wilson. 'Who the hell's that?'

Another door slammed.

'Derek, lights, for God's sake!'

More by good luck than careful selection, Mr. Wilson, junr., found the right switch and flooded the stage with light.

'Who the hell was that?' asked Mr. Wilson.

'There's no one in the theatre, except the cleaners and the stage-doorkeeper and the three of us,' said Herbert. 'I know that for certain, sir.'

'That was no cleaner ... nor the old boy at the stage-door, from the pace he was moving at. Derek!'

'*Adsum,*' said Derek.

'Go round to the main entrance and see if anyone's gone out past the cleaners.'

'The life you policemen lead...' said Derek. 'I don't know how you find time to do anything, you're so busy giving orders. All right, I'll go.'

'Queer, sir,' said Herbert.

'Damned queer.'

'Can I come down now, sir?'

'Eh? Oh yes, come on down. You've been a great help, Herbert. I'll see you get a peerage for this.'

'Thank you, sir,' said Herbert. 'They've been given for less, I've no doubt, sir.'

'Hey!' said Derek from the other side of the curtain.

Mr. Wilson poked his face round the curtain. The theatre itself was still in darkness. He could just make out the figure of his son and heir leaning against the brass rail of the orchestra pit.

'Well?' said Mr. Wilson. 'Anything?'

'Yes. A man went out of the main entrance at a hell of a lick. The chars are all het up about their lovely clean marble slab. They didn't have time to take the fellow in, but they think he was a tall thinnish bloke in a light-grey overcoat and a dark felt hat!'

'That might be Mr. Douglas, sir,' said Herbert, appearing suddenly around the curtain. 'Except that he's fat.'

'It might be Ramsay Macdonald,' said Mr. Wilson. 'Except that he wears horn-rimmed glasses and is at Geneva at the moment.'

'But hey!' said Derek. 'That's not all, folks. Come down here. I've had an idea.'

'You ought to print that in your paper as Today's Colossal Sensation,' said Mr. Wilson, climbing over the conductor's desk and out into the auditorium. 'What is it?'

'Do you see what I see?' asked Derek.

'It all depends,' said Mr. Wilson. 'Probably not.'

Ever noticed, when a curtain in a theatre

52

doesn't quite fit, or has been pulled off the straight, or is rather the worse for wear, how very clearly you can see the goings-on on the stage through the little slice of brilliant light that comes through? A pair of dancers' shoes, a chink of scenery, something like that? It is the invariable habit in amateur theatricals for the members of the cast to have a squint through the curtain to see if their sisters and aunts are in their seats yet. They can't possibly be seen, they think; yet if only they could see themselves as the audience sees them! The glare of the stage-lights reveals everything in a curtain that isn't altogether protective.

'I see,' said Derek, pointing to where the two halves of the curtain met in the centre of the stage, 'a small round hole. And ... just a minute, while I climb up. Yes. If that isn't a bullet-hole, then I'm a Nazi!'

'Very interesting,' said Mr. Wilson, climbing after his offspring and inspecting the hole carefully. 'You're right, for once. It is a bullet-hole.'

'Gosh!' said Derek. 'Don't you see, nit-wit? The shot was fired from the audience. By someone who knew the play, who knew that a shot was going to be fired at Brandon Baker during the play, by someone who synchronized his own shot with the one fired by the Foster fellow. Gosh!... What a story!'

'It's not a story,' said Mr. Wilson. 'It's a myth. Derek, you're raving. You seem to forget that when Brandon Baker was murdered the curtain was up.'

'Oh,' said Derek. 'Yes, there is that to consider, isn't there? Hell and blast!'

'Exactly. But you've got us moving, at any rate. Herbert ... could you pull the curtains along, please? Right along, just as they would be when the murder took place. Thanks ... now, Derek, come on up on the stage.'

The curtains rolled smoothly along, their folds billowing until they anchored safely at each side of the stage.

'Right, Herbert,' said Mr. Wilson. 'Stand just where you are for the moment, will you? That's just about where Baker was standing when he was shot. Now, let's see...'

Mr. Wilson produced his favourite pipe from his jacket pocket. Instead of going through the usual rites of cleaning and filling and lighting, he held it by the bowl at about the level of his shoulders.

'Look along there, son,' he said. 'We could go through all our little performance with the string again, but it's hardly necessary. Even a youth of your intelligence can tell that three very important things – the mark where the bullet landed in the proscenium wall, the position occupied by the late Brandon Baker's heart, and the little round hole in this curtain – are all as near as dammit in a straight line with this pipe. Substitute revolver for pipe, and what have you?'

'My God!' said Derek. 'You mean – Brandon Baker was murdered by someone standing in this spot?'

'I didn't say anything of the kind,' said Mr. Wilson. 'But I do say that at some time in the history of this theatre a man (or a woman) has stood concealed behind this curtain and fired a bullet straight across the stage so that it buried itself in the wall of the proscenium opposite. And I should be very much surprised if it didn't happen at exactly the moment when the unfortunate Mr. Foster fired *his* little revolver from the Heights of Abraham yonder. It would be much the most convenient time to choose, don't you think?'

CHAPTER FOUR

Keeping well to the true theatrical traditions to the bitter end, the funeral of and inquest on Mr. Brandon Baker clashed magnificently on the following Friday. The funeral (memorial service at St. Oswald's, interment afterwards at Gloucester Street Cemetery) and the inquest (at the Craven Street coroner's court) were both timed for eleven-thirty. It is really rather wonderful how the people of the Theatre manage these things.

Mr. Douglas B. Douglas had postponed the first night of *Blue Music* from the previous Thursday (when it would have clashed with the opening of *Never A Care* at the Ambassador's, a show in which Mr. Douglas had a fair amount of money) until the Tuesday (when it clashed splendidly with the first performance of *Brothers And Others* at the Duke of York's, a show in which Mr. Douglas had no money at all). Not that the public objected to the clashing; they went, of course, to *Blue Music,* and the play at the Duke of York's had to be papered so liberally that it began to look like a wallpaper emporium.

The Friday clash of funeral and inquest was a much more serious affair. The Brandon Baker Gallery Club went practically delirious over it, and went so far as to present a petition to the Craven Street coroner demanding that the inquest on their late idol be postponed until a quarter to one, in order to give them a sporting chance of doing both shows.

In vain; and the problem was settled satisfactorily only by those families who numbered two or more members of the Gallery Club in their ranks. In these fortunate cases, Cissie went to the inquest and Agnes to the funeral, and met for tea and kippers at four in the afternoon to exchange their eyewitness accounts.

It also bothered the Wilson family quite a lot. Not because the Wilson family was at all desirous of attending either proceedings, and being crushed to a state worse than death in order to bring home a copy of the order of service for the funeral as a souvenir, or to listen to Mr. Halliwell Ogle, the Craven Street coroner, shedding wisecracks all through in the inquiry into Brandon Baker's death. But Mr. Wilson, senr., made a point, whenever possible, of putting in an appearance at the funerals and inquests of any unfortunate folk whose departure from this life he was investigating. And Mr. Wilson, junr., had been commanded to show his face and note-book at both performances by an editor who – as editors will – saw no reason why one reporter should not be in more than one place at one time.

'There's only one thing for it,' said Mr. Wilson,

junr., caught once again in the act of stoking himself with coffee and grapefruit. 'Toss.'

'Toss?' said Mr. Wilson, senr.

'Toss,' said Derek. 'It's the only satisfactory way of settling anything in this house. Got half a crown on you?'

'Why half a crown?' asked Mr. Wilson, producing the coin named.

'It's much the best coin for tossing' said Derek. 'Now, listen. Heads you go to the funeral, tails I do. Heads you give me a two-column report of the farewell performance for the *Gazette*. Tails you give me a half-page verbatim account of what happened at the inquest. Heads I tell you anything that I heard at the inquest that might be in your line. Tails I tell you if I've seen anyone behaving suspicious-like at the graveside. Understand?'

'Not a word of it,' said Mr. Wilson. 'But never mind. Toss.'

Mr. Wilson, junr., tossed.

'What does that mean?' said Mr. Wilson, senr., removing the half-crown from a perfectly vertical position in the butter-dish and wiping it with his napkin. 'Do we both go to both?'

'That was a little slip,' said Derek. 'We try again, like Bruce and the burnt cakes. Keep your hand over that pot of marmalade. There ... heads. You for the funeral – me for the inquest. Thank God. I haven't a black tie to my name.'

'You'll be able to buy one now,' said Mr. Wilson, noticing his half-crown disappear slickly into the pocket of his son and heir's dressing-gown. 'Righto. I'll go and put on the sad rags. I've got to go along to the Yard after it's over, and see old

Anderson about the bullet they pulled out of the plaster. We'll meet here for a spot of food at sevenish and swap stories, eh?'

'Remember you're covering the funeral for me,' said Derek. 'Don't miss anything. What all the actresses were wearing, who was sobbing hysterically, all that bunk. Seven o'clock here. Oke.'

'Please...' said Mr. Wilson in a pained voice. 'Not oke, Derek. Okay, if you really must give way to these vulgar Americanisms. But not oke.'

'Okay,' said Derek obligingly, and went upstairs to finish his dressing.

From the fortunate position in which we are situated, we can follow both Mr. Wilson, senr., to St. Oswald's, and Mr. Wilson, junr., to the Craven Street police court.

Wilson *père*, then, followed his son upstairs, dressed himself tastefully in black jacket, striped trousers, hard collar, black tie, and bowler hat, and went out to the memorial service looking rather like a stockbroker who had just been the victim of a strong bull movement. He arrived outside the church at ten minutes to eleven, exactly forty minutes (if our mathematics are still functioning correctly) before the rites were due to begin. 'Outside the church' is perhaps an exaggeration, for Mr. Wilson was unable to get anywhere nearer the main entrance of St. Oswald's than some fifty yards further south on the opposite pavement.

The membership of the Brandon Baker Gallery Club was reckoned to be slightly over two hundred thousand persons at the last census, and it seemed to Mr. Wilson that every man, woman and child of that two hundred thousand were trying to get inside St. Oswald's at the moment, having brought with them their husbands, wives, sisters, and next-door neighbours to share in the fun. Mr. Wilson had once had to carry out an investigation during the last day of a remnant sale in a London store, and from what he could remember of it that experience was about as quiet and unexciting (in comparison to this) as a Sabbath evening at the North Pole. He edged his way skilfully through the crowd and arrived on the correct pavement with only his bowler hat missing.

Here, Mr. Wilson found that most of the Metropolitan Police Force had been brought on the scene, and were managing by sheer brute strength to keep a narrow gangway clear leading up to the church door. Mr. Wilson at this point had a heated altercation with a small woman carrying a string-bag, who said *(a)* that she'd come all the way in from Golder's Green to see the funeral; *(b)* that she'd seen every show poor dear Brandon ever acted in; *(c)* that it was a crying shame if a lifelong supporter of poor dear Brandon couldn't even get inside the church; *(d)* that there was no need to push like that; and *(e)* that this was no place for a man, anyway, and Mr. Wilson would be better employed doing a bit of honest work than wasting his mornings looking at funerals.

Mr. Wilson could have said quite a lot in reply to this last line of argument, but thought better of it and continued to wedge his way towards the cordon of bobbies. Arriving there eventually with his collar and tie pulled out of all connection

59

with each other, Mr. Wilson tapped the nearest bobby on the shoulder and said, 'Excuse me.'

'No good, sir,' said the constable. 'Church full. Only them what has tickets allowed in now.'

'I'm Inspector Wilson of Scotland Yard,' said Mr. Wilson. 'I'm in charge of this case. Don't you think I really ought to be allowed in?'

'Insp – why, so it is, sir,' said the constable. 'Didn't recognize you, sir. Lost your 'at, 'aven't you, sir? Certainly, sir. Step underneath, sir.' And *pianissimo:* 'There's a block of seats still vacant under the west gallery.'

'Thank you,' said Mr. Wilson, and stepped under the arms of the law and into the church.

'That's Douglas B. Douglas, the perducer,' said a large woman, swaying against the police cordon as he passed.

'Don't talk barmy,' said her neighbour, a complete stranger. ''Enry Hainley, that is. I'd know 'im a mile orf.'

Mr. Wilson walked past, impressed by the second woman's intelligence. The church was already practically full, though, as the constable had said, three rows of seats were still vacant under the west gallery. Mr. Wilson sat down as reverently as possible in a corner of the back pew, and took a look round. It was certainly going to be a very good funeral. The church was decorated in a lavish fashion with arum lilies, scarlet carnations, and white lilac – all three of which, Mr. Wilson gathered from conversation going on round about him, had been dear Brandon's favourite flower.

The more expensive wreaths had been grouped tastefully around the altar to add colour to the scene, and were being photographed in close-up by a quick succession of Press photographers. *From D.B.D., in affectionate memory of a long and valued acquaintanceship. From the Grosvenor Theatre staff, in appreciation. From Gwen, with all my love.* Mr. Wilson recognized a number of well-known stage and screen personalities sitting in what he thought would be better described as the stalls than the pews. There was no mourning – Brandon wouldn't have liked it – and this had given the audience-congregation an opportunity of displaying their latest and loudest in the way of hats and dresses. Altogether, Mr. Wilson decided, Brandon Baker's last performance was much more brilliant than his unfortunate first London performance in the musical comedy *Blue Music*.

The service droned on and finished at last. Mr. Wilson thought he was going to be very sick at what happened after that. The clergy had hardly billowed out through the door leading to the vestry at the end of the service, when the animal instinct in the Gallery Club members who had obtained admission to the church came up to the very top. It could never, Mr. Wilson thought, have been very far down. They stormed the pews like a mass attack going over the top in the trenches. They ripped the church bare of its lilies, carnations and lilac inside a couple of minutes. Not content with the flowers and the order of service pamphlets, they removed large chunks from the prayer-books and hymnals strewn on the pews. Mr. Wilson, at one time, caught sight of fifteen different celebrities signing fifteen different autograph books in front of the altar. The woman who had recognized him as Henry Ainley must have found or forced her way into the church, she came storming down the aisle and found her victim sitting in a dazed condition at the end of his pew. 'Please – there's a duck,' she said, thrusting her album in front of Mr. Wilson's nose.

'Delighted,' said Mr. Wilson, and signed it gravely.

'Thanks, ever so,' said the woman, and shot off to conquests new. Mr. Wilson hoped that she would not read what he had written until she got safely home. He waited in his seat until the church had emptied, which it did speedily, the Gallery Club remembering suddenly that they simply mustn't miss seeing the cortège leave the side door on its way to the cemetery. Mr. Wilson got up sadly, looked for his bowler hat under the seat, and then remembered that it had gone for all time in the big push. He was half-way up the aisle when he noticed that the church was not yet completely empty. A little woman in black was sitting at the end of one of the side pews. Mr. Wilson did not like to look too closely, but imagined that she was crying.

'Not pretty, was it?' said Mr. Wilson.

'No,' said the woman. 'Not a bit pretty.'

'Did you know him?' asked Mr. Wilson, not quite knowing why he was asking such a question.

'Not well,' said the woman. 'He was my husband.'

Mr. Wilson saw no answer to this at all. He walked quietly out of the church, and commiserated with the caretaker whom he met at the entrance on the results of the battle.

'Give me weddings,' said the man vehemently. 'Every blasted time. I used to think that filthy confetti was the last word. But give me weddings rather than this. Any damned day!'

Mr. Wilson agreed that a wedding, even with the many drawbacks, of which confetti is perhaps the least, would have been preferable to the ceremony just ended. He then bought a new bowler and went to the Yard in a very bad temper.

'Jackson,' said Mr. Wilson to the first person he saw on arriving at the Yard, 'do you know what I've discovered this morning?'

'No, sir,' said Jackson. 'What, sir?'

'We arrest all the wrong people.'

And Mr. Wilson shot off to meet Mr. Anderson, the noted expert on firearms, leaving Jackson to puzzle out this remark.

So much for the funeral. They say a celebrity cannot call his life his own. If the case of Brandon Baker is anything like a typical case, it is quite certain that no celebrity would wish to call his death his own.

On to the inquest.

Now an inquest, like a plate of sago, is a dull thing. The reasons for this fact being twofold. One, the regrettably unoriginal way in which most people put an end to their lives. And two, the regrettably unoriginal way in which most coroners conduct their enquiries. Nothing, it seems, can be done about the first of these two, short of inventing a poison which turns you tartan, or a new kind of bullet which makes you swell for a fortnight and then burst. But something can be most definitely done about the second. And was done, in the case of Mr. Halliwell Ogle, the Craven Street coroner.

Mr. Ogle used to preside over a stuffy little courtroom in the wilds of Northumbria, where nothing more exciting happened than a motor-cycle smash or a death from using methylated spirits – as a lubricating rather than a cleansing fluid. Even to these paltry affairs Mr. Ogle managed to bring a nice wit, a twinkling eye, a merry wisecrack, and a delightful ingenuity in introducing his own caustic opinions on the world in general, no matter how little they had to do with the case in hand.

He was obviously wasted in Wooler (the village in Northumberland where he held sway). Wasted – until one lucky day a Power That Was happened to enter Mr. Ogle's little courtroom to give evidence in an inquest where his Daimler had been regrettably bruised and a yokel unavoidably massacred. The Power at once saw how wasted Mr. Ogle was in his present position, went back to London at once, and pulled several strings in several different directions. The result of which string-pulling being that Mr. Ogle was transferred from his stuffy court in Wooler, Northumberland, to a rather stuffier one in Craven Street, London. To the annoyance of Wooler, but to the intense delight of the London Press, who – whenever they had a dull day – went along to Craven Street in a bunch to pick up a few of Mr. Ogle's witticisms for their middle pages. 'London Coroner's Amusing Sallies.' 'Coroner's Pungent Views on Modern Girl.' 'Coroner's Wit Enlivens London Inquest.' You see that sort of thing in half-inch headlines nearly every day now, and ten times out often it refers to Mr. Halliwell Ogle.

Derek Wilson had nearly, but not quite, as much trouble getting inside the Craven Street court buildings as his father had had getting inside St. Oswald's church. He had a good deal to say later in the day when his father suggested that all the two hundred thousand of the Gallery Club were present at the memorial service, for it was perfectly obvious that nearly a hundred and fifty thousand of the poor saps were here at Craven Street.

'Press,' said Derek, having at last reached the door.

'Press?' said the constable on duty wittily. 'I should ruddy well think it is a press. Never seen nothing like it no time, I haven't! Press, indeed … gorblimey, I've been at Arsenal matches what was nothing to this. I should ruddy well think it is a press, and no mistake!'

'Very amusing,' said Derek, and forced his way inside to join the other reporters at the I-should-ruddy-well-think-it-is-a-press benches.

Mr. Ogle appeared punctually at eleven-thirty. He looked benignly round the court. A full house. Newspaper men here in full force. Very satisfactory. A very good opportunity for getting rid of that pithy little soliloquy on the Betting Laws that had come to him suddenly in his bath that morning. Yes, vote of thanks to Mr. Brandon Baker for passing away in his district. First witness, please.

First witness, Mr. John Hackett. Brother of the deceased. A tall, thin man with a moustache which would have been mistaken for an error in shaving if it had been one hair less.

'I was asked to go to Craven Street mortuary on Wednesday morning to identify the body of the deceased. I identified the body as that of my brother, Ernest Hackett, professionally known as Brandon Baker.'

'Why did your brother change his name when he went on the stage, Mr. Hackett?' asked Mr. Ogle for no good reason.

'I don't know, sir,' said Mr. Hackett. 'Hackett isn't a very suitable name for an actor, I suppose, sir.'

'Oh, I don't know,' said Mr. Ogle, beaming. 'What about Tod Slaughter?'

(Laughter in Court.)

'It's the same *rough* idea, surely?' continued Mr. Ogle, well pleased with the house's reception.

(Renewed Laughter in Court.)

Next witness, Dr. Armitage. Slow and dull. Next, Mr. Douglas B. Douglas himself. Mr. Douglas had been called away to the inquest in the middle of launching rather tricky negotiations with a Broadway musical-comedy star to take the leading part in *Blue Music* when the show was revived. He was in no mood for Mr. Ogle.

'You are, I believe, connected with the theatrical profession?' asked Mr. Ogle serenely.

'I am the theatrical profession,' said Mr. Douglas.

'Were you at the theatre on the night of the occurrence?'

Mr. Douglas laid his chin on his knuckles and looked Mr. Ogle straight in the eye.

'Considering that I had put over fifty thousand pounds of my own hard-earned money into the show,' said Mr. Douglas, 'considering that I had travelled over twelve thousand miles to secure the right cast and scenic designers and composer for the show; considering that I had worked fourteen hours a day for seven days a week during the rehearsals of the show; considering all that,' said Mr. Douglas, rather out of breath, 'it is not surprising that I *was* present on the opening night of *Blue Music.*'

'Quite,' said Mr. Ogle, rather taken aback. 'Now would you tell us what you saw, please? Without, perhaps, quite so much consideration.'

'I saw the beginnings of a damn' fine show,' said Mr. Douglas, realizing that even an inquest can be good for the box-office.

'I mean – what you saw of the actual happening with which we are concerned?'

'Oh!' said Mr. Douglas. 'Well, I was in a box. A stage-box, the one on the prompt side.'

'So termed, I understand, because its occupants invariably arrive late?' observed Mr. Ogle.

'I had a party of five with me,' said Mr. Douglas, ignoring the coroner. 'At the beginning of the second act of the show there was a big ensemble number by the chorus. Then Mr. Baker and Miss Turner were left alone on the stage. Mr. Foster had to enter from the O.P. side–'

'The what side?' asked Mr. Ogle.

'B.F.,' said Mr. Douglas tersely.

'Quite,' said Mr. Ogle, not quite knowing. 'Continue, please.'

'–And fire at Mr. Baker with a revolver. The gun he used was supposed to be a dummy one; the report was made by someone off-stage. Mr.

Baker was supposed to receive only a flesh wound; he had to fall on the stage, raise himself on to his knees, draw his own revolver, and shoot at Mr. Foster as he was escaping.'

'But this did not actually happen on the night in question?' said Mr. Ogle.

'Considering–' began Mr. Douglas, and realized the futility of it. 'No, it didn't. Mr. Baker fell on the stage. I realized something was the matter when he didn't get up right away. Then I saw a little blood ooze out on the stage. I went round to the wings and found he'd been killed. That's all.'

'And quite enough, so far as Mr. Baker was concerned, I'm sure,' said Mr. Ogle. 'Have you known the deceased long, Mr. Douglas?'

'Forty-two years,' said Mr. Douglas.

'Forty-two years,' echoed Mr. Ogle. 'I understood that Mr. Baker was what is known as a juvenile lead?'

'Doesn't mean a thing,' said Mr. Douglas cruelly.

'Surely to say that a man of over fifty was juvenile leading was – if I may say so – definitely juvenile misleading?'

'I've a cabaret on at the Troxy,' observed Mr. Douglas chattily. 'We need a good low comedian. Care to come along?'

'Next witness, please,' said Mr. Ogle sternly.

Next witness, Miss Eve Turner (Coletta, a Native Dancer). Corroborated previous witness's evidence re shot, fall, scream, oozing blood. Added that she'd never been so cut up in all her life, and that her legs went all wonky when she realized what had happened. Asked by Mr. Ogle

68

to give a demonstration of Native Dancing, replied archly that the witness-stand was hardly a suitable place for same, but hadn't she heard something about coroners having private rooms away at the back of the court somewhere?

After Miss Turner, Herbert. Corroborated Mr. Douglas's and Miss Turner's evidence. Added that he had personally dropped the curtain, sent for a doctor, cleared the stage, kept the show going, summoned Mr. Douglas, revived the leading lady, got hold of a police inspector, wiped up the mess on the stage and closed the theatre for the night.

'A useful man,' said Mr. Ogle. 'You should play Pooh-Bah.'

'Thank you, sir,' said Herbert, clicking his heels, turning smartly, and exiting in a military manner.

Next witness, Mrs. Mary Johnson, née Mary Foster, sister and only living relative of the late J. Hilary Foster. Questioned about her brother's relations with Brandon Baker, said she knew of no possible reason why Foster should kill Baker. They had worked together for a good many years, and so far as she knew there had never been any quarrel or enmity between them. No, her brother had not behaved in any way out of the ordinary recently, though she had not seen him for some weeks before the happening. He had been rather worried during the past few months, but that was due to purely personal reasons and had nothing to do with his stage career. No, he did not keep a revolver; at least, she had never seen such a thing in his possession. The whole thing was a complete mystery to her; she was quite certain that Hilary had not killed Brandon Baker intentionally.

'Thank you, Mrs. Johnson,' said the coroner.

Next and last witness, Sir Basil Bone. Well-known post-mortem expert. Explained, in a few well-chosen but rather too-technical phrases, exactly how Brandon Baker had met his end. During this recitation, Mr. Ogle shut his eyes and stroked his chin thoughtfully, remembering how simply that old doctor in Northumberland used to say exactly the same thing.

'Quite so, Sir Basil,' said Mr. Ogle. 'From your examination of the body, there is no doubt that the bullet which killed Brandon Baker was fired from the position occupied by the man Foster – as described by the previous witnesses?'

'None whatever,' said Sir Basil.

'It is impossible that the shot was fired from any other part of the stage or theatre?'

'Absolutely impossible.'

'Thank you, Sir Basil. That is all, thank you.'

'One in the eye for old man Wilson,' said Derek to himself.

'Pardon?' said his neighbouring journalist.

'I was wondering whether old Basil's hair is all, part, or none his own,' said Derek.

'Part,' said the other reporter. 'Down to about square-leg, I should say. I was at a murder trial once when the rest slipped off.'

'Thanks very much,' said Derek. 'So nice to know.'

Mr. Ogle summed up wittily, bringing in the bit about the Betting Laws without the slightest difficulty.

'The finding of this Court is that Brandon

Baker died as the result of a wound in the heart, caused by a bullet fired by Hilary Foster.'

The courtroom emptied. From the remarks of two passing members of the Gallery Club, Derek decided that it was a good thing for J. Hilary Foster that he was not in a position to enjoy a lynching. 'The brute,' said Gallery Clubber number one. 'The great brute! I never liked that man. I saw him years ago at the Empire in *Here's A Howdydoo!* – we were in the very front row of the pit, and we couldn't hear a word he said.'

'Such a face he had, too,' said Clubber number two. 'Evil, that's what it was. 'Course he only got the villain parts. Killing poor dear Brandon in cold blood, like that. It's awful. There'll never be another to take his place. They say that new Hungarian actor at the Metropole's terribly good-looking. Seen him?'

The chatter in the court died away. Derek and his reporter colleague stayed behind for a moment, engaged in a slight controversy over the spelling of 'indisputably'. Having settled this at last, they turned to leave the court. There was only one other person left in it. A small woman in a dark navy costume. She was crying into a lamentably inadequate handkerchief.

'There's a story in that,' said Derek.

'You talk like the pressmen on the talkies,' said the other reporter.

'Just a minute. You go on ahead.'

'Exclusive Scoop by *Daily Gazette* Cub Reporter. I want my lunch.'

'God bless you,' said Derek.

The woman in the navy costume had got up to

71

leave the court, still dabbing at her eyes.

'Excuse me...' said Derek.

'Well?'

'Anything I can do? You look a bit upset.'

'It's nothing, thanks. Nothing at all.'

'Was he ... was he a great favourite of yours?' asked Derek, thinking of the business the laundries would have this week, with two hundred thousand weeping Gallery Club members.

'Not exactly,' said the woman in navy. 'He was my husband.'

CHAPTER FIVE

'The funeral service for the late Brandon Baker,' said Mr. Wilson, setting sail on his promised account for his son's newspaper, 'was one of the most disgusting, repulsive exhibitions of ill-breeding seen in London for many years. At times strongly reminiscent of scenes of the Ypres salient, it–'

'All right, all right,' said Derek. 'That's enough of that. Please remember there must be about a hundred thousand members of the Gallery Club in our circulation.'

'They should all be shot at the first convenient dawn,' said Mr. Wilson. 'Both for reading your paper and for the way they behaved this morning. Of all the obnoxious exhibitions I've ever seen–'

'All right,' said Derek. 'Keep calm. What was

Gertie Gibson wearing?'

'I neither know nor care,' said Mr. Wilson. 'What is much more important is that I was wearing a bowler hat that cost every penny of twenty-one shillings when I set out for the church, and was bare-headed when I landed there. And I was also mistaken for Henry Ainley.'

Mr. Wilson, junr., collapsed on a suitable armchair.

'By an hysterical female,' added his father.

'Hysterical is right,' said Derek, recovering his power of speech. 'I mean, Henry Ainley!... If it had been one of the Four Marx Brothers, I could have understood it. Whoops! I think I'll put that in our Bubble and Squeak page. "A well-known London police inspector was the victim of an amusing case of mistaken identity at yesterday's fashionable funeral of Brandon Baker. Several autograph-hunters, under the impression that the inspector was Greta Garbo, demanded his signature and presented him with a bouquet of lilies-of-the-valley. The inspector's feet are thought to be the cause of the girls' mistake—"'

'Idiot,' said Mr. Wilson.

'Did you find out anything at all, then?' asked Derek.

'Not a thing. I was so scunnered, to use a good Scots word, at the whole blessed proceeding, that I didn't look for anything. All I wanted was to get outside and meet some normal people again.'

'Me, for instance.'

'Oh, there was one thing. I waited in the church until the mob had cleared out. There was a little woman left behind. I think she was praying. I had a word with her, and she said she was Brandon Baker's wife.'

'What?' said Derek.

'Brandon Baker's wife. I never knew he had such a thing.'

'Listen, you. I was about the last to clear out of the inquest, and there was a small dame left sitting all on her own in the public seats, and I had a word with her, and *she* said that *she* was Brandon Baker's wife.'

'Odd,' said Mr. Wilson, senr.

'Damned odd,' said Mr. Wilson, junr.

'What was your one like?'

'Small and thin,' said Derek. 'Dressed in a navy-blue costume with a blue hat. And sniffing into the smallest hankie I've ever seen. What's yours?'

'Double whisk – oh, the woman ... no, it couldn't have been the same. Mine was in black, and she had quite a sensible handkerchief. And needed it.'

'Added to which, you saw yours at St. Oswald's not more than half an hour before I saw mine at Craven Street Police Court. Distance from St. Oswald's to Craven Street, three and three-quarter miles approx. Time taken to traverse same in series of lousy buses, half an hour at the very least. Possibility of your woman getting from St. Oswald's to Craven Street in half an hour, changing her costume and hat and getting a clean neb-wiper en route, definitely nil. Elementary, my dear Watson.'

'Thank you,' said Mr. Wilson. 'I didn't suggest for a minute that it was the same woman. I have heard of members of the theatrical profession taking unto themselves more than one soul mate in the course of their lives, haven't I? Or haven't I?'

'You have,' said Derek.

'Only this morning, in your disgusting *Gazette,* I read about Miss Polly Vavasour, well-known Hollywood and Broadway beauty, married at Pennsylvania yesterday to Mr. Mortimer Murray, famous star of silent-picture days. It gave a list of Polly's and Mort's past conquests – neatly tabulated side by side down the column. Polly was leading by two up and three to play with, if I remember rightly. Brandon Baker may have just been another of the same.'

'Too true,' said Derek. 'Did you get her address?'

'No,' said Mr. Wilson. 'I didn't, now I come to think of it.'

'Sap!' said Derek expressively.

'Did you get yours?'

'No,' said Derek, 'I didn't, now you mention it.'

'Sap,' said Mr. Wilson tersely. 'Anything else interesting at the inquest?'

'Not a thing. D.B.D., Herbert, the girl that was on the stage when it happened, and Foster's sister – rather a nice-looking woman – all gave evidence. Oh, and Sir Basil Bone, the post-mortem lad, knocked all your bright little ideas about the shot being fired from the wings right on the head. He said that the direction in which the bullet entered the heart showed that it could only have been fired from the position taken up by Foster on the mountains.'

'A pity,' said Mr. Wilson, lighting a cigarette. 'A great pity...'

'Coroner Ogle made a few snappy wise-cracks and refused D.B.D.'s invitation to join the show as a low comedian. The verdict, of course, made out that Brandon Baker was murdered by Hilary Foster.'

'That,' said Mr. Wilson, 'is a lie.'

'What makes you so damned positive?' asked Derek. 'It'll take a fat lot of proving that that wasn't what actually did happen. Listen, you. Bloke A shoots Bloke B in full view of two hundred thousand spectators. Bloke B falls dead. Bloke A does a bunk and is found half an hour later swinging on a rope in his dressing-room. As I keep on telling you, the thing's as plain as your face.'

'Thank you,' said Mr. Wilson. 'Only this afternoon the Commissioner was saying how strongly you resembled your father.'

'God forbid,' said Derek fervently.

'I entirely agree,' said Mr. Wilson. 'God forbid. And I agree, too, that on the face of it the thing looks pretty straightforward. But just consider what kind of a bloke Bloke A was. He definitely wasn't the sort of man who would murder a fellow human. Certainly not the way Brandon Baker was murdered. I had a long crack with Herbert at the theatre this afternoon about this man Foster. "Quiet, respectable sort of cove, sir," said the bold Herbert. "Not the sort of gent you'd ever take to be a nactor, sir. I can't think what took him, sir." That's what the bold Herbert said. And the bold Herb is a pretty good judge of character, if I'm any judge of character myself.'

'Which you're not,' said Derek. 'Remember that time you opened your heart to a most respectable old gentleman in connection with the Masters case, and the most respectable old gentleman turned out to be the dirty swine who'd bumped off old Masters with a poisoned whisky?'

'There's no need to go into all that,' said Mr. Wilson hurriedly. 'Herbert's all right. And I'm quite sure, from what he said, that Foster wasn't the kind of man to commit murder.'

'May I ask a question?' said Derek.

'It's a waste of time,' said Mr. Wilson. 'I know all the answers. But go ahead.'

'Does a man who *hasn't* committed murder dash off and commit suicide?'

'No,' said Mr. Wilson slowly. 'But a man might commit suicide if he *thought* he'd committed murder.'

'Explain yourself,' said Derek. 'In less than one hundred and fifty words, using one side of the paper only.'

'Suppose Foster and Brandon Baker were known to be enemies. Suppose, for the sake of argument, that Foster had been heard by some third party to say, "I'd like to kill you for so-and-so, Baker" – the way people are always saying things like that in the detective novels. Suppose that third party, having heard that remark and knowing the relationship between the two men, had taken advantage of the facts to get rid of Brandon Baker. Suppose he had substituted a pukka revolver for the dummy one that Foster was to use in the play, and Foster had been *made*

77

to murder Brandon Baker. Suppose all that. Wouldn't a string of events like that, if they all came off, be enough to drive a man to the brink of suicide, if not over the brink?'

'Good God!' said Derek. 'And d'you think that's what happened?'

'Not for a moment,' said Mr. Wilson in an aggravating manner. 'I'm much too fond of my bullet-in-the curtain theory to drop it at this stage of the proceedings. But it makes quite a good little story, doesn't it? Well, Martha?'

The reason why Martha, cook-general-cum-housekeeper-cum-valet-cum-general-factotum to the Wilson family, has not appeared earlier is due to the fact that Martha was continually having the day off to visit her married sister in Golder's Green. Martha's married sister in Golder's Green had been on the verge of passing away with asthma ever since the Wilsons had taken her into the bosom of their flat. The number of times that Mr. Wilson (senr., or junr.) had arrived home and found cold ham and salad on the table, no Martha, and a note saying, *Jessie is took bad again, but hope to manage back to-night,* must have been well into the three-figure figures. Mr. Wilson, senr., suspected Martha's absences of being caused by devotion to the cinema rather than the sister. Mr. Wilson, junr., put it down to gin. But when present Martha was a good soul, a grand hand at an omelette, and very good at putting buttons on the Wilson pants.

'Well, Martha?' said Mr. Wilson. 'How's Jessie?'

'Bad,' said Martha. 'Right bad. Wheezing awful. I really feel she needs me, sir.'

'What on earth will you do with your time when she pops off, Martha?' asked Derek callously.

'I wonder at you saying such things, Mr. Derek,' said Martha. 'Retire, I hope. After all the trouble she's been to me, it'd only be right. It's all right me having the evening off, is it, sir?'

'Yes, Martha,' said Mr. Wilson. 'Give Jessie my love.'

'That won't help her, sir,' said Martha. 'She's too far gone for that kind of thing. Oh, there's a woman here. I clean forgot.'

'A woman?' said Derek.

'Yes, sir. But it's the master she's after. A Miss Davis, sir.'

'What's she like?' asked Mr. Wilson, who always made a point of getting a pro-forma invoice where women were concerned.

'Bit loud, for my liking, sir. Lips, you know. About my build.'

'My God!' said Derek.

'Show her in, Martha,' said Mr. Wilson.

'Okay, sir,' said Martha, and disappeared.

'Okay...' said Mr. Wilson, wincing. 'Not only one's son, but also one's housekeeper... Oh, Miss Davis?'

Miss Millicent Davis had, as Martha had mentioned, a figure built on the same lavish lines as that of Martha herself. It was a little better controlled, perhaps, in places where control was necessary, but it had the same general spreading tendencies. She was smartly dressed and overpowdered. Mr. Wilson recognized her at once as the member of the *Blue Music* company who had kept an eagle eye on the young ladies in Abdul

79

Achmallah's harem in Act One, and who had put across a number called 'Girls Fight at Me, Men Fight for Me' with a fair amount of zest and abandon.

'Inspector Wilson?' asked Miss Davis. 'I'm sorry to trouble you – I understand you're in charge of the Brandon Baker affair?'

'That's right,' said Mr. Wilson. 'At least, I was.'

'Why – aren't you now?'

'It appears to be closed now,' said Mr. Wilson.

'That's just why I came to see you,' said Miss Davis. 'I'd like a word with you – alone, if you could.'

Miss Davis cast a meaning eye at Mr. Wilson, junr.

'My son and heir,' said Mr. Wilson. 'He's on a newspaper, but you can trust him for all that. Sit down, won't you?'

Miss Davis chose the best armchair and crossed one shapely and expensively clad leg over another of the same.

'My name's Davis – Millicent Davis,' she said. 'I was in the show *Blue Music–*'

'I remember,' said Derek pleasantly. 'You were the lady who did that tap-dance on the revolving stage, weren't you?'

'No,' said Miss Davis. 'That was Miss Owens. Thanks for the compliment, all the same. But my tap-dancing days are over. I was Madame du Cregne, of the Harem. You remember?'

'Perfectly,' said Mr. Wilson. 'I enjoyed your performance tremendously.'

'Thanks,' said Miss Davis. 'It's about this verdict at the inquest to-day. It's all wet.'

'Wet?' said Mr. Wilson.

'She means it's all bolony,' explained Derek.

'Hilary Foster no more murdered Brandon Baker than the cigarette-box on that table.'

'You see?' said Mr. Wilson to his son. 'What did I tell you? How d'you know he didn't, Miss Davis?'

'I don't know. I just know he wasn't that kind of man. He hadn't the guts, for one thing. He was scared stiff of even having to hold a dummy revolver, let alone a real one.'

'You seem to know a good deal about Mr. Foster,' said Mr. Wilson.

'Course I know a lot about him. He – he was my husband.'

'Really? I'd never have thought so,' said Mr. Wilson, referring presumably to Miss Davis's complete absence of mourning.

'Well, when I say he was my husband,' said Miss Davis a little uncomfortably, 'I mean – well, hardly anyone knew that we lived – very few people knew about it, you understand?'

'Perfectly,' said the Wilsons, senr., and junr., in unison.

'Well,' said Miss Davis, 'I know he wouldn't do a thing like that. He hadn't a grudge in the world against Brandon Baker. They hardly knew each other. Baker was a top-liner and he knew it. He hardly spoke to any of the small-part people in the show. That's the way he was. I don't expect Hilary and he spoke more than a dozen words to each other in their whole lives. The whole dirty business was a rotten frame-up.'

'Frame-up?' said Mr. Wilson.

'That bullet was planted in the revolver. He was *made* to kill Brandon Baker.'

'You see?' said Derek. 'What did I tell you, Inspector?'

'But the – the unfortunate happening afterwards, Miss Davis?'

'I know. It's difficult to explain that. But ... well Hilary was in a hell of a mess one way and another. Money, principally. Other things, too. He'd threatened once to do himself in when I was over at his flat – when he was with me, I mean. His nerves were all to hell over it all. A thing like this, happening all of a sudden as it did – it would be enough to send him nuts, you understand?'

'Quite,' said Mr. Wilson. 'Nuts?'

'Loopy,' said Derek. 'Batty. Dippy. Gaga. Mental.'

'He'd be out of his mind, you understand, Inspector ... he wouldn't know what he was doing – all he'd realize was that he'd shot a man dead. So he went and–'

'I see,' said Mr. Wilson. 'So you think the revolver was tampered with before the scene commenced, do you?'

'I don't think,' said Miss Davis – 'I know. And I know who did the tampering.'

Mr. Wilson, senr., and Mr. Wilson, junr., said, 'Who?' again in perfect unison.

'The stage manager,' said Miss Davis coolly. 'Herbert.'

'What?' said Mr. Wilson.

'Herbert. The stage manager. I was in Hilary's dressing-room in the interval between the first and second acts. I used to go there a good deal

82

because – well, you know. Herbert came in and said he wanted all Hilary's props ready in the wings. He'd gone on without the gun one night in Manchester. He was always doing that kind of thing. Just before the second act began he handed the gun back to Hilary – the gun, and a dagger thing he had to carry in his other hand. It wasn't the same gun. I'm sure of that.'

'Very interesting,' said Mr. Wilson.

'Don't you see? He'd changed the dummy revolver for a real honest-to-goodness one, and given it back to Hilary so that when he shot at Brandon Baker it would mean – amen. If only I'd realized that at the time – I never thought–!'

'Why didn't you realize and think in time to give evidence at the inquest?' said Mr. Wilson. 'It might have helped, you know.'

'I know,' said Miss Davis. 'I'd been thinking it over since it happened. There didn't seem any use – I mean, Brandon was dead and Hilary was dead. And I didn't want to get mixed up in anything – you know. And then I saw the verdict in to-night's paper – "Murdered by Hilary Foster" And it kind of got me all het up. I couldn't let that go by without doing something about it. Because it's a rotten, lousy lie!'

'All right,' said Mr. Wilson, who had a rooted objection to women when they started to scream. 'All right. I'm very glad you've come and told me this, Miss Davis. I'll probably want to have another chat with you some time. Where can I find you?'

'Two hundred and thirteen, Lancaster Avenue.'

'Thanks very much. You just leave this in my

hands. If I don't settle it, my son will. Good night.'

'Good night,' said Miss Davis. 'It was that man Herbert, Inspector ... I'm certain of that...'

Mr. Wilson closed the door thoughtfully.

'Startling Developments,' said Derek. 'Inspector Wilson is believed to be in possession of new and sensational developments in the Brandon Baker case, and an arrest is thought to be imminent.'

'Arrest Herbert?' said Mr. Wilson. 'Derek, in the language of our departed guest, you're all wet.'

'Thank you. What d'you think of her?'

'Nothing,' said Mr. Wilson. 'Nasty stink she's left behind her. You'd get precious little sympathy and understanding out of that lady, I'm thinking. No tears for Hilary, were there? Even if they were only living together ... and the idea of fixing the thing on Herbert, of all people–'

'Listen,' said Derek. 'Cut out the exchange of revolvers theory for a minute. Who was standing in the wings when it happened – in exactly the spot where you stood that time and held your pipe as if it were a revolver? Go on, answer me – don't stand there like the Statue of Liberty.'

'Well – who was?' demanded Mr. Wilson.

'Herbert,' said Derek. 'Who called the late Brandon Baker several kinds of dirty names and said he was the sort of thing you found when you changed the stones in the rockery? Herbert. Who was so damned quick at cleaning up the mess and so damned eager to help with the murder-from-the-mountain idea? Herbert. Who was it that–'

'Derek,' said Mr. Wilson, 'shut up. And go and

answer the telephone. It's been ringing for the last two minutes.'

Mr. Wilson, junr., shut up and answered the telephone as directed. He was away for rather less than a couple of minutes, during which time Mr. Wilson, senr., went through his usual methodical rites of cleaning and filling and lighting his briar pipe, wasting a great many matches and strewing the carpet with surplus tobacco in the process.

'Who says policemen have no sex-appeal?' demanded Derek on his return.

'Who was it?' said Mr. Wilson.

'What is it about you, I wonder, that's made you so popular with the fair sex all of a sudden? Is it those strong, manly features, do you think? Or those large, manly feet? Or...'

'*Who was it?*' asked Mr. Wilson, thoroughly peeved.

'Gwen Astle. The leading lady herself. Was that Inspector's Wilson's house? It was, sez I. Was Inspector Wilson at home? He was, sez I. Could she speak to him for a minute – very important, it was? Inspector Wilson speaking, sez I.'

'Derek!'

'Well, there didn't seem any point in getting you to the 'phone. It's not every day a young lad like me gets the chance of chatting to a musical-comedy star – henna or no henna.'

'What the blazes did she want?'

'You,' said Derek dramatically.

'Me?' said Mr. Wilson, leaping from his chair like a man impaled.

'She wants to make a date with you, at least. Really, you modern parents ... Miss Astle – Gwen

85

to you – would be very much obliged if Inspector Wilson could come round to her apartment this evening, as she has something to tell him about the Brandon Baker case that she thinks might be important.'

'The devil she has!' said Mr. Wilson. 'What's the address?'

'Three hundred and eighteen, Chalmers Street, N. Top flat.'

'And what time?'

'Any time to-night, she said. She's staying in the whole evening for you. I don't know what things are coming to – first of all the Head Girl of the Harem drifts in here, and now you're spending the night with the leading lady.'

'If I go now,' said Mr. Wilson, rising with some dignity, 'there will be no necessity to spend the night. Boy, my hat!'

'What about me?' said Derek.

'Well – what about you?' asked Mr. Wilson.

'Hard words from a father to his only son. I mean – what about me coming along with you?'

'Were you invited?'

'No ... but I don't like the idea of you alone in the top flat with Gwen. If it had been the second top flat or the bottom flat I shouldn't have worried at all. But the very top flat...'

'Idiot!' said Mr. Wilson. 'All right, come along.'

The Wilsons arrived at Chalmers Street at a quarter past eight, having taken rather more than one hour over the journey. Mr. Wilson, under the impression that he knew the locality off by heart, had insisted on taking the tube to some practically obsolete station which (so Mr. Wilson said) landed you bang opposite No. 318. Mr. Wilson, junr., who gave the impression of having lived in and around Chalmers Street since early childhood, recommended a bus, changing from this to another bus at the corner of East Trevor Street, and walking the rest of the way – a mere yard or so, Mr. Wilson, junr., said. After a fairly thorough trial of both bus and tube services, Mr. Wilson, senr., lost his temper and hailed a taxi. It was much the best idea of the night.

No. 318 Chalmers Street turned out to be a large block of very modern service-flats. Mr. Wilson knew at once that they were very modern, for all the chromium-plated nameplates at the main entrance were devoid of capital letters. 'mr. anthony messingham' said one. 'mr. and mrs. john vanzimmer', remarked another. 'mr. noel arkwright, osteopath and manipulative surgeon', announced a third. And high up on the door-jamb, 'miss gwen astle', said a fourth.

There was, of course, a lift. It took some time to collect anyone to work the lift, and when this was eventually done it proved to be a gentleman in a navy-blue uniform with red collar and cuffs. Derek put the age of the gentleman down as roughly one hundred and fifteen, and that of his uniform at perhaps ten years less. It is a peculiar thing about these ultra-modern service-flats that they go in for such ultra-antique and unserviceable porters. The lift, however, behaved excellently once the porter had been persuaded to start it, and Mr. Wilson and Derek were shot up to the top flat at a fine speed.

'That there,' said the porter, pointing to the

door opposite. 'Not that there. That there.'

And, having settled this satisfactorily and beyond any possible argument, the centenarian shuffled back inside the cage of the lift, closed the doors tenderly, and vanished downstairs.

'Bright lad,' said Derek. 'Another fifty years and he'll be making way for the younger blood. Snappy line in carpet slippers, hadn't he?'

'Ring the bell,' said Mr. Wilson.

Derek rang the bell. Mr. Wilson waited patiently. He heard the lift arrive at the end of its journey far below, listened to the doors being opened and shut. Then the ultra-modern block of service-flats was wrapped in ultra-silence.

'Ring again,' said Mr. Wilson.

'Aye, aye, sir,' said Derek, and rang again. While the first attack on the bell had been a mere prod, this was a good, honest bit of work, reminiscent of Wagner at his most boisterous moments. Nothing happened.

'Ring again,' said Mr. Wilson. 'And knock.'

Derek rang again, this time more in a musical-comedy strain, in the hope that it would appeal more to Miss Astle's ear. He also knocked. Several times. Still silence.

'What is the date, anyway?' said Derek.

'June twenty second. What the hell has that to do with it?'

'I thought it might be April first. What a shame – the first time in our innocent young lives that we get a chance of spending an evening with a Real Live Actress, and it all turns out a bum.'

'*What* an expression!' said Mr. Wilson. 'You'd better go down and get hold of that hall porter, if he's still alive.'

'Just a minute,' said Derek. 'After ringing and knocking, always try the handle. Failing that, enter by lavatory window. Rules for Would-Be Journalists, Number Seven. There you are!... What did I tell you?'

The door to Miss Astle's apartment was unlocked. Mr. Wilson, junr., stepped neatly inside.

'You ought to have a warrant for doing this,' said Mr. Wilson, senr. 'If anyone comes, I can arrest you for housebreaking. Dear me!'

Mr. Wilson's expletive (if 'Dear me!' can be reckoned as such) was caused by the fact that the hall of Miss Astle's flat was in a state of what is called, in European politics and other circles, flux. Or chaos. Three chairs lay upturned on the carpet. The contents of a large table standing against one wall were scattered across the hall. A slightly suggestive alabaster statuette lay at the foot of the staircase, broken in two places at a most important junction of its anatomy. Lying beside it was what Mr. Wilson diagnosed as one of Miss Astle's new Paris gowns.

'Early for spring-cleaning, isn't it?' said Derek.

'Late, you mean,' said Mr. Wilson. 'Come on in here.'

Miss Astle's sitting-room was rather worse than Miss Astle's hall. A meal had been set on a small table near the fire. The past perfect is the right tense to use, for it seemed that someone in a moment of pique had taken a tight hold on a corner of the table-cloth and pulled in a highly successful manner. There was a lot of what seemed to have been an omelette lying in spilt

89

coffee all over the fire-place. There was also a good deal of ink. Ordinary blue-black ink. Mingling with the omelette and the coffee, it provided an even brighter colour scheme to the tiles of the fire-place than had originally been the case.

'Why ink?' said Mr. Wilson thoughtfully.

'She'd been writing,' said Derek brightly.

'You amaze me,' said Mr. Wilson. 'So she had. Isn't that it, on the carpet?'

Derek stooped down and rescued the half-sheet of notepaper from any danger of a spreading lava of omelette. Not that much more could have been done to the paper, for quite seven-eighths of it was covered in an enormous blot where the ink-pot had misbehaved itself.

'Hey!' said Derek. 'Have a look at this.'

There were four words only written on the sheet of paper. The rest was blot. Mr. Wilson read the four words slowly.

If Inspector Wilson comes–

'Aggravating,' said Mr. Wilson. 'Very aggravating.'

CHAPTER SIX

'Derek,' said Mr. Wilson, 'go and fetch Methuselah up here.'

Fetching Methuselah up here turned out a much trickier job than it sounded. Derek landed on the ground-floor level at the exact moment when the electric clock on the entrance hall took it upon itself to announce – by one of its ultra-modern clucking noises – that the time was exactly eight-forty-five. Exactly eight-forty-five happened to be the hour at which Mr. Bowker (that being the hall porter's name) went down to the bowels of the building, untied his bootlaces, removed his red-and-navy jacket, and called loudly for a spot of grub. His wife Agnes had just taken a well-laden plate of steak and chips from the gas stove and planted it in front of Mr. Bowker when Derek appeared on the scene.

'Hoi!' said Derek. 'Hey, you!'

Mr. Bowker was not in the habit of young men appearing suddenly and saying, 'Hey, you!' when he was on the verge of getting going with his sup-per. He gave a grunt of displeasure, and stacked a neat pile of chips on the edge of his knife.

''Smatter?' asked Mr. Bowker. 'Can't you see when a bloke's busy?'

'I want you,' said Derek. 'Upstairs. Top flat. At once.'

Mr. Bowker steered his knifeful of chips safely through the undergrowth of his walrus mou-stache, masticated loudly for a moment, and then said, 'What for?'

'Never mind what for. My old man wants to see you on the top flat. Right away. Come on – rally round. Shove the old chips back in their news-paper and they'll be nice and hot for you when we've finished.'

Mr. Bowker wiped his moustache and said that it was a bit thick and no mistake. If a hard-work-ing man of his age couldn't take a half-hour off to have his supper and a read at the evening paper without a continual stream of complete strangers barging into his kitchen and forcing him to go up to the top floor, then there was something wrong somewhere. Mr. Wilson, junr., agreed affably, plucking a loose chip from Mr. Bowker's plate and putting it neatly away. Mr. Wilson, junr., added that it might be of interest to Mr. Bowker to know that the tall gentleman with the large feet who was waiting on the top landing was a detective from Scotland Yard, and that if he didn't get a move on and stop stoking chips inside him he was liable to find himself eating his next meal inside a prison cell. Where, Mr. Wilson, junr., concluded, steak and chips were rarely, if ever, found on the menu.

Mr. Bowker shot from his seat.

'Detective?' he said.

'Scotland Yard?' said the wife Agnes.

'Strange, but true,' said Derek. 'Are you coming or are you not?'

'Coming, sir,' said Mr. Bowker, already half-way to the kitchen door and still with his boot-laces flapping in the breeze.

''Arfaminute,' said Mrs. Bowker, shoving the steak and chips back in the oven. 'I'm coming too. What's happened, eh? What's wrong? What's she been doing now, eh? We don't know anything about her. She's only been here six months...'

The Bowkers and Derek squeezed inside the lift. There was, literally speaking, a slight hitch when Mr. Bowker's loose bootlaces became en-tangled between the cage of the lift and the out-side world, but once this had been settled in a businesslike way by Derek's pocketknife the cage shot upwards at a goodly speed and deposited the trio on the top flat.

'My name's Wilson,' said Mr. Wilson. 'Inspector Wilson, Scotland Yard.'

'Yes, sir,' said Mr. Bowker, trembling already.

'I thought you said Miss Gwen Astle was at home?'

'So she is, sir.'

'Prevaricator,' said Mr. Wilson tersely.

'He means you must have been mistaken,' said Derek, putting in a rough translation for the benefit of the Bowkers.

'Ain't she in, sir?' said Mr. Bowker.

'She is not,' said Mr. Wilson. 'Come in and see for yourself.'

The Bowkers filed gingerly into the hall, Mr. Bowker tripping over several of the odds and ends that were strewn over the carpet, and Mrs. Bowker's eyebrows going a shade further up with every step she took.

'Gorblimyluvaduck!' said Mr. Bowker, using one of his favourite expletives.

'Well!' said Mrs. Bowker, finding her tongue at last and proving straight away that once the thing was found it took some losing. 'Well! A nice state of things, I must say, and no mistake, I don't think. If she imagines for one moment that I'm going to waste my time going round after her clearing up messes like this, then all I can say is she's very far out. Look at that carpet ... she can get down on her knees and have a shot at getting them inkstains out of there, for I'm blessed well sure I'm not going to do it. And will you look at that fireplace? Can you imagine me wasting a

93

solid half-hour getting the bisom's tea ready for her, and all the thanks and gratitude I gets is to see the whole thing scattered all over the blessed fireplace. Well, this kind of thing's happened before, but it's the last time it'll ever happen, you mark my words. The very first thing to do to-morrow morning, Albert Henry Bowker, is to put on your coat and hat and go straight round to Mr. Tiffen and tell him what's happened. I'm proper fed up with it, that's what I am. Either that woman clears out of here or I do. If she thinks that I haven't anything more to do than–'

'Quite,' said Mr. Wilson, edging in cleverly. 'Quite so. It must be extremely annoying.'

'Annoying!' said Mrs. Bowker, who had several more suitable descriptions for it on the very tip of her tongue. 'Annoying? It's more than that, Inspector. It's–'

'Quite,' said Mr. Wilson, once more damming the tide with difficulty. 'If you'd be so good as to let me say a few words for a change–'

'That's right, sir,' said Mr. Bowker, who had felt that way about Mrs. Bowker for the last forty-eight years. 'Aggie, shut up. Let the inspector say what he wants to say.'

Aggie shut up, pursing her lips.

'When did you last see Miss Astle?'

'Eleven o'clock this morning, sir,' said Mr. Bowker.

'Just after four this afternoon,' said his consort.

'Going or coming?' asked Mr. Wilson. 'I mean, was she leaving the flat then or coming into it?'

'Going out. She said she'd be in again for tea about five, and that she wanted supper at eleven-thirty. For two, of course. She was one of them women who don't count it a decent meal if they has to eat it alone.'

'And you didn't hear her come back at five o'clock?'

'No, sir.'

'Miss Astle had a key of her own, sir,' said Mr. Bowker, 'and she knew how to work the lift herself and let herself in and out and all that. More often than not she used the lift herself or went up by the stairs rather than trouble me, me getting a bit on in years, as you might say, sir. Very good that way, was Miss Astle, I must say.'

'She was a brazen-faced, painted hussy,' said Mrs. Bowker, who apparently wished to hear no good spoken of Miss Astle.

'Tell me – how long has Miss Astle lived here?'

'Nigh on six months, sir,' said Mr. Bowker. 'It was the day I was took right bad with my rheumatics that she came in, sir, I mind that fine. That was just before Christmas, sir. I mind that, because I got a letter from our Jackie, and he only writes us once a year, just a bit before Christmas. As near as makes no odds, sir, it must have been about the–'

'All right, all right,' said Mr. Wilson. 'Thanks very much. Six months. That's quite near enough. She's always lived alone here?'

Mr. Bowker allowed his right foot to fiddle with the stray end of lace on his other boot. Mrs. Bowker pursed her lips a shade tighter. A moment before you would not have thought such a thing possible, but Mrs. Bowker was a grade A purser. The last vestige of blood vanished, leaving only a thin, grim line.

'Well?' said Mr. Wilson.

'Well, sir,' said Mr. Bowker, playing with his moustache in an embarrassed fashion and discovering a lone chip marooned on the outskirts, 'well, sir, she lived alone and she didn't live alone, in a manner of speaking, as you might say, if you follow what I mean, sir.'

'I don't,' said Mr. Wilson.

Mrs. Bowker unlocked the lips.

'There's no use hiding things what didn't ought to be hid,' she said. 'Especially not from the police, there isn't. Inspector, it's not for me to speak ill of nobody, however much trouble they may cause you in your life, what with expecting me to run after her night and day and clear up all her dirty litters and…'

'Yes?' said Mr. Wilson. 'But…?'

'That Gwen Astle was one of Those Women,' said Mrs. Bowker impressively.

'Ah,' said Mr. Wilson. 'Tut.'

'Mind you,' said Mrs. Bowker, folding her arms across her ample bosom. 'Mind you, I'm broad-minded. No one couldn't say as how I wasn't that. And I've had a fair bit of experience with these here actresses, and knows what to expect. But that there Gwen Astle was just a bit over the score, if I may say so, Inspector. If she's had one man inside this here flat since she came here six months ago, she's had millions.'

'Millions?' said Mr. Wilson.

'Millions,' said Mrs. Bowker. 'Not that I objects for one moment to a tenant keeping company, and, as I says, you expects a bit of carrying-on from a nactress. But the length that woman carried it to – it gave the place a right bad name, it did. We had a very respectable party took the flat opposite this only last month – a Mrs. Bottomly, sir, what had been sent home from India on account of her husband and the rainy season, sir, and–'

'I'm really not interested in–'

'–And she was here less than a fortnight when she gave in her notice and cleared out. Mind you, sir, there wasn't no unpleasantness, sir, Mrs. Bottomly merely saying as how it was the noise of the traffic in the street outside what didn't suit her, but I knows perfectly well what the trouble was. It wasn't the traffic in the street, sir. It was the traffic in here, sir. At all hours of the night and morning, may Gawd strike me down where I'm standing if I'm so much as exaggurating a single sentance.'

Mr. Wilson said 'Tut!' again.

'She used to bring them back from the theayter, sir, after the show was finished. Squads of them. Had Albert here and me running after them until two in the morning many a time, sir. "Get some sandwiches, Mrs. Bowker. Enough for a dozen, there's a lamb." That's the kind of thing we'd get thrown at us when it was high time any decent person was in their bed. And the times Albert here has had to go along to the "Hen and Chickens" at the end of Chalmers Street and in by the back door and come staggering back laden with beer–'

'Aggie!' said Mr. Bowker in a worried voice. 'The gent's a detective, remember.'

'All right,' said Mrs. Bowker. 'They can't get you into no trouble for it – it was that hussy's doing, and the man at the "Hen and Chickens's" stupidity for serving you out of hours. And the time they went away, Inspector–'

'When they *did* go away, Inspector,' put in Albert archly.

Mr. Wilson did not wish to 'Tut!' again, so contented himself by clicking his teeth in a slightly shocked fashion.

'I've seen me going my rounds at a quarter to six,' said Albert, 'like I does every morning and have done for the past thirty years and hopes to do as long as I'm spared, sir, and when I comes to collecting the boots and a-polishing of them – what d'you think, sir?'

'I haven't the slightest idea,' said Mr. Wilson truthfully.

'Outside her door, sir, as bold as brass, if you please a pair of shoes what would never have fitted her not in a week of Wednesdays, sir.'

'Dear me,' said Mr. Wilson. 'Tell me – in all this steady flow of male company that you and Mrs. Bowker talk about – was there any particular man?'

'No man what kept company with that there woman could be particular,' said Mrs. Bowker cleverly.

'Quite so,' said Mr. Wilson. 'What I meant was – was there any one man who came here often? A habitual visitor, I mean?'

'Can't say as how there was, sir,' said Mr. Bowker. 'They came late on, sir, and they left Gawd knows when, sir. I didn't see many of them. Not so as I'd recognize them or remember them, as you might say, sir.'

'You haven't ever seen a tall young man – wearing perhaps a very light-grey overcoat and a black felt hat?'

''Smatterofact, sir,' said Mr. Bowker, 'now you come to mention it like, there was a bloke of that description called here this afternoon. But she wasn't in then, so he just cleared off. It mightn't have been the gent you mean, sir, of course; I couldn't say for sure from the description.'

'Yes,' said Mr. Wilson, 'it is rather a loose description, I'm afraid.'

'That's the way as how I'd describe the lot of them, I would,' said Mrs. Bowker, pursing again.

'How?'

'Loose,' said Mrs. Bowker snappily.

'H'm ... yes,' said Mr. Wilson. 'Did either of you know Brandon Baker by sight?'

'Of course,' said Mrs. Bowker. 'Everyone knew Brandon Baker. Poor dear. What a question!'

'Was he a ... did he ever visit Miss Astle here?'

'Yessir,' said Mr. Bowker. 'I've seen him come home with her quite a lot recently. Just within this last three weeks, it was, sir. I remember saying to the missus as how I wouldn't be a bit surprised if Miss Astle and Brandon Baker pulled it off one of these fine days. And the words were hardly out of my mouth when I read in the papers about him being shot.'

'And a tall, very thin man – grey hair, small grey moustache, hooky kind of nose, very thick eyebrows – dark, not grey, the eyebrows were. Ever seen anyone like that here?'

'No, sir,' said Mr. Bowker. 'Can't say as how I have. What about you, Aggie?'

'Don't think so,' said Mrs. Bowker. 'He must be about the only one I *haven't* seen, though.'

'Well,' said Mr. Wilson, apparently satisfied, 'thank you very much. Both of you. You've been a great help. It's so nice to find people who aren't afraid to talk. I'd like to have another look round, if I may. Don't bother to stay up here, though. We'll let ourselves out all right.'

'Thank you, sir.'

'If Miss Astle should turn up after I've gone, would you let me know? Central two-one-three-three-seven. That'll get me. Or at New Scotland Yard – Whitehall one-two-one-two. And thanks very much for all your help. Good night.'

'Good night, sir,' said the Bowker family, and disappeared into the lift and down to a completely ruined plate of steak and chips.

'What d'you mean – thanks for the help?' asked Derek when they had gone.

'Points for Progressive Policemen, Number Seven – Politeness Pays,' said Mr. Wilson, lighting his pipe. 'Always thank people for nothing. They may give you something next time. The Bowker clan don't seem to have a very high respect for our Gwendoline, do they?'

'Less than the dust,' said Derek. 'And probably quite right. I don't hold with actresses who ring up newspapers when they change the colour of their hair. And that's what Gwen did. What were all those deep questions about the blokes who'd signed the Astle visitors-book?'

'Didn't you recognize the descriptions?'

'Number one – the man who did a bunk from the Grosvenor Theatre that morning you were messing about with the lights. He wore a light-grey overcoat and a black felt hat, you remember. He may have been here this afternoon, according to Mr. Bowker, but I've no doubt there are quite a lot of men going about London in light grey overcoats and black felt hats. Not much help there. Still, the fellow who was in the theatre may have been one of Gwen Astle's boy-friends, and may have been the man who was looking for her this afternoon. Number two, Brandon Baker.'

'I gathered that. You mentioned him by name.'

'So I did. He definitely was one of the boy-friends. Number three, Hilary Foster. If the Bowkers are any good at recognizing descriptions and remembering appearances, the said H.F. was *not* on the calling list.'

'So what?'

'So nothing. But I'm beginning to think that Brandon Baker's sudden end was the result of something happening to that old geometrical figure the eternal triangle. Perhaps the square on the side opposite the hypotenuse got a bit fresh with the angle at the base of the triangle, and the sum of the other two angles didn't quite approve. Perhaps not. But I'm sure of this, if there was a triangle, angle A was Gwen Astle, angle B was Brandon Baker, and angle C was our friend in the light-grey overcoat and dark felt hat.'

'From the Bowkers' chatter, it sounded more like a polygon than a triangle.'

'Maybe. Come on – let's have another look round.'

The Astle flat was furnished just about as tastefully as a flat with modern tendencies can be. There were four rooms on the first-floor level, and a short staircase leading to two smallish bedrooms in the attic of the building. Mr. Wilson picked up the two sections of the alabaster statuette, rejoined them and placed the complete article carefully back on the hall table. It is surprising how so much amusement can be got out of the simple things of life. A statuette broken and placed together the wrong way round is a fairly good example. Mr. Wilson, junr., collapsed in a hysterical fashion against the opposite wall. Mr. Wilson, senr., took his pipe out of his mouth and smiled in a whimsical way.

'It's a very good thing our backsides are at the backside, isn't it?' said Mr. Wilson, junr.

'Don't be childish,' said Mr. Wilson, senr., 'You take the low road and I'll take the high. Have a good look round.'

'Does it occur to you that it's usual to have a search-warrant to do this kind of thing?'

'It does. And I have. I always carry half a dozen, just in case.'

Mr. Wilson went upstairs to the attic bedrooms. The one which he diagnosed as Miss Astle's own boudoir was in a state of eruption which made the downstairs part of the house look as if it had been recently spring-cleaned. A suitcase lay open on the bed, with a fairly exhaustive selection of ladies' undergarments oozing out of it and over the quilt. Mr. Wilson inspected them gravely, wondering why it was that the fair sex wasted so much time and money on garments that none but the owner would have the pleasure of seeing. Carrying the idea a bit further, Mr. Wilson decided that if all the Bowkers had said were true there might be something, after all, in what seemed such unnecessary extravagance. He crossed to the large triple-mirrored dressing-table, and toyed for a moment or two with the vast range of aids to Miss Astle's complexion.

He opened a drawer. There were a few letters lying loose on top of a conglomeration of gloves, handkerchiefs, and other odds and ends. 'My Darling...' the top one began. Mr. Wilson had no desire to read what anyone had written to their darling. He contented himself with a glance at the last line of the last page, and even in doing that his conscience gave a fairly hefty prick at the idea of snooping around a lady's private correspondence. The way in which the letter ended made Mr. Wilson pull his nose thoughtfully for quite a minute – a sign, in Wilsons, that the grey matter slightly above the nose was working pretty vigorously.

Mr. Wilson took a look into the other room. Peace, quiet, and order. He came downstairs.

'Anything?' he asked.

'Not a thing,' said Derek. 'Except omelette and ink.'

'Right. Come on. I think I've seen enough of the leading lady's lair for one night. Just a minute!...'

'What's the matter?'

Mr. Wilson crossed to the wall at the door of the sitting-room. He appeared highly interested in the pattern of the wallpaper. Being an ultra-modern flat, it was an ultra-modern wallpaper, and not the sort of thing one would have imagined anyone wishing to study at close range for any length of time.

'What's the matter?' repeated Derek.

'That's a queer thing to write on a bit of wallpaper, isn't it?' said Mr. Wilson.

'If you'd get out of the way, I might be able to pass an opinion,' said Derek. 'Why should anyone write anything on wallpaper, anyway? Perfectly good box of notepaper over there on the desk. What is it?'

'C-R-A-I-L-E,' said Mr. Wilson.

'Craile?'

'C for catarrh. R for rheumatism. A for adenoids. I for ingrowing toenails. L for leprosy. E for elephantiasis. Craile...

'What is Craile, when it's at home?'

'I haven't the foggiest,' said Mr. Wilson. 'Craile...'

CHAPTER SEVEN

At this stage of the proceedings it might be as well to follow the example of Lot's unfortunate wife and take a look back over our shoulder at things.

Mr. Ivor Watcyns – but before going a syllable further, do you remember who Mr. Watcyns was? Of course you don't. How true the newspapers are when they say that the Memory of the Reading Public is Notoriously Short-Lived. Look back, then, as Mrs. Lot looked back, to the first-night programme of *Blue Music*. The chances of being turned into a pillar of salt for doing so are extremely slight. You will find, if nothing saliferous happens, that Mr. Watcyns was the gentleman responsible for the words and music of *Blue Music*. Settled? Splendid...

On the morning of the day which included, inter alia, Brandon Baker's inquest, Brandon Baker's funeral (these two reported in huge headlines on the front pages of the evening papers), Hilary Foster's inquest, Hilary Foster's funeral (these two tucked away in tiny paragraphs on the back pages of the same evening papers), Mr. Wilson's visit from Miss Davis, and Mr. Wilson's visit to Miss Astle's flat – on the morning of the day when all that happened, Mr. Watcyns wakened with a brute of a head. The daily religious service broadcast by the B.B.C. was launching into the second verse of its first hymn. Or, to be more concise, it was just after ten-fifteen. Mr. Watcyns, sitting up in bed in a pair of black-and-yellow pyjamas and scratching his hair vigorously, is not altogether a pleasing sight. It would be much better if we waited until he has got out of bed, stretched himself, drunk a tumblerful of orange-juice, slipped on a dressing-gown, steeped for half an hour in a bath heavily laden with salts which bear suggestive Continental titles, dried himself, poured his elegant figure into a lounge suit with a waist that would put any average hour-glass to shame, had his nails manicured, attended to his hair with *(a)* a brisk dry shampoo, *(b)* a quick run-through by the Branewave Electric Comb, and *(c)* a liberal douche of Itfixis, the Hair Tonic of Quality, slipped on another violent dressing-gown, and tripped along to the sitting-room for his iced grapefruit. It will be a longish time to wait, but undoubtedly it will be worth it.

Mr. Watcyns was a remarkable young man. It seemed only yesterday that the shiny seat of his blue-serge trousers was perched on a high stool in the general office of Trewitt and Trevor, Ship-brokers and Shipping Agents. In those days Mr. Watcyns was twenty-one and earned the same number of shillings per week. Mr. Watcyns stayed on his little stool for six months, at the end of which time Mr. Burton (assistant secretary to the firm of Trewitt and Trevor) passed suddenly away as a result of leaving a tin of canned salmon open for a fortnight and then eating the contents in the form of salmon sandwiches. Mr. Watcyns re-moved the seat of his pants from the stool, knocked at the private office door of the senior partner, and recommended himself for the job. He got it.

It was a good thing, for the blue-serge seat was by now dangerously transparent. With the job he got a rise of ten shillings a week and a room of his own. The room of his own was the important thing. Once installed in it, Mr. Watcyns settled down to work with a goodly amount of vigour. Not, it must be admitted, on anything to do with Messrs. Trewitt and Trevor, but rather on the first act of a play called *Infernal Triangle*. He finished the play inside a month, using a great deal of the firm's foolscap in the process. He then paid a sec-ond visit to the senior partner's private sanctum, and suggested that he would be able to get through the invoices much quicker if he had a typewriter of his own. After a spot of humming and a little hawing, he got a second-hand portable. *Infernal Triangle* was typed and checked in another three weeks, this time on the firm's quarto paper.

There remained only the little matter of getting it produced, and Mr. Watcyns did not expect any difficulty about that. He bound it neatly in one of Messrs. Trewitt and Trevor's filing folders, took the afternoon off, and parked himself at the stage-door of the Ambassadors Theatre. The show at the Ambassador's at that time was a farce called *What Bloomers!* and contained Miss Vivienne Sinclair in the leading part. Mr. Watcyns couldn't see why Miss Sinclair should go on wasting her time and talents in a play like *What Bloomers!* when there was a gem of a part for her in his own *Infernal Triangle*. His plan of campaign was, roughly speaking, to thrust the play at Miss Sinclair as she left the theatre and sign a fairly fat contract the next morning. Unfortunately, Miss Sinclair was unavoidably absent from this performance owing to a sudden indisposition with a stock-broker at Brighton. Fortunately, the matinée audience that afternoon contained no less a person than Mr. Douglas B. Douglas, the well-known theatrical producer. Mr. Douglas had heard that there was a pair of highly commendable legs with two lines to say in *What Bloomers!* and had come along to give them the once-over on the off-chance that they might come in handy for his next musical show. Mr. Watcyns seized both his opportunity and Mr. Douglas's elbow,

107

shoved his masterpiece into the theatrical magnate's fist, and said, 'I'd like you to produce that. It's a very good play.'

Infernal Triangle was not a very good play. It was a very bad play, which was just what Mr. Douglas B. Douglas was looking for at the moment. Its entire action took place on a heavily upholstered settee which was the main attraction of Jimmy Weldon's country-house at Maidenhead. For the work of a young shipping clerk, it was fairly incandescent. Many of the situations were of the kind that are only allowed to be performed in London on Sunday evenings. Much of the dialogue was the sort of thing that made Mrs. Patrick Campbell's remark in *Pygmalion* sound merely like 'Bother!' or 'Tut!' The point is that Mr. Douglas read it and pronounced it good. *Infernal Triangle* was put on at the Ambassador's as soon as *What Bloomers!* stopped blooming, and ran for three hundred and eighty-seven performances, wearing out five complete settees in the course of its run. Mr. Watcyns went back to Messrs. Trewitt and Trevor, but only to collect a month's salary that happened to be due to him and to tell the senior partner, somewhat ungratefully, to go to hell.

Since when there has been nothing at all Lot's-wifish about Mr. Watcyns. He followed up *Infernal Triangle* with two more plays which had the same plot and characters but which were carried out not on a settee, but in a ship's cabin and the dormitory of a girls' convent respectively. He then wrote a one-man revue for Mr. Douglas in which he not only wrote the book, composed the music, concocted the lyrics, designed the scenery, played

108

the leading part, produced the production and trained the chorus, but also wrote most of the notices himself for the London papers.

Mr. Watcyns was made. His last musical show was transformed into an unrecognizable American talkie for which he received two hundred thousand pounds. His last straight play has been a sensation in every country in the world except Tibet. And still the man wakened on this particular morning with a head. Odd.

'Good morning, sir,' said Mr. Watcyns' man Williams.

Mr. Watcyns grunted.

'I trust you slept well, sir?' said Mr. Watcyns' man Williams.

'Then put your trust in something else,' said Mr. Watcyns. 'I didn't even sleep badly.'

'Indeed, sir,' said Williams. 'A pity, sir. Iced grapefruit, sir, provides a refreshing *apéritif* after an evening marred by insomnia.'

'Lead me to it,' said Mr. Watcyns.

Mr. Watcyns was in the habit of breakfasting alone, enjoying a cigarette, and then pushing the bell for one of his three stenographers to break the calm. The morning mail had to be attended to. It is a peculiar fact that the more celebrated a celebrity becomes the duller and more uninteresting becomes his correspondence. In the old blue-serge-trousers days, Mr. Watcyns received an average of two letters a week, one from his mother in Peebles every Monday, and another every mail day from his married sister in Waterville, Maine. And the letters of those days fairly throbbed with interest. Never a Monday went by

109

without Mrs. Watcyns' daily help giving notice or Mrs. Watcyns' Persian cat having kittens. Never a mail day passed without Mr. Watcyns' married sister's house being engulfed in a tornado, or Mr. Watcyns' married sister's husband's employer decreeing a ten per cent. salary cut all round. Or something of the sort.

Nowadays, if Mr. Watcyns received less than fifty letters in the morning he was forced to the conclusion that Sir Kingsley Wood was not trying. And, as a rule, only about one out of each fifty contained any atoms of either interest or intelligence. If it wasn't letters from passionate females in Rochdale demanding his autograph, then it was letters from passionate females in Wolverhampton beseeching his photograph. Or more probably letters from passionate females in Dundee asking for both. Mr. Watcyns' three stenographers attended to these, ordering a thousand more photos when the supply ran dry, and signing 'Very truly yours, Ivor Watcyns' on countless albums without a tremor of their consciences. That kind made up about seventy-five per cent. of the Watcyns post, and the other twenty-five consisted of letters from his agents advising him of the sales of his latest published play, receipts of the tour of his last musical comedy, cheques for the foreign translation rights of his last farce, and Press notices about his latest revue. All terribly boring. Mr. Watcyns looked at the pile of letters on the table in front of him and agreed with the fellow Byron when he talked about the martyrdom of fame.

'Williams,' said Mr. Watcyns, 'get Miss Briggs

in, will you?'

'Certainly, sir,' said Williams, and got Miss Briggs in.

Miss Briggs was Mr. Watcyns' second-best stenographer, and arrived with notebook poised at the alert and pencil stuck in her hair.

'Photograph...' said Mr. Watcyns, on the lines of the film-star in the Noel Coward revue. 'Photograph... Tell them no, as politely as possible... Photograph... Ask them to draw up a contract on the lines suggested... Photograph... Photograph... What the hell's this?'

Mr. Watcyns read the letter in his hand several times.

'Williams!' he said.

'Yes, sir?'

'Get the car out at once.'

'Yes, sir.'

'And pack a suitcase.'

'Yes, sir.'

'I may be going away for the week-end.'

'Yes, sir.'

'And answer the rest of that muck as you think fit, Miss Briggs.'

'Yes, sir.'

'And get out of the way, Williams.'

'Yes, sir.'

Mr. Watcyns went back to his bedroom in a hurry. He had the outspoken dressing-gown off and his overcoat and hat on in its place within thirty seconds. Another thirty to collect gloves and stick and arrive at the door of his flat. Fortunately the car had been just as speedy in getting out of the garage. Mr. Watcyns slipped into the driving-seat.

'If anyone calls, tell them I'm in Czechoslovakia,' he said.

'Yes, sir,' said Williams. 'Czechoslovakia, sir. It shall have my attention, sir.'

Mr. Watcyns was at Mr. Douglas B. Douglas's offices in Great Kempton Street on the stroke of twelve.

It was Mr. Douglas's habit to arrive at his office shortly before that time. Anything earlier than eleven-thirty was a phenomenon. Consequently the staff of Douglas B. Douglas Productions, Ltd., had got a nasty jar when their lord and master clocked in at nine-thirty that morning. They were busily engaged with the racing pages, the society gossip, and the football news of the *Daily Gazette,* according to their individual tastes, at the time, and Mr. Douglas said just what he thought of them in a few well-chosen sentences. He then shot into his private office and slammed the door. At ten o'clock Mr. Douglas put through a transatlantic 'phone call to Middleschmidt and Jacobson, Theatrical Agents, New York City. At ten-thirty-five the call came more or less through. The noise in Mr. Douglas's right ear was not unlike Niagara after a particularly heavy year's rainfall. 'Hullo,' said Mr. Douglas. 'Is that New York? Hullo. Hullo? Hullo, hullo, hullo. Hell. Hullo! Is that Middleschmidt and Jacobson, New Ork? Douglas B. Douglas speaking from London. Listen. I have a big musical show opening here in three weeks. I want a leading man, and I want him badly. Needn't be an actor within the meaning of

112

the act, needn't have a voice, but must be able to dance. Name and personality essential. Grand part for the right man. I understand you've got a fellow of the name of Elmer Clarkson doing nothing at the moment. Listen, then.

'There's a boat leaves New York at midnight tonight. Gets in to Southampton Saturday midday. I want that bird Clarkson on the stage of the Grosvenor Theatre, London, England, by ten o'clock Monday morning. And I won't take no for an answer. Is that perfectly clear?' New York, after a brisk bout of atmospherics, said, 'Pardon?' Mr. Douglas mopped his brow and repeated the recitation more or less verbatim. New York then said, 'Sorry. Line's bad. You'd better cable us. So long.' Mr. Douglas jammed back the receiver and swore several times in three languages. He then selected a cigar from the large box on his desk, removed the band, spat the end accurately across the desk and past a secretary on the other side and into a waste-paper basket standing against the wall opposite, and tried Paris. Was there such a thing as a leading man doing nothing at the Folies Bergère at the present moment?

Paris, needless to say, said no – there being precious few moments when men, leading or led, are wasting their time doing nothing at the Folies Bergère. Berlin, Mr. Douglas's next port of telephone call, merely said, *'Es tut mir leid'* over and over again in a highly exasperating fashion. Mr. Douglas swore again and champed the remains of his cigar into an ashtray. At twenty to twelve Mr. Douglas had another go at New York. He had just got through when Ivor Watcyns burst on

113

the scene.

'Shut up,' said Mr. Douglas. 'Shut up and sit down.'

The atmosphere over the Atlantic seemed to have cleared up a little as the day went on. It was now rather less like Niagara and rather more like the resumption of work on the giant Cunarder.

'Hullo,' said Mr. Douglas. 'Hullo? Hullo. Hull–Middleschmidt and Jacobson? Fine! Douglas B. Douglas speaking from London. I want a leading man for a new musical show opening here in three weeks. How about this fellow Elmer Clarkson?'

'Glad to get rid of him,' said New York.

'Fine. Boat leaves New York to-night, arrives here Saturday. Put him on board. Rehearsal ten o'clock Monday, Grosvenor Theatre, London. All set?'

'Oke,' said New York. 'Hey!...'

'What?'

'What's the salary?' asked New York in a mercenary way.

'Um ... four hundred a week,' said Mr. Douglas.

'Dollars?'

'Pounds,' said Mr. Douglas, biting his upper lip in agony. He had intended to leave it an open question, but New York had said that 'Dollars' in a very superior sort of way.

'Not a chance,' said New York.

'Make it four-fifty.'

'Don't make us laff.'

'Five hundred a week. Get him here by Monday morning.'

'Huh!' said New York.

114

'What was that you said?'

'We said "Huh!" There's a new show opening on Broadway in six weeks. We got Elmer under option for the leading part at six thousand dollars a week. Sorry. So long.'

Mr. Douglas threw down the receiver and chose another cigar.

'Look here...' said Mr. Watcyns.

'Do me a favour, Ivor. Go quietly away for a Mediterranean cruise or something. Any other time I'd have been crazy about seeing you. There's a lot of things I want to talk over with you before the show reopens. That third act's got to be re-written. And a lot of Brandon's songs taken out. But just now I'm rather busy, see? Brandon Baker was never much use as an actor when he was alive, but he's a damn' sight less use now he's stiff. And I've got to find someone to take his place, you see? So run along, Ivor, and leave me to it.'

'What's this about Gwen Astle throwing up her part?' asked Mr. Watcyns, refusing to run along.

'What?'

'She's walking out on the show. I had a note from her this morning.'

'What does she think this is, eh – an epidemic? What's she think a contract is, eh? Dammit, it's not a peace treaty, you know. You've got to take some notice of a contract. What's biting her, eh?'

'She's got the jimjams. Over this Brandon business. Says she can't carry on with her part. Listen, D.B.D. – you've *got* to make her play her part, understand?'

'I've got to?' said D.B.D. 'Listen here. My hands are going to be plenty full finding another leading man without bothering about leading ladies. If Gwendoline wants to clear out, she can clear. There were eighty-nine actresses sitting on my doorstep when I was casting that part, and I don't expect all the other eighty-eight have got jobs by this time. You can tell Gwen Astle with my compliments that she can get out and stay out, for all I care. And that is that.'

Mr. Watcyns leaned over the desk and gripped Mr. Douglas by the lapels.

'She's not going out of this show, do you understand? She's playing her part as though nothing had happened. And you've got to make her.'

'What's it matter to you?'

'Never mind.'

'Oh...' said Mr. Douglas. 'Well, if it's for purely personal reasons, go and make her yourself. I'm not caring two lashes of a donkey's tail whether Gwen Astle or any other actress plays lead in *Blue Music*. For once I'm not interested in women. What I'm after is a man. Ivor!...'

'What?'

'Of all the half-baked, semi-conscious nitwits ... here am I wasting pounds, shillings, and pence telephoning all over the world for a leading man for *Blue Music* and all the time right in front of my horn-rimmed specs... Ivor, take a tight grip on that fountain-pen.'

'What for?'

'You're going to sign a little contract. That's what for.'

'Me? Take Brandon Baker's part?'

'Of course. Why not? You can sing. Brandon couldn't. You can act. Brandon would have liked to, but something always got in the way. You can dance. The thing's a cinch. Will you do it?'

'No,' said Mr. Watcyns. 'I wouldn't take Brandon Baker's part for all the gold in Christendom.'

'Why the hell not? Afraid you'd get murdered like he did?'

Mr. Watcyns went rather white.

'Never mind why,' he said. 'I won't do it, that's all. But you've got to do this for me, D.B.D. You've got to insist that Gwen plays her part.'

Mr. Douglas lit a third cigar.

'I tell you, it's a matter of complete indifference to me whether Gwen Astle, Mary Queen of Scots, or Boadicea plays the part,' he said. 'As a matter of fact, I'm not so sure that the other two wouldn't make a darn' sight better shape at it than that hennaed hussy. Pity they're not available. They had better legs, I'm sure, and Mary had a pretty snappy soprano, I've heard. Which your Gwen certainly hadn't. I tell you, I don't care whether she stays in or walks out. If you want her to stay in, use your sex-appeal about it. I'll save mine for something more important. All I want is a definite yes or no from the good lady by this time to-morrow. Excuse me … that's probably New York, climbing down…'

Mr. Douglas snatched the telephone receiver.

'Yes… Hullo? … Douglas B. Douglas speaking… Who?… Oh, is that so?'

'Who is it?' asked Mr. Watcyns.

'Your Gwendoline,' said Mr. Douglas grimly. 'Well, what's the matter?… Oh?… You don't think so, don't you?… Well, well, well, well… Quite so… I understand perfectly, my dear… Of course, if

117

that's the way you feel about it... Yes, my dear, I quite understand... I know how it is... Quite... Inconvenience?... No inconvenience at all, I assure you, my dear ... I can get hundreds as good any day... I'm sorry – liver troubling me a little this morning... Yes... What?... Contract?... Don't let a little thing like a contract worry you, my dear... Not a bit – tear it into a lot of little pieces and light the fire with it in the morning... Yes, isn't that what contracts are for, after all?... What's that?... I know I'm sweet. Good-bye... And if ever you want another part, just you come along and ask me ... yes, come along and ask me... You've got about as much chance of getting it as a lump of lard has of lasting ten minutes in hellfire. Good-bye ... God bless you.'

Mr. Douglas put back the receiver on its stand. It was the first satisfactory thing that had happened that morning.

'That's Gwendoline back in the shop window, anyway,' he said. 'A pity. I liked that girl.'

'You mean – she's through?'

'Her own wish entirely, my good man. Who am I to thwart a girl's inner feelings?'

'Damn you, Douglas,' said Mr. Watcyns. 'Listen. I'm going to see her now. She'll stay in the show when I've talked to her. Don't do anything about the part until you hear from me. Promise?'

'Like white mice, I never keep 'em,' said Mr. Douglas. 'Good morning.'

Mr. Watcyns left in a hurry and banged the door.

'Why the blazes,' said Mr. Douglas to his secretary – 'why the blazes should Ivor Watcyns be so keen about keeping Gwen Astle in the show?'

'I've no idea, sir,' said the secretary.

'I didn't suppose for one moment you would have,' said Mr. Douglas. 'Get me New York again....'

Outside the Douglas offices, Mr. Watcyns lost no time in pressing the self-starter and the accelerator. He kept his foot just exactly where it was on the latter. He was in Chalmers Street, N., inside twenty minutes, and inside the entrance hall of Number 318 within twenty-one. Mr. Bowker was polishing the brass fittings of the lift doors.

'Arfternoon,' said Mr. Bowker.

'Good afternoon,' said Mr. Watcyns. 'Take me up to Miss Astle's flat, will you?'

'Waste of time,' said Mr. Bowker. 'She's out.'

'Out?'

''Sright. Went out arfanour ago, she did, sir.'

'Did she say where she was going?'

'Yes, sir. That she did. She said as how she might be taking a bit of a stroll in Hyde Park, seeing as how it had cleared up the way it has after looking so bad all morning, sir. And she said if she didn't go to Hyde Park she might slip into a cinema for an hour or two, sir, just to pass the time of day, as you might say, sir. And just as she went out the door, sir, she said something about buying honey and going to Whipsnade to feed the bears.'

Mr. Bowker had expected all this information to be greeted with profound gratitude. He was wrong. The gentleman didn't seem grateful in the least.

119

'A hell of a lot of help that is, isn't it?' said the gentleman.

'As a matter of fact, sir, I have known her take the tube down to—'

'All right,' said Mr. Watcyns, not wishing to hear any more alternatives. 'It doesn't matter. Did she say when she'd be back?'

'No, sir,' said Mr. Bowker. 'But I expects she'll be in to tea, sir. She'd have said if she wasn't going to be, sir.'

'Thanks very much,' said Mr. Watcyns. 'I'll probably ring her up later. Good afternoon.'

''Arfternoon, sir,' said Mr. Bowker, and breathed damply on the brass fittings.

Mr. Watcyns went out into Chalmers Street again. He put his hand on the door of his car, and then apparently thought better of it. He walked along the full length of Chalmers Street, displaying a great interest in the contents of the modiste's window at the corner. He then crossed the street and walked back on the opposite pavement. On arriving opposite Number 318, he lit a cigarette and sauntered across the street in a casual manner. There was no sign of Mr. Bowker in the hall. The Brasso and cleaning-rags were still lying on the floor. Mr. Watcyns hung around for a moment, and then heard the lift doors slam two floors above. The lift was coming down. He made his mind up quickly and ran silently upstairs. He met no one en route. Mr. Watcyns reached the top flat rather short of breath, and let himself into Miss Astle's flat with one of the many little keys on the ring which reposed in his left trouser pocket.

He took a quick look round the flat and satisfied himself that, apart from Ivor Watcyns, it was quite empty. He seemed to have a fairly thorough knowledge of the geography of the place, for his first action was to make a bee-line for the cocktail cabinet which stood in a corner of the sitting-room. He poured himself out a large whisky and drank it neat. He poured out another of the same, added a suspicion of soda for the sake of appearances, and sat down on the settee to wait.

He was still in the flat when Mrs. Bowker arrived with tea at four-thirty, although the good lady was not aware of the fact. He heard her say vehemently, 'Well, if it's dead cold it's not my fault!' and waited until she had slammed the door before coming out from behind the bay-window curtains.

He was still there when Miss Astle came home at five-to-five, having gone to neither Hyde Park nor the cinema nor Whipsnade nor the tube, but having, in fact, spent two hours wandering round and round an uninteresting block of office buildings in a rather queer manner. She let herself in with her own key, threw off her hat and gloves, and walked into the sitting-room.

'Oh, God!' said Miss Astle. 'What are you doing here?'

And at a quarter past five, when Mr. and Mrs. Bowker were enjoying a stimulating cup of tea in the cellars of Number 318 Chalmers Street, a man and a woman left the building in rather a peculiar way. The man went down to the ground level himself, entered the lift, and returned inside it to the top storey. He then carried the limp body of a well-dressed young woman inside the

121

lift and dumped her on the floor. Getting to the end of the lift's little journey, he opened the doors cautiously and peered out. There was no one in sight. He walked quickly across the floor of the entrance hall and took a look up and down the street outside. Chalmers Street, like the Bowkers, was busy at its tea.

The man ran back to the lift, collected the limp figure lying on the floor of the cage, and half dragged her out of the hall, across the pavement, and into the car. The last thing he did was to pull down the blinds of the car's back windows and drive off at a goodly pace.

It may be of interest to note in passing that the man was wearing (inter, of course, alia) a very light-grey overcoat and a black felt hat.

CHAPTER EIGHT

Mr. (Derek) Wilson was solving a crossword with a fair amount of success. Not an ordinary crossword; not one of those affairs where five thousand pounds is given to the person who puts 'rat', 'crash' and 'exclaim' in the squares where several million poor mutts have put 'cat' 'clash' and 'declaim'; not even a puzzle with any attendant prize at all. On the contrary, a highbrow affair altogether. An affair with no black squares, but a number of provoking lines. An affair in which most of the clues were quite unintelligible, many of them reversed, not a few written in Latin, and all of them in verse. The younger Wilson was doing pretty well against odds as heavy as these; already he had pencilled in 'cablegram' as a result of pondering since ten past nine over the clue 'A healthy weight here proves to be, A message sent when on the C.' And in a moment of inspiration the word 'legend' had gone boldly in for 'A tale passed down throughout the years, As (mis-pronounced) a foot appears.' Derek lit his second cigarette of the morning and looked at the completed squares with a good deal of satisfaction. Twenty-three across, 'A musical composer this, Without, one fears, his good-night kiss.' A blighter, that. Decidedly nasty. Mr. Wilson, junr., laid the newspaper on his knees, placed both feet on the tiles of the fireplace, stuck his pencil in his hair, and closed his eyes. A pleasant air of peace and calm settled over the Wilson family seat. Disturbed only by the behaviour of Wilson *pére*.

'Craile...' said Mr. Wilson, senr., to himself, rising suddenly and setting out on a series of little walks from the fireplace to the door and back via the sideboard. 'Craile ... Craile? ... Craile!...'

Mr. Wilson, junr., opened his eyes slowly and listened carefully for a moment. He decided that this was something not at all unlike the Writing on the Wall. When a man – hitherto perfectly sane and normal in every way – suddenly begins to pace the sitting-room carpet in a diagonal and agitated manner, muttering to himself a word that isn't even in the Oxford Dictionary – when that kind of thing happens, it is only a question of time before the person concerned runs amok with the breadknife or refuses to sit down on anything but

123

a half-slice of toast in the firm conviction that he is a poached egg. Mr. Wilson, junr., allowed his eyes to return for a minute to his crossword. The clue that caught the said eyes remarked mysteriously, 'This preacher's behaviour was rather eccentric, So for a physician his relatives sent quick.' It was neither good verse nor good sense – even for this particular brand of crossword puzzle – but it seemed to Mr. Wilson, junr., to be a fairly neat summing-up of the present situation.

'Hi!' he said.

'Craile...' said Mr. Wilson, senr., stepping out of the groove he had made for himself and stopping to gaze sadly out of the sitting-room window at a passing plain van. 'Craile? ... Craile...'

'Are you crooning?' asked Derek.

'I'm thinking,' said Mr. Wilson.

'Then you can't be crooning,' said Derek neatly. 'No one who stopped to think would croon, and no one who croons can ever have stopped to think. Do you know that Muttering to Oneself is the first sign of senile decay?'

'I was not muttering,' said Mr. Wilson with a fair amount of dignity.

'Pardon me. If it's not muttering when a man spends the entire morning stampeding up and down a room saying, "Craile, Craile, Craile," over and over to himself, then I don't know muttering when I hear it. What is Craile, anyway?'

'That's what I want to know,' said Mr. Wilson.

'But where d'you get hold of the word? There's no such word in the language. Cradle, a crib or small bed. Crave, to beg or desire longingly. Cranium, the skull or brainbox. But craile ...

124

definitely no.'

'You have a memory like a flowerpot,' observed Mr. Wilson pleasantly. 'One small hole in the bottom, through which anything can trickle freely. Don't you remember what was written on the wall of Gwen Astle's sitting-room?'

'Good Lord, yes ... Craile!'

'It's alive,' said Mr. Wilson. 'Light has dawned in the valley of the shadows. As you say, Craile. And what I want to know is – who is Craile? What is Craile? Why did Gwen Astle write the word Craile on the wall of her room? Where is Gwen Astle? What happened in her flat after she rang me up? Why didn't–'

'All right, all right,' said Derek. 'All orders executed in strict rotation. What's it matter, anyway?'

'It matters a good deal, I think,' said Mr. Wilson. 'Gwen Astle knows something about the Brandon Baker business. I'm as sure of that as I'm sure that you're my legitimate offspring, God forgive me. And Gwen Astle's vanished. And the last thing she did before vanishing was to write this damned word on the wallpaper of her sitting-room.'

'You don't know that,' said Derek. 'She may have written it months before. You've no proof that she wrote it that day. Or that she wrote it at all. It might have been Methuselah or the female Bowker.'

'Not a bit of it. That writing was recently done. A day or two would have rubbed the loose bits of lead away. They were still there. It was written within an hour of our arriving at the flat. Why in the name of heaven should anyone want to leave a bit of wallpaper scribbled on for months on end? Damn it, it's not a natural thing to do – to go writing things on wallpaper. Is it?'

'I used to play noughts and crosses in the bathroom. But that was distemper. Quite different.'

'Quite,' said Mr. Wilson. 'So were you. No, whoever wrote that word wrote it out of dire necessity. I'm sure of that. They wrote it there in the hope of someone seeing it, and because they couldn't write it in any other place. From the writing I'm not so sure they didn't do it behind their back – to prevent someone else in the room seeing them at it. And I'll bet a thousand pounds to the bottom button of my waistcoat that it was Gwen Astle who did the writing.'

'The bottom button of your waistcoat,' said Derek, 'is missing. You've lost the bet.'

'Is it? Dammit. Martha!' said Mr. Wilson.

The Wilson factotum appeared in a bleary fashion at the doorway, having had an all night sitting at the bedside of her married sister in Golder's Green.

'Yessir?' said Martha.

'This waistcoat. Practically falling to bits. Bottom button. And the second bottom button, I see. *And* the top one. Thanks very much. And would you bring in the telephone directory, please?'

'I'll try,' said Martha.

'What d'you mean – you'll try?' asked Mr. Wilson.

'If you'd put in a night like what I put in last night, sir, you wouldn't feel too sure of being able to fetch anything, sir.'

126

'Tut,' said Mr. Wilson. 'On the skite, eh?'

'May God in Heaven forgive you, sir,' said Martha. 'And me up with Effie from nine o'clock at night until a quarter past five this morning, and her breathing her last, sir–'

'What is it? Cirrhosis of the liver?'

'No, sir. Asthma. Something chronic, she has it.'

'I see,' said Mr. Wilson. 'Well, the waistcoat and the directory, if you can manage them, Martha.'

'I'll try, sir,' said Martha, and dropped out.

'Why cirrhosis?' asked Derek.

'You get it from over-indulging in gin,' said Mr. Wilson. 'And Martha's married sister seems to need ginial companionship as well as spiritual companionship. That was a joke, for your information. She had a breath about as strong as Carnera this morning. Ah ... directory. Thank you, Martha.'

'I was wondering, sir...' said Martha.

'Afternoon off?' said Mr. Wilson. 'Certainly. I know the feeling. The afternoon following the morning after the night before is always the worst time. Yes, that's all right, Martha. My love to Effie.'

'Thank you, sir,' said Martha the factotum, and disappeared.

'Why the directory?' asked Derek.

'I'm looking up Crailes. It must be someone's name, I suppose? I wonder if Douglas B. Douglas or anyone at the theatre could help us? It may be some man she has been running around with ... Craile ... Craile ... Craik. Craig. Craile. Ah!'

'Is there such a being?'

'Yes. One of the clan, only. Craile, Major-General Sir Arthur, thirteen Townsend Avenue. West three-nought-eight-seven. Derek, ring up the Major-General.'

'Okay,' said Derek.

'Well?' said Mr. Wilson, on the return of the son and heir.

'Not too successful. A valet or secretary or something answered the 'phone, and led me to believe that Sir Arthur was in his bath. On hearing a muffled voice exclaim, "Ask who the hell it is, you silly fathead," I insisted on conversing with the Major-General in person. I said that it was *(a)* a matter of grave national import, *(b)* a topic of far-reaching effect, and *(c)* a question of life and death. Somewhat impressed by this, the fathead handed over the 'phone to the Major-General in person. And although I brought all my tact, personality and well-known charm into the conversation I was unable to make any impression on Sir Arthur. In fact, I was told in a Major-General sort of way to go to hell and stay there.'

'What did you ask him?'

'I asked him if Gwen Astle, the musical-comedy actress, spent the night with him last night. Answer yes or no, I said, and write clearly in block capitals.'

'Ass!' said Mr. Wilson. 'Blithering, unadulterated ass. Still, I don't suppose he had anything to do with it.'

'He doesn't sound as though he had the least interest in the affair,' said Derek. 'Well, Martha?'

'A gentleman to see the master,' said Martha

'What's his name?' asked Mr. Wilson.

'Gent called Jenkinson, sir.'

'Jenkinson?'

'That's what he said, sir,' said Martha, standing her ground firmly.

'There was a fellow I knew at school,' said Derek, 'who always made a habit of putting garden worms in the house tutor's bed on the last day of term. But his name was Jackson. He–'

'Shut up!' said Mr. Wilson. 'Right, Martha. Show him in here.'

Mr. Jenkinson, shown up, proved to be Herbert and none other.

'God bless my soul!' said Mr. Wilson. 'I'd forgotten all about sending for you, Herbert. Didn't recognize the description. That woman called you Jenkinson or something.'

'That's me, sir,' said Herbert, sitting respectfully on the extreme edge of a chair. 'Herbert Jenkinson, sir. You didn't think I'd just been christened Herbert and it left at that?'

'No,' said Mr. Wilson. 'But if you'd just said plain Herbert to Martha I'd have known at once who you were. I was beginning to think it was a Fresh Development.'

'I did, sir,' said Herbert in an apologetic manner. 'When your maid asked me my name I said to her, "Just call me Herbert," and she says to me, "I'm not in the mood for freshness this morning, me lad." Quite sharp, she was, sir. What was it you wanted to see me about?'

'Hilary Foster's revolver,' said Mr. Wilson.

For the first time since the Wilsons had made Herbert's acquaintance, he looked slightly flustered.

'Revolver, sir?' he asked.

'Yes. Why did you change Hilary Foster's revolver just before he went on in the second act?'

'Here ... Mr. Wilson – what are you getting at, sir?'

'Never mind,' said Mr. Wilson. 'Why did you?'

'Because I was told to,' said Herbert.

'Who by,' asked Mr. Wilson, forgetting his prepositions.

'Mr. Douglas, sir.'

'But I went to Mr. Douglas's office yesterday and asked him if he'd given instructions for the revolver to be changed. He said no, he hadn't. What d'you make of that?'

'It's ... he's mistaken, sir. Honest to God he is. He must have forgotten. I got the instructions sent backstage to me at the end of the dress rehearsal.'

'What d'you mean – sent backstage? Mr. Douglas didn't come and tell you himself?'

'No, sir. The boss always sits in the stalls during a dress rehearsal, sir. He has a secretary alongside of him, sir, and she makes a note of all the things he wants altered and it gets sent up to me when the rehearsal's finished. There was about fifteen or twenty things he had me change before the first night. This blood – blooming revolver was one of them. I can remember what he said on the note – clear as anything, sir. "Change Foster's revolver to something that looks like a revolver." That's what it said, sir, and that's what I did.'

'I see,' said Mr. Wilson. 'It's a bit awkward, isn't it?'

'I should think it is, sir. Funny – it never struck

me that way until last night. I went all sweaty at the idea, sir. I mean – me planting a new revolver just a few minutes before Mr. Baker was shot. I thought to myself, 'It's a ruddy good job this didn't come out at the inquest.'

'It ought to have been out at the inquest, Herbert,' said Mr. Wilson.

'I know, sir. But somehow I never connected–'

'Where did you get the new revolver from?'

'Hamilton and Innes, gunsmiths, Upper Kent Street. They supply all firearms and that kind of thing for our shows.'

'And ... the ammunition?'

'Ammunition, sir? There wasn't no ammunition, sir. Good God, sir, you're not trying to plant this on me, are you?'

'No,' said Mr. Wilson. 'Certainly not. Ninety-nine out of a hundred other men in my position would, though. You change a dummy revolver for a pukka one fifteen minutes or so before a man is shot – seemingly with the revolver you've just provided. You say you were acting on orders given you by Mr. Douglas, and Mr. Douglas flatly denies this. It's your word against his, Herbert.'

'What are you going to do, Mr. Wilson?' said Herbert.

'Nothing at all. I'd arrest you on the spot, I think, if I weren't so damned positive that Brandon Baker wasn't shot by the revolver held by Hilary Foster at all.'

'What, sir?'

'I don't believe Hilary Foster had anything to do with it. I believe he was made to *think* he had killed Baker. Just as I made you think just now

131

that you were responsible for the death of Brandon Baker. But I'm too fond of another little theory of my own to waste time trying to find out whether it's Douglas B. Douglas or you that's lying. By the way, were there other people in the theatre at this rehearsal?'

'Yes, sir. Any amount. Newspaper men, and a whole lot of the boss's friends, and Mr. Watcyns and Mr. Carlsson, the authors of the show, and a whole crowd more.'

'Who handed you the note of the things Mr. Douglas wanted changing?'

'One of the theatre pages, sir.'

'And this secretary who took down Mr. Douglas's instructions. Can I get hold of her anywhere?'

'Yes, sir. She works at Mr. Douglas's office when he's not at the theatre.'

'I'll look her up' said Mr. Wilson.

'So will I,' said Derek. 'If D.B.D. chooses his secretaries from the same formula as he picks his chorus, she ought to be worth looking up.'

'Right, Herbert,' said Mr. Wilson. 'That's all for the present. And cheer up. After all, I haven't arrested you.'

'No, sir,' said Herbert. 'Thanks very much, sir.'

'Oh … Herbert!' said Mr. Wilson.

'Yes, sir?'

'You don't happen to know anyone called Craile, do you?'

'Craile, sir?'

'Yes. C-r-a-i-l-e. Craile. A friend of Miss Astle's, it might be.'

'No, sir. Never heard of anyone of that name. I

132

never thought it was the name of a *person* before, as a matter of fact.'

'It is,' said Derek. 'Maj.-Gen. Arthur Craile, M.C. His vocabulary–!'

'Quiet,' said Mr. Wilson shortly. 'What did you think it was the name of, Herbert?'

'Why, a place, sir, of course,' said Herbert. 'Craile's the place where Mr. Watcyns goes for his hinspiration, as he calls it. He wrote nearly all of *Blue Music* there, sir. It's a village up in Buckinghamshire, I think, sir. He goes and stays at a pub up there for the peace and quiet and–'

'Herbert,' said Mr. Wilson, 'God bless you. If you gave my one and only child here a kettleful of arsenic and made him transparent with bullet-holes, I wouldn't arrest you even then. You've set us on the trail at last. Didn't I offer you a peerage once? Make it a couple of peerages! And now get out.'

'Yes, sir,' said Herbert, rather dazed. ''Morning, sir.'

'Good morning,' said Mr. Wilson. 'Derek, the gazetteer. Wasting the whole morning ringing up Crailes when all the time it's a village in Buckinghamshire! Found it?'

'Keep calm,' said Derek. 'Craile. Vill. Six miles fr. Aylesbury. R.S.: P.O. Eliz. ruins. Early-cl. Wed. Pop. Six-six-seven.'

'What does R.S.: P.O. mean?' asked Mr. Wilson.

'Rural scenery perfectly odious,' said Derek. 'Alternatively, it's a snappy way of telling one that Craile is fitted with all modern conveniences, including a railway station and a post office.'

133

'Yoicks!' said Mr. Wilson. 'Get me a first-class return ticket to Craile, Derek.'

'What on earth for?'

'I'm going there. Not for the benefit of my health. Not to swell the pop. to six-six-eight. Not to gaze at the Eliz. ruins. But to find Gwen Astle. And, unless I'm pretty far mistaken, Ivor Watcyns.'

'Just a minute,' said Derek. 'Not so fast, old man. You know, if you suddenly barge into Craile, people'll start talking.'

'That's what I want,' said Mr. Wilson. 'I want Gwen Astle to start talking and not to stop until I ask her.'

'No. No. But you'll ruin the whole thing. Famous Detective Arrives Mysteriously in Old-World Village. You know what'll happen. They'll have the red carpet and the local brass band out to meet you, and before you're there the birds – to mix a metaphor – will have folded their tents and crept silently away.'

'I thought of going disguised as an artist,' said Mr. Wilson. 'Or an author in search of local colour.'

'With feet like those – impossible, said Derek. 'You're a policeman, and Willie Clarkson himself couldn't make you look anything but a policeman. But if I went...'

'You?' said Mr. Wilson with a snort.

'Why not? If you go, you'll have everybody within twenty miles chattering. Nobody knows me. I can go and have a preliminary skirmish, anyway. As an ordinary common or garden hiker.'

'A hiker?' said Mr. Wilson.

'That's what I said. Wandering rough-shod o'er Bucks. Stopping at Craile overnight to give the Eliz. ruins the once-over. Perfectly simple.'

'You couldn't persuade anyone you're a hiker,' said Mr. Wilson. 'If I can't disguise myself as a painter, it's no use you trying to make people believe you're a hiker. You've got quite respectable legs, for one thing.'

'Give me half an hour,' said Derek. 'I'll show you.'

Mr. Wilson, junr., put on his hat and went out on a shopping expedition with five pounds in his notecase. After a bit of meandering, he hit exactly the right kind of emporium. G. Daniels, Cyclists' and Hikers' Outfitters. Camp Requisites at Bargain Prices. Step Inside and Look Round. No Obligation to Purchase. Mr. Wilson, junr, stepped inside and looked round. He also purchased, though (as Mr. Daniels had promised) not under any obligation to do so.

'Good morning,' said Mr. Wilson, junr., 'A pair of shorts, please.'

'Yes, sir.'

Brief argument re waist and buttock measurements now follows.

'And a khaki shirt, please. With a zip fastener.'

'Certainly, sir.'

Remarkable range of zip-fastened shirts produced. Mr. Wilson, junr., slightly carried away, rejects such a prosaic idea as khaki and selects material of royal-blue colour and emery-paper texture.

'And a haversack, please. And a saucepan, I think.'

135

'Certainly, sir.'

'One of those oilskin capes, I think. Yes, the yellow one.'

'Yes, sir.'

'And a beret.'

'Yes, sir.'

'How much is all that?' asked Mr. Wilson, junr., fluttering his fiver.

'Um ... three ... seven-and-six ... fifteen-and-six sixteen-and-ten ... twenty-two-and-three ... twenty-three shillings, sir.'

'Good Lord,' said Derek. 'Is that all?'

'Call it twenty-two-and-six, sir, for cash down,' said Mr. Daniels.

'In that case,' said Derek, in a flash of genius, 'I'll take a bicycle.'

'Certainly, sir,' said Mr. Daniels, washing his hands vigorously with invisible soap.

'And I'd like to change here,' said Derek, 'and put the things I'm wearing just now inside the haversack. May I?'

'Certainly, sir,' said Mr. Daniels once again. 'This way, sir.'

Mr. Wilson, junr., came 'this way' and made a transformation scene inside two minutes that would have put any pantomime to shame. The sun was shining fairly strongly outside the shop, but Mr. Wilson, junr., ignored it altogether and girt himself in the oilskin cape. It put, he thought, a final touch of authenticity to the ensemble. Mr. Daniels seemed satisfied rather than ashamed at what he and his emporium had accomplished, and arranged Mr. Wilson, junr., and his haversack, more or less tidily on the bicycle.

136

'Going a cycling tour, sir?' inquired Mr. Daniels pleasantly.

'No,' said Mr. Wilson, junr. 'Swimming the Channel.'

He reached the Wilson family seat with a minute of his half-hour to spare. He felt that, with the exception of the two occasions when he had parted company with the cycle at corners, the whole proceeding was a particularly neat bit of work.

'My God!' said Mr. Wilson, senr.

'Tricky, don't you think?' asked Derek. 'Beret on the small side. Shirt slightly itchy. Otherwise O.K. Right. Give me five pounds, will you. I'm off. The wanderlust has claimed me. A bar of chocolate and an orange and I'm all set for Craile, Bucks., pop. six-six-seven. I'll let you know if anything happens.'

'In that rig-out anything might happen,' said Mr. Wilson. 'Cheerio!'

'Cheerio,' said Derek. 'Now, which way does Bucks lie, anyway?'

As the gazetteer had been good enough to point out, Craile lies about six miles from Aylesbury in the county of Bucks. Nothing wrong with that; six miles from Aylesbury in the county of Bucks is just about as sensible a place to lie as any. The snag about it is that Aylesbury in the county of Bucks lies itself a good many miles from London. Especially on a bicycle. Mr. Wilson, junr., set off with a light heart and haversack.

At Willesden the heart was still much the same weight as before, but something had happened to the haversack. At Edgware, Mr. Wilson, junr., dismounted, bought an orange, and asked several policemen several questions. A little further on, Mr. Wilson, junr., threw away the haversack into a passing pond and was extremely surprised to see that it floated. A mile or two more and Mr. Wilson, junr., developed acute shooting pains in the behind. Another half-mile, and he had a brief but animated argument with a four-ton lorry which seemed to be carrying not only several hundred sheep to the slaughter, but also a quantity of bedroom furniture to the sales. There is a sort of discrepancy between a four-ton lorry and a pedal-cycle that makes a meeting of the two rather one-sided. Mr. Wilson, junr., picked himself off the highway, dusted himself carefully, and decided that this was the last straw.

The humorous side of the escapade, which had been fairly well developed at the start, had now completely evaporated. He lifted his right leg carefully and lowered himself tenderly on to the saddle. Like the haversack, something had happened to the saddle. To a tender behind, it now felt much more like an idea of the Spanish Inquisition than a well-shaped piece of leather. Mr. Wilson, junr., pedalled grimly on.

Arriving with a sigh of relief at Watford, he purchased a single ticket to Craile for self and cycle and sat down on an upturned milkchurn to wait for the next sensibly directed train. It came in an hour. Mr. Wilson, junr., parked the wretched machine in the luggage van and himself in the corner seat of a third-class smoker, stretched his legs, lit a cigarette, and felt a little more at ease with the world.

This state of affairs was not allowed to last for long, as it happened, for a couple of heavily built females bounced into the carriage just as the train was leaving, sat down on the opposite cushions, and started to talk in a pointed way about modern hikers who hiked by rail. After ten minutes of this, Mr. Wilson, junr., not unnaturally took the dialogue to refer to himself, and changed his carriage at the next station. He reached Craile at a quarter to five, after one of the most regrettable days in his young life.

A deceptive little place, Craile. The gazetteer put down the pop. as 667, you remember. It may be quite right, of course; but coming into Craile for the first time you would be forgiven at once for assuming that the gazeteer had made a mistake and put in a 6 too many. Or, if the figure was correct, that something ought to be done at once about the over-crowding in rural areas. Or, again, if 667 was not a misprint, that there had been a surprising emigration to the Colonies on the part of the younger Crailers since the taking of the last census.

Take, for instance, the Main (and only) Street of Craile. There are not more than a dozen houses on each side of its meandering and rut-ridden route. Well, allow for the fact that Craile may be very fond of children, and give each of the funny little cottages six inhabitants apiece. And that's only a hundred and forty-four all told. The rest may be crowded inside the big house at the very end of the village, but, as a matter of fact, they aren't; old Lady Bunsen and her servant Sarah and her spaniel Agnes are the only folk up there. They may

139

be, then, living at 'Craile Arms', half-way along the Main Street on the side opposite the pump (water, not petrol, thank God). But if they are, surely it's a bit unfair to include inn-dwellers in a census. And that's absurd, anyway; there cannot possibly be four hundred guests packed inside that little hostelry, with its one entrance for the bar part, and its other entrance for the hotel part, its bay windows stacked with geraniums and lace curtains and its odd attic windows poking out of the roof every yard or so. Mr. Wilson, junr., hoped that it was impossible, anyway, for he very much wanted a bed for the night.

He propped the cycle up against the 'Craile Arms' and noted with a certain amount of satisfaction that it had contracted a slow puncture in the luggage van. He hoped it hurt it. And giving the punctured tyre a vicious little kick, he went in by the bar entrance, ordered a bottle of beer from what was obviously the village idiot, drank it at a gulp, came out into the street again, gave the cycle another kick, and re-entered the 'Craile Arms' by the hotel entrance.

There was a complete absence of life about the place, unless you count a number of stags which looked down glassily from their wooden plaques on the walls of the entrance hall, and a stuffed salmon in a glass case. Derek peeled off his cape and draped it over the salmon. He then caught sight of a leather-bound visitors' book lying on the hall table. Suddenly remembering what he had come to Craile for, he opened it and took a look at the last page. *Mr. and Mrs. Smith* was the final entry, written in a neat, unashamed handwriting.

It might be; and again it might not. Noticing that the date when the Smith family had stayed at the 'Craile Arms' was May 1, 1927, Derek decided that it probably was not. When he saw that Mr. Smith had written *Meagre and thin we entered in, Contented and stout we staggered out,* in the Remarks column he was quite sure that it wasn't. And still no sign of life apart from the deer and salmon. Derek found a bell-push and pushed.

'Was you wanting something, sir?' said a small maid with very prominent front teeth, appearing suddenly round a door.

'Yes,' said Derek, 'I was.'

''Igh tea, or just plain, sir?' asked the maid.

'As a matter of fact, I wanted a room for the night.'

But this was outside the small maid's province, for she ogled at Derek for a moment as though he had asked for a loan of a zeppelin, and then said, 'I'd better fetch the missus, sir.'

The small maid exited and was heard calling 'Missus!' in a shrill soprano all over the 'Craile Arms'. Mr. Wilson, junr., went and had another beer while the hunt was on. When he came back to the hotel proper he found what he presumed to be the proprietress waiting with a teapot in one hand and a clean towel in the other.

'Was it just for one night, sir?' said the woman.

'Yes ... I think so. I'm just passing through. I say!...'

'Yes, sir?' said the proprietress.

Mr. Wilson, junr., realized with a bit of a jolt that he was talking to the little woman he had met after the inquest. Brandon Baker's wife, in fact.

CHAPTER NINE

Meet, at this rather late stage, Miss Prune. You come out of the 'Craile Arms' by either the wet or the dry exit, you turn left, you march a hundred yards or so down the Main (and only) Street, you pass the pump, and you stop at a microscopic shop with a small-paned bay window. And in case you are in any doubt about it, you cock your head upwards and read on the green wooden sign over the shop entrance, 'Craile Post Office, Ethel Prune, Postmistress, Public Telephone Inside, Money Order Business Transacted, Licensed to Retail Tobaccos, Boarders Kept, Mineral Waters, Picnic Parties Catered For.' Yes, all that; every word of it.

And inside the shop there are a great many more notices, 'Choice Bon-Bons, 4d. per qtr.', and 'Local Views 1d. Each' and 'Suits and Costumes Cleaned and Dyed, Mod. Charges, Returned in Four Days as Good as New'; and something about the Shop Acts Of 1923 forbidding Miss Prune to sell Postal Orders (but allowing her to sell Choice Bon-Bons) after two o'clock on Thursdays.

Wasn't it Lord Dunsany who wrote a queer play about an odd little shop where the customers came to exchange their private troubles across the counter? One came in and handed over his toothache and got back someone else's nagging wife in exchange. Well, Miss Prune's establishment was run on rather similar lines to that. At five to ten it was Mrs. Twigg for a packet of Lux and a two-shilling postal order. In exchange for which, Mrs. Twigg parted with two-and-sevenpence and the latest news about Matilda Martin and that new policeman at Aylesbury. At ten past ten it was Mrs. Haliburton in search of a two-shilling book of stamps, some toilet soap, and a fresh lettuce. All of which were handed across the counter plus the Matilda-policeman gossip as a sort of free gift; and Mrs. Haliburton gave back in exchange three shillings and twopence and the very latest about that painter person who had taken Hawthorn Cottage for the winter. Stuffing her purchases in her string-bag, Mrs. Haliburton left the post office, having a difficult job to negotiate past the vicar's sister in the narrow doorway. Notepaper and the *Christian Herald* and a packet of hairpins for the vicar's sister, getting both the Matilda-policeman and the Hawthorn Cottage stories as a bonus, and giving (as her own small contribution to the feast) the text of her brother's sermon for the following Sunday morning. And so on. *Bureau de Change* ... that was the name of Dunsany's play. Well, Miss Prune was a sort of *proprietrix de bureau de change* in the village of Craile.

Mr. Wilson, senr., had been born and bred in a village with a pop. not much larger than that of Craile. Almost the last thing he said to his oilskin-clad son and heir as the latter cocked his leg over the saddle of his cycle was, 'There's sure to be an inquisitive bisom at the local post office. Don't 'phone unless you have to. And don't send post-cards unless you've nothing to say. And if you

143

telegraph, use fictitious names if you find out anything.' Which more or less accounts for this series of highly provoking (to Miss Prune) telegrams which began to shoot briskly back and forwards between the village of Craile and the city of London shortly after the arrival of Derek Wilson in the first-named place:

(i)

Handed to Miss Prune at 9.10 a.m. on the morning after Derek's arrival:

Arrived safely but aching in all possible limbs hotel mattress composed entirely barbed wire also no grapefruit proprietress turns out Nebuchadnezzar's wife whom met at inquest Derek

(ii)

Handed in at London an hour later:

Sorry hear aches mattress grapefruit try pumping proprietress any signs Belshazzar Salome Dad

(iii)

Handed to the Prune just before lunch the same morning.

Proprietress gives many interesting sidelights Nebuchadnezzar's private life Henry Eighth family man in comparison Belshazzar Salome both here but Salome returning London this afternoon send ten quid

144

incidental expenses beer excellent Derek

(iv)

To the Prune's younger sister, the Prune herself being away at the midweek meeting of the Dorcas Society:

Belshazzar Salome had hell of row hotel lounge Salome not returning London after all quite certain Belshazzar mixed up Nebuchadnezzar's death suggest search his flat Derek

(v)

In London early the next morning:

Searching of Belshazzar's flat somewhat hampered by Belshazzar not being at Craile but in London all the time suggest you visit oculist oftener and hotel bar rather less Dad

(vi)

To the Prune, immediately on receipt of this.

Thanks ten quid cannot understand your last telegram Belshazzar definitely here all night stand by for possible further developments immediately Derek

(vii)

Half an hour later, to the Prune:

Absolute sensation here come at once Derek

(viii)

In London again:

*Sorry cannot get down to-day Chief holding confer-
ence re new designs constables helmets will try tomorrow what has happened anyway Dad*

and (ix)

To the now hysterical Prune, 11.30 that morning:

*Your presence here essential on my way to local gaol
arrested by nitwit policeman Derek*

Now, you cannot send a series of telegrams like
that in a small village like Craile without causing
a fair amount of discussion and eyebrow-
elevation. Even in busy, sophisticated London
telegrams (iv) (vii) and (ix) created something of
a stir among those officials of the General Post
Office who had to do with their reception and
dispatch. But in Craile the whole series was a riot.
   To begin with, the idea of substituting certain
Old Testament characters for the names of Mr.
Baker, Mr. Watcyns and Miss Astle turned out
not nearly so simple a matter as it had seemed
before Derek Wilson left London. This was
chiefly due to the fact that on the one day of the
week when she was not serving inhabitants of
Craile with postal orders, lettuce, and Lux, Miss
Ethel Prune attended divine service at the local

parish church at intervals from eight a.m. on-
wards and spent her Sabbath afternoons presid-
ing over the infant class in the Sunday-school.

Miss Prune consequently had a pretty fair
knowledge of matters Biblical. She knew perfectly
well, for one thing, that Nebuchadnezzar be-
longed to quite a different generation than either
Belshazzar or Salome, and that these three per-
sonages had no right at all to figure in the same
telegram much as though they were bosom pals.

'Nebuchadnezzar?' said Miss Prune, coming up
gradually from the level of her counter.

'Nebuchadnezzar,' said Derek firmly. 'N for
pneumonia, e for eucalyptus, b for bisurated
magnesia, u for...'

'Thet's quaite all raight, sir,' said Miss Prune
sternly. 'Ai'm perfectly well aware of the spelling.
Only it's rether an unusual word for a telegram,
is it not, sir?'

'Not at all,' said Derek. 'Nebuchadnezzar?
Personal friend of mine. Dear old Nebby.'

'Quaite, sir,' said Miss Prune. '...Nebuchad-
nezzar's waife whom met at inquest – Derek. Two
shillings and eightpence, if you please, sir.'

'Good morning, sir,' said the Prune, and was
left to brood over this extraordinary telegram and
to wonder whether it was blasphemy or merely
the high spirits of the modern youth. Certainly it
was very odd. 'Proprietress turns out Nebuchadnezzar's wife...' That was presumably the proprietress of the 'Arms' for Mrs. Twigg had
mentioned that this young hiking gentleman had
arrived there last night. But the proprietress of the
'Arms' had been known and respected as a single

147

woman for twelve years now, hadn't she? And Nebuchadnezzar, of all people. Miss Prune sent telegram (i) on its first hop towards Mr. Wilson in London with an uneasy feeling that she was conniving at something that wasn't altogether naice.

Outside the post office, Derek inspected the pump. And a sort of mental telepathy functioned suddenly as he realized that if you lowered the handle sufficiently far, then sure enough a miserable little trickle of water came out of the spout on the other side and dribbled down into the gutter. 'Try pumping the proprietress' Mr. Wilson, senr., was going to write in telegram (ii), and Mr. Wilson, junr., gave the pump-handle a last vicious jab and set off to anticipate his father's suggestion.

He found the proprietress of the 'Craile Arms' in the act of going over the carpet of No. 7 bedroom with a 'Kleenkwik' vacuum cleaner. He noted that when she had finished with No. 7 she passed No. 8 bedroom respectfully and went on to knock hell out of the commercial room carpet. On the mat outside No. 8 there still lay one pair of gentleman's shoes and one pair of lady's ditto. Derek followed the lady of the house into the commercial room and said, politely enough, that it was a fine morning for the time of year.

'I wondered when you'd start,' said the proprietress.

'I beg your pardon?' said Derek.

'You're a journalist, aren't you? You're the young man who came up and spoke to me at the inquest. Well, carry on now you've found me out. I can't think why you people have to ferret folk

148

out after anyone famous dies, though.'

'Look here,' said Derek. 'You've got me all wrong. Honestly. I am a journalist. It's a dreadful confession to make, I know, but I admit it freely. But I'm not down here on business. I'm on holiday. Look at these trousers – you don't think I'd wear things like these if I were working, do you?'

The proprietress stopped her vacuum manœuvres and inspected the trousers carefully for a moment.

'Why did you speak to me that day?' she asked. 'I've often wondered that.'

'Well – you seemed to be about the only person in all that crowd who really cared.'

'I expect I was,' said the proprietress, and sat down on one of the commercial room armchairs as though sitting down was both a luxury and a rarity.

'I suppose you wouldn't like to tell me something about it?' asked Derek.

'Front page a bit bare?' said the proprietress.

'I wish you'd forget that idea. I'm not after news – really. Only somehow I got the idea you are rather anxious to get it off your chest. Wrong again, it seems, I'm sorry.'

'No,' said the rather tired-looking woman, 'you weren't wrong. I would like to talk to someone about it. No one down here knows anything about it at all...'

'Well?' said Derek, feeling rather uncomfortable at the success of the pumping operations.

'I met Brandon Baker first in 1909. We were both on the stage. At least, I don't know if you would call it being on the stage. It was mostly

149

concert-party work at the seaside towns. I was a soubrette and dancer in a troupe – "The Merry Monarchs" we called ourselves. Brandon joined the troupe at the beginning of the season. He was a light baritone and dancer – pretty bad at it, too. I expect I was pretty bad as well, but I certainly didn't think so then...'

'Yes?' said Derek, realizing that a little careful prompting was going to be necessary to keep the proprietress away from that vacuum cleaner.

'We got married in August at Eastbourne. They gave us a benefit-night. We got eight pounds ten, I remember. We were terribly happy and absolutely broke. Just before Christmas we signed on with a touring company of a musical comedy – I forget the name. *The Girl from Somewhere-or-other*. We were both in the chorus, but Brandon was understudy to the juvenile lead. The juvenile drank an awful lot – fortunately for Brandon. We were up in some dreadful town in the Midlands when he had rather more than he could hold and broke his leg trying to climb down from a hansom. Brandon got the part, and he did it pretty well. At least, it seemed pretty well in comparison with the other fellow. When the tour ended he was offered the lead in another musical show. After that he got a leading part in London. Twelve quid a week. We could hardly speak for happiness. We took a flat in London, and Brandon went into the rehearsal, and I gave up the show business and started to learn all about boiling eggs and having babies and that kind of thing. Then the trouble started.'

The tired little woman's eyes roamed back in

the direction of the vacuum, and Derek put in another 'Yes?' to egg her on with the story.

'There was a woman in the show – Doris Fraser. Brandon fell in love with her. I got to know all about it, but I didn't say anything until one night I heard that things were getting a little too warm to be comfortable. We had a pretty good row about it, and Brandon promised that he would never see her again. A week later he told me he was leaving me.'

Feeling that 'Yes?' had been overworked by now, Derek made a series of clucking noises with his teeth.

'They lived together about a year. Then she left him. I think that sort of embittered Brandon. It changed him, anyway. After the War, when he came back into musical comedy and got right up to the top of the tree, he led a pretty hectic life. He hadn't a very good reputation, I'm afraid, right up to the time of his death. Not that that's any business of mine. Or of yours, Mr...'

'Hopkinson,' said Derek.

'Oh, Hopkinson? It looked like Hepplewaite in the register.'

'Thank you,' said Derek. 'And did you never see Brandon Baker after you – after he left you?'

'Oh, yes. Often. As a matter of fact, we got to be quite good friends. It's funny, that, but we did. I worked with him in a lot of shows – he in the leading parts and me in the chorus. And then I got a bit old and a bit short of wind and my figure started running away with itself, and I decided to chuck the stage and settle down. I'd managed to save a little money, and I bought this place up

151

cheap and started to lead the simple life. Brandon was very kind. He tried to help me with money when the hotel wasn't doing too well at the start, but I always managed to get along without it. There was an awful lot of good in Brandon Baker, Mr. Wilson, though you mightn't think it. It's funny, that, isn't it? – that there's usually a lot of good in bad people?'

'Quite,' said Derek. 'Er – have you heard anything about him recently. Before his death, I mean?'

'I hadn't seen him for over three years when I read about his death in the papers. But I'd heard a good deal about him. I used to hear from one or two friends who are still on the stage, though they oughtn't to be, poor dears. He wasn't behaving himself very well, I'm afraid. Drink – and women. Now I've taken up quite enough of your time, Mr. Wilson, and in any case I don't hold with speaking that way about the dead.'

'Just one other thing,' said the persistent Mr. Wilson. 'Did you ever hear Brandon Baker's name linked with that of ... Gwen Astle?'

The proprietress got up from the chair and set off on a renewed attack on the commercial room carpet.

'Brandon was living with Gwen Astle at the time of his death,' she said over her shoulder.

'Then...' said Derek. And stopped.

The commercial room door opened suddenly. A head of unbelievably golden hair shot around it, followed by a pair of large eyes framed in carefully groomed lashes, a small nose, and a brace of brilliantly scarlet lips. Miss Gwen Astle, celebrated musical-comedy star and late leading lady of the Douglas B. Douglas production *Blue Music.*

'Hi!' said Miss Astle through the wheeze of the vacuum. 'Is everyone dead in this place? I've been ringing the bell in my room since ten past nine, and nothing's happened so far. What's on to-day, eh? Everyone away at the local flower show, or what?'

'I'm sorry, Mrs. Wright,' said the proprietress, stopping the wheeze. 'I think something's wrong with the bell in Number eight. Were you wanting something?'

'Was I wanting something?' said Mrs. Wright *née* Astle. 'What the hell d'you think I've been keeping my finger on the ruddy bell for, eh? Listening to the pretty music, eh? I want a taxi for two o'clock and a double gin-and-ginger right now.'

'Yes, madam,' said the proprietress. 'I'll tell Willie to bring the drink up to your room.'

'Oh, never mind,' said the leading lady, changing her mind as leading and other types of ladies will. 'I'll go down and get it myself. Don't you forget that taxi now. Two p.m. on the dot. And choose one with a cushion. It's got to take me all the way back to London.'

'Mr. Wright and you leaving, madame?' asked the proprietress.

'I'm leaving,' said the lady at the doorway. 'Mr. Wright can stay here and rot for all I care. But I'm going back to London just as soon as I've got my scanties packed. And that's that.'

And that, apparently, was that, for the hair, eyes, nose and lips withdrew and the commercial-room door shut with a slam that very nearly wakened Willie the oaf in the bar parlour below in time to have Miss Astle's drink ready before she asked for it.

'Not the usual type of visitor we get here, Mr. Wilson,' said the proprietress apologetically.

'Do you know who that was?' demanded Derek.

'Yes, sir. A Mrs. Wright. Her husband comes here quite a bit, but it's the first time she's been here. And he's such a nice, quiet–'

'Mrs. Wright my Great-aunt Maggie,' said Derek. 'That hennaed hussy was Gwen Astle, the musical-comedy star.'

'Oh no, sir,' said the proprietress. 'You're mistaken, I'm sure, sir. I've never seen Gwen Astle on the stage, but I've seen her pictures in the papers many a time, and that's not her, sir. 'Why, she's real pretty – Gwen Astle, I mean, sir.'

'Did you ever see a photograph of an actress that was anything like the original? If that isn't Gwendoline Astle then I'm Nazi and you're a Storm Trooper.'

'I'm sure you're wrong, sir. That woman's not a bit–'

'What's the man like who's with her?' said Derek.

'Mr. Wright, sir?'

'Mr. Wright, if you like it that way.'

'Quite young, sir. Tall and thin. Good-looking, in a way, sir. And travelled, sir, to judge from all the labels on his suitcase. Well dressed, sir. Nice grey double breasted suit–'

'Light-grey overcoat and black felt hat?'

'Yes, sir. I think so, sir. How did you know that?'

'Saw them hanging in the hall downstairs,' said

154

Derek. 'Right, Mrs. Baker, I mustn't keep you any longer. Thanks very much for telling me what you did.'

'That's the first time I've been called Mrs. Baker for ten years, I think,' said the proprietress. 'My, it did sound queer. And you won't put anything in the newspapers, sir, will you?'

'I promise,' said Derek. 'You're the first actress or ex-actress who has uttered such an extraordinary statement, but I promise not to. Cheerio.'

'Good morning, sir,' said the proprietress, and roused the vacuum once again into a pitch of excitement.

Outside the door, Derek collided with Willie the oaf.

''Nuther tellygram, sir,' said Willie.

Sorry hear aches mattress grapefruit try pumping proprietress any signs Belshazzar Salome Dad

'Is that you, Willie?' said the proprietress, peeping her head out of the commercial-room door.

'Yes, mum. Tellygram for the gent, mum,' said Willie.

'Go round to Thompson's and order a taxi for two o'clock. It's to take Mrs. Wright to London.'

'Can't, mum. She's down in the bar mopping 'em up fast as I can turn 'em out. I'll send Jackie, mum.'

The oaf shambled off downstairs. Derek put telegram (ii) in his pocket, where there would be no chance of anyone reading the words 'try pumping proprietress'. He did not approve of pumping people, especially when the pumping

155

was as easy and as successful as had been the case this morning. 'Any signs Belshazzar Salome?' Signs of Salome, anyway. And if he didn't hustle and send off telegram (iii) the signs would have vanished in the direction of London. And ten to one Belshazzar too. Derek set off downstairs. He had gone half-way down when he turned suddenly, ran back to the top landing, and opened the door of No. 8 bedroom.

'What the hell do you want?' asked Ivor Watcyns, sitting on the edge of his bed pulling on a rather gay silk sock.

'I'm sorry,' said Derek, in what he hoped was a hiking accent. 'Isn't this Number ... oh no, neither it is ... I say, I am sorry ... I'd no idea... Mine's across the landing ... I *am* sorry... Good morning.'

'Good morning,' said Mr. Watcyns viciously.

Splendid. Both Belshazzar and Salome on the premises. Salome leaving for town at two o'clock. Belshazzar presumably staying on. Cue for telegram (iii).

Miss Prune recognized him with a slightly nervous smile. 'Proprietress gives many interesting saidelaights,' she read, 'Nebuchadnezzar's praivate laife ... Nebuchadnezzar's praivaite laife, sir?...'

'That's right,' said Derek. 'The same chap as before. Nebuchadnezzar. Neb. to you. Carry on, brightness.'

'Praivaite laife,' Miss Prune carried on. 'Henry Eighth ... words or figures for thet, sir?'

'Figures, I think,' said Derek. 'He would have liked it that way, don't you think?'

'Pardon?' said Miss Prune.

'I mean he was rather hot on figures, wasn't he?'

'Pardon?' said Miss Prune.

'Never mind,' said Derek. 'Don't worry. It doesn't matter. Put it in words.'

'Quaite, sir,' said Miss Prune. 'Henry Eighth femily men in comperison Belshezzar Selome both here but Selome returning London this aefternoon send ten quid incidental expenses beer excellent Derek... Three-and-a-penny, if you please, sir.'

'Three-and-a-penny? There's three-and-six. Give me the *Daily Gazette*, will you?'

'Certainly, sir. Fourpence change, sir. Good morning.'

'Good morning,' said Derek and negotiated himself past a barrel of apples and a rack of Local Views and out into the street.

Left alone, Miss Prune decided it was neither blasphemy nor high spirits, but just sheer common or garden lunacy. Extremely good for business, all the same. There hadn't been two telegrams of over a shilling sent from Craile Post Office in the same day since that time when the Colonel's steward wired the Colonel about the Colonel's cattle having anthrax.

Derek sauntered back to the 'Craile Arms' and ordered a pint from William. Expressing the opinion that it was rather stuffy in here, and that he would prefer to drink his beer outside if William had no objections, Derek left the bar parlour and parked tankard and self on the wooden bench which ran outside the front of the hotel. He was flanked on either side by two local gentlemen who were obviously rivals for the honour of being Craile's Oldest Inhabitant. Derek was not particularly interested in the conversation of these two lads, which seemed to run on two tracks only, *(a)* that Lunnon must Be a Rare Place and No Mistake, and *(b)* that Them There Motor-Cars were Fair Stomach-Turning and No Mistake. Nor was he really anxious to sit beside the 'Craile Arms' while he wrapped himself around his beer, for the wind was chilly and the wooden bench exceedingly hard.

The real reason for sitting on this uncomfortable bench, drinking beer in the presence of a couple of centenarians, was that Derek wished to have a ringside seat from which to view the departure to London of Miss Astle, alias Mrs. Wright. At what the wireless people tried to make us call thirteen-forty-five, he began to realize that something had gone wrong with the arranged departure. Either Miss Astle had changed her mind again. Or Mr. Watcyns had changed it for her. Or the taxi had developed carburettor trouble before reaching the hotel. Or the exit had been made by the back of the hotel. Or something. Derek got up, assured the two centenarians once and for all that London was one of the dullest spots on earth and that the motorcar was one of the most praiseworthy inventions of modern civilization, bade them a polite goodday, and went to seek out the proprietress. He found her in the hotel kitchen, in a thick haze which smelt strongly of both tomato soup and steak and onions.

'What's happened to Gwe – to the lady in Number eight?' he asked. 'She doesn't seem to have left as she arranged.'

'No, sir,' said the proprietress. 'She's not going now, sir. Mr. Wright came down and got her out of the bar and took her upstairs. An awful scene they made, sir. Locked her in the bedroom, and her screaming fit to wake the dead, sir, so Matilda here tells me.'

'Fit to wake the dead, sir,' corroborated Matilda, appearing gradually through the soup haze. 'He's a-beating of her, sir, that's what he's doing, sir. It made my blood run cold, sir, so help me Gawd if it didn't.'

Derek, having pushed away as much of the atmosphere as possible with a wave of his hand, decided – on inspecting Matilda – that her blood had probably seldom run very hot and that she might be a good teller of tales but a bad relater of facts.

He went into the dining-room and had lunch. Tomato soup (canned). Steak and onions or cold roast and beetroot. Pears (tinned) and cream (canned). After a spot of bother through asking for black coffee (an unheard of commodity in the village of Craile), he trotted back to the post office to seek out the Prune for telegram (iv). As you already know, the Prune was not to be found, being away at the Church Hall for the midweek meeting of the Dorcas Society and very busy indeed, putting elastic in a pair of knickers destined eventually to cover part of a young lady in the Fu-Chow Mission Field.

Apparently Miss Prune had not had time to

159

instruct her younger sister in the strange ways of the young man who kept on sending Biblical telegrams to someone in London, for Derek had to start all over again at the beginning and spell Nebuchadnezzar to the younger Prune.

'Two z's,' said Derek patiently. 'One for zebra. And then another one, just like the first, for Zambuk. And after that it gets easy again. Z-z-a-r. Nebuchadnezzar. There.'

'...Nebuchadnezzar's death suggests search his flat, Derek,' said the younger Prune. 'Two shillings and sevenpence, please, sir. Thank you. Good afternoon, sir.'

'Good afternoon,' said Derek, wondering if there was any chance of Sir Kingsley Wood reintroducing the penny post as a result of all this sudden rush of business.

From that moment on Derek behaved rather more like the hiker he appeared to be than the journalist son of a detective that he actually was. Roughly speaking, his time-table for the rest of the day ran something like this, 3 p.m., leave Miss Prune's shop and visit Eliz. ruins; 3.30 p.m., sit down on Eliz. ruins and sleep; 5.15 p.m., return to 'Craile Arms' for high tea (finnan haddock); 6.30 p.m., conversation in bar with William and two centenarians about the Battle of Waterloo and present state of potato crops; 8.45 p.m., supper; 9 p.m., witnessed departure of Mr. Watcyns and Miss Astle (or Mr. and Mrs. Wright) in high-powered car, presumably to London; 9.20 p.m., surprise return of Mr. Watcyns alone. Gathered from conversation in bar that Mr. Watcyns had put Miss Astle on the London train, but was

160

himself staying on at Craile for some days; 9.30 p.m., rather dull symphony concert on wireless set in hotel lounge; 10.50 p.m., walk through village before turning in – somewhat surprised to notice Mr. Watcyns' car standing alone and neglected at entrance to Craile Woods, a mile or so out of the village. And 11.45 p.m., contact with the barbed-wire mattress.

A dull afternoon and evening, you say. And dull it certainly was compared with the evening put in by the chambermaid Matilda and her lover, Police-constable Lightfoot, of Aylesbury. First of all there was the business of Getting Out, this not being Matilda's official night off and the missis being that strict about that kind of thing. The lavatory window and the co-operation of William had to be brought into use before the escape was successfully managed. Then there was the meeting. This took place by arrangement behind the larger of the Colonel's two cowsheds, and lasted a little over an hour and a quarter. Police-constable Lightfoot was a slow mover in matters of the heartbeats, as well as ordinary beats. And then there was the question of Where To Go. Matilda, it seemed, favoured Craile Woods. And P. C. Lightfoot, it seemed, was all for the Eliz. ruins., it being rather damp underfoot. But Matilda won the night, saying that the ruins were far too bare and open and you never knew who would be coming on you suddenly, and anyway she felt like the woods to-night. So the woods it was. What these two young people did, or thought, or said is none of our business. Indeed, if you make it your business to be your business you would find it all

161

extraordinarily dull. The main thing is that they enjoyed themselves.

At ten to twelve Police-constable Lightfoot said, 'Time we was getting along, love.' He had been saying this at intervals since about a quarter to eleven, but this time he apparently meant it. He pushed Matilda's head from the position it had taken up round about the second and third buttons of his tunic, and he buttoned the top button, and straightened his hair, and found his helmet, and removed a slug from the lining of the helmet, and got up stiffly, shook himself, and pulled Matilda up after him. Matilda shook herself, and found her beret, and pulled it on, and powdered her nose, and pulled down her skirt, and put her arm round P. C. Lightfoot's ample circumference, and together the love-birds set off on the homeward track, deciding to go back through the short cut by the side of the little brook which ended up by being a water-supply for the Colonel's livestock. Because there was something about moonlight shining on the water (although the brook happened to be completely dried up at the moment), and, in any case, it took nearly a quarter of an hour longer if you went back to the village by the short-cut instead of by the ordinary path through the woods.

On they went, then, in a completely satisfied silence. They had been meandering along for five minutes or so, when P. C. Lightfoot's anything-but-light feet tripped over something at the side of the brook, and he thundered to earth like a ton of coals being shot down a chute. He brought Matilda down with him, and the pair of silly young asses lay for quite a time in the long grass giggling happily. And then P. C. Lightfoot picked himself and the future Mrs. P. C. Lightfoot up, and fumbled for his lantern, and switched it on to see whether it was a tree or a log or what that he had tripped over. And Matilda's giggle changed suddenly to a high-pitched shriek that wakened a family of crows in the trees above and sent them cawing in a complaining and irritated manner. It was not a tree. Nor a log. It was the body of a dead woman.

CHAPTER TEN

Mr. Wilson, senr., arrived in Craile by car at eleven-fifteen the following morning. Being July, precious little water had flowed under the inadequate little bridge which crossed the river at the entrance to the village. On the other hand a great deal of things had happened in the village itself. By eleven-fifteen Miss Prune was in a state of complete and utter collapse, being revived by smelling-salts in the back room of her shop. Having led a calm unruffled life for every morning of the past fifty-eight years, it had all been too much for Miss Prune. First of all the news of the Murder. Miss Twigg had brought that in a hazy version at first, when she looked in for lettuce at a quarter past nine. There had been a murder last night in Craile Woods. 'Oh, good God!' Miss Prune said – the first time she had used the name of the Deity outside the scope of her work as a member of the church choir and a teacher of the Sunday-school infant class. But who? Or whom, or whatever it was? An Unknown Female, said Miss Twigg, and dashed off to ferret for further details, forgetting her lettuce in the heat of the excitement. Then there had been the vicar's sister. But the vicar's sister had been most disappointing, not knowing a thing about the Murder, not knowing even that such a thing had taken place, and merely expressing the opinion, when Miss Prune told her the news, that she hoped it was an ill-founded rumour, as it was things like that which gave the village a bad name. Miss Prune had been pretty peeved by the lack of interest shown by the vicar's sister, had given her half a dozen of the doubtful eggs that she had intended sending back to Mr. Mitchell at the dairy, *and* a penny short in the change, and had bundled her out. And then, only ten minutes later, there had been the strange young man who was stopping at the hotel and who had kept on sending these weird telegrams full of people in the Old Testament.

The strange young man hadn't heard, either. In a way that was a disappointment to Miss Prune, although it was nice to be the first to break the news. Miss Prune, somehow, had been quite sure that the strange young man was mixed up somewhere in the business. In fact, she'd been rather surprised at seeing him bounce into the shop like that at all, for Miss Prune had inwardly put him down as the Man Who Did It, and had imagined him well away from Craile by this time and on board a ship on his way to the Continent.

She would have to give evidence at the inquest, she supposed, 'Yes, your Honour, or your Worship, or whatever it was, he came repeatedly into my shop and sent strange telegrams to an address in London. In code, I think they were. Yes, sir, raight from the start I was suspicious of him. He was dressed laike a haiker, but he didn't talk the least bit laike one. I've hed a great deal of experience with haikers in my shop in the lest few years, and you cen't deceive me.' Yes; at the inquest she would wear her navy-blue velour. (At the trial, if they got him...) But in bounced the strange young man at twenty to ten, looking really very nice and clean and attractive and not a bit like a murderer. So Miss Prune passed on the news, partly because that was what news was for, and partly to note his reactions (was that the right word?). He had, of course, heard about the dreadful affair last night? No?

Well, they've found the body of an Unknown Female lying dead in the copse at the back of Craile Woods. And reaction? Wagon-loads of the stuff. The strange young man had stopped twiddling with the rack of Local Views, one penny each, and had stared at Miss Prune and shot out the word 'Murder?' Yes, murder, Miss Prune had repeated. And then there had been a perfect salvo of questions flung over the counter at Miss Prune, to very few of which she knew the answer, but to all of which she managed somehow to reply.

Who was it? An Unknown Female, that was what Miss Twigg had said. And who had found her? Well, Miss Prune wasn't quite sure, but she thought it had been the girl Matilda Mowitt, the maid at the hotel. And when? Oh, but Miss Prune really had no idea, but it must have been pretty late, because she understood from what Miss Twigg had said that the girl Matilda was ... er ... enjoying the evening with her fiancé, who was a policeman in Aylesbury. And it was on their way home that they just happened to come on the body suddenly, you see, so that would be either just before midnight or just after midnight, because the girl Matilda was one of those modern girls, and many a time she'd had her aunt in the shop complaining about the hours she kept when she was out with men.

And where was the body now? the strange young man had demanded. Well, Miss Prune had really no idea at all, but she imagined the police-station – wouldn't that be the usual place to take the ... er ... the deceased? Right, then where was the blessed police-station, the young man had asked – quite snappily, as though his life and death depended on knowing. Miss Prune's suspicions soared again. She must remember every detail of this conversation for the inquest. 'He appeared haighly egitated, sir, and when I pointed out the police-station to him he left the shop at once and disappeared in the opposite direction at a great speed.' But as a matter of fact, he didn't. He said, 'Thanks very much,' and, 'Here – send this wire, same address as before,' and out of the shop and across the street and over the little gate at the foot of P. C. Root's garden without even bothering to unlatch the latch and open it, and up the drive, and was both ringing a bell and knocking a knocker before Miss Prune could find her long-distance glasses to bring him back into focus. And, what's more, inside P. C. Root's cottage, alias the police-station.

Miss Prune was left with telegram (v):

Thanks ten quid cannot understand your last wire Belshazzar definitely here all night stand by for possible further developments immediately Derek

Not that that told you much. 'Possible immediate developments', though. Promising, that. And sure enough within another ten minutes the strange young man shot out of P. C. Root's cottage, and took the gate in a leap, and bounded across the road into the shop again. With P. C. Root standing at the door of his cottage shouting, ''Ere, 'ere, 'ere, 'ere, 'ere!' over and over again.

'Another telegram,' said the young man. 'Come on, get a move on!'

Miss Prune got a move on.

Absolute sensation here come down at once Derek

The poorest so far by a long way from the financial point of view, but definitely the most exciting of the series. '*Ebsolute sensation*' read Miss Prune, her hand shaking just a little. 'Is anything wrong, sir?' 'Nothing,' said the young man, with one of his attractive smiles, 'Nothing at all. One-and-a-penny? Thank you so much.' And out of the door again, and off along the Main Street in the direction of the hotel as fast as his legs could carry him. And, 'Millicent!' Miss Prune had yelled –

167

'Millicent, come and mind the shop!' and had followed the young man out (the first time in her life she could remember being seen in the village without her hat on), and had crossed over to P. C. Root's cottage and done her level best to get something out of that massive lump of the law. Unsuccessfully, though, for P. C. Root was obviously in one of his aloof moods and was giving nothing away. Indeed, he managed to get rather more out of Miss Prune than Miss Prune got out of him.

'Do you happen to have any idea as to who that man what was inside of your shop just now is?' asked P. C. Root laboriously.

'No,' said Miss Prune. 'Yes. At least, he's a young man staying at the "Arms", I understand. What has happened? Is he mixed up in this ghestly business, Constable?'

'I'm not so sure as how he isn't,' said P. C. Root.

'But tell me – is it true, really? Have you any idea, Constable, as to who the unfortunate woman may be?'

'Maybe I have and maybe I haven't,' said P. C. Root.

'Is the ... is she inside?'

'I'm not saying as how she is or isn't,' said P. C. Root.

'Well,' said Miss Prune, exasperated, 'why on earth don't you go efter that young man? Stending there shouting, "Here, here, here," laike thet!... *Do* something, man!'

'All right, all right,' said P. C. Root. 'They'll be plenty doing when things start doing, don't you fear, P. C. Lightfoot's gone down to Aylesbury on his bike to get up the Inspector. Then I suppose Scotland Yard'll be in on it. We'll all be in the papers to-night, you see if we're not, Miss Prune.'

'Do you heppen to know how the person was ... er ... killed?' asked Miss Prune.

'Maybe I does. And maybe I doesn't. None of your business, that, if you don't mind my saying so. What was that young man after in your shop, Miss Prune?'

'He gave me a telegram.'

'Tellygram, eh? And what was the wording of same, might I enquire?'

'I really have no raight to tell you, Constable–'

'Come on, come on, come on!'

'Ebsolute sensation here come down at once Derek.'

'And who was the tellygram addressed to, Miss Prune?'

'To – oh, dear, this is all against the regulations, Constable – to Wilson, Fifty-eight Park Terrace, London. He's sent quaite a number since he arraived yesterday – all to the same men. It's may belief that he's in league with–'

'Maybes,' said P. C. Root, retiring inside his cottage. 'And maybes not. I shall probably require you again for interrogation, Miss Prune, when I am able to leave the cottage–'

'I see,' said Miss Prune, going rather pale. 'You've got to stay and keep guard over the ... the Body. Thet's it, isn't it?'

'Maybes,' said P. C. Root heavily. 'In the meantime, kindly let me know if any further happenings ... er ... happen,' ended the constable rather lamely.

There had been all that excitement, then. And then – good gracious, it made her go quite faint to think of it – there had been the reappearance of the young man. About an hour and a half later, that must have been; but the time had simply flown, for there had been one customer after another, and the story to tell to them all, for most of them had seen Miss Prune talking to P. C. Root and just dropped in to get the real story. Then the young man. Looking very worried, Miss Prune thought, and not a bit like himself, quite stern and never smiling at all. Hadn't there been any answer to his last telegram? No, not yet. But at that very moment the 'phone had rung and the answer come through, and here it was,

Sorry cannot get down to-day chief holding conference re new designs constables helmets will try tomorrow what has happened anyway Dad

Miss Prune couldn't make head nor tail of it, but it had a dreadful effect on the young man. 'Hell!' said the young man. 'Hell and damn and blast the ruddy conference!' said the young man. And then, 'I'm very sorry. I beg your pardon. Could I use the telephone, please?' said the young man politely, as though language like that could be cancelled out merely by a smile and an apology. And inside the telephone-box he'd stepped and put through a trunk call to London. Miss Prune heard him distinctly, because the door of the telephone-box didn't close properly unless you gave it

170

a good bang, and Miss Prune had never had it attended to because it was rather interesting to...

'Whitehall one-two-one-two. Personal call for Detective Inspector Wilson, of the Criminal Investigation Department...' Miss Prune dusted the pyramid of soap packets busily, her best ear towards the 'phone-box. 'That you, Dad?'... And then the young man on the other side of the glass door had given her *such* a look and banged the door shut, and that had been the end of that. But not the end of the day's excitements. Good gracious, no!

Enter P. C. Root while the young man was still busy inside the telephone-box. And P. C. Lightfoot of the Aylesbury Constabulary. And another P. C. whom Miss Prune had never seen before. 'Good morning,' said Miss Prune weakly, 'And ... er ... what can I do for you, gentlemen?' Doing her best to appear as though she thought it was postage stamps or even Choice Bon-Bons that had occasioned the invasion of the law into her shop. But knowing perfectly well that it wasn't, even before P. C. Root said heavily, 'That's all right, Miss Prune. We're not requiring you at the moment. It's this young gent here as what we're after.' And then... Oh, dear. More smelling-salts, quickly, Millicent, *please*.

For out came the young man from the telephone-box, looking much more pleased with life than when he had gone in. And, 'I'd like a word with you, sir,' P. C. Root had said.

'Splendid!' said the young man. 'First of all, I'd like one with you. My name's Wilson. My father is Inspector Wilson of Scotland Yard. He sent me down here to look into a matter that he's rather interested in at the moment – look into it in quite an unofficial kind of way. Well, it's ended up rather differently to what we expected, see? And at present you don't know who the murdered person is, do you? And you definitely don't know who the murderer is, do you?'

''Ere, 'ere, 'ere–' said P. C. Root.

'I must warn you that anything–' said P. C. Lightfoot.

'Never heard tell of such a thing,' said the anonymous member of the trio.

'Shut up!' said Derek. 'And stay shut up. Here's a bit of news for you. I know who was the woman who was found dead in Craile Woods last night. And I know who the man was who killed her.'

''Ere, 'ere–'

'Exactly. Hear, hear. Glad you agree with me.'

'Come on, then, young fellow-me-lad,' said P. C. Lightfoot, taking charge. 'Who the 'ell are they, then – you that knows everything?'

'Under the circumstances, I'm not going to tell you that.'

'Oh,' said P. C. Lightfoot. 'Oho. Refuses to give the information when I requested so to do eh? Come along, come along.'

'There's only one way of getting actual proof of this murder, and that is to do nothing. Just carry on being your own sweet selves without an idea in your three heads.

'There's more in this business than just finding the murderer of the woman whose body you found last night. Much more.'

'Do you know that Scotland Yard are coming

down here right away?' asked P. C. Root viciously. 'Doing nothing, indeed!'

'No, they're not,' said Derek. 'I've just been speaking to Inspector Wilson of Scotland Yard, and they're doing nothing of the sort.'

'Are you trying to make out that you're Inspector Wilson's son?'

'There's no need to try to make it out, my good man. Nothing like that in our family. I *am* Inspector Wilson's son.'

'Then why are you registered at the "Craile Arms" under the name of J. Hopkinson?' demanded P. C. Root.

'For perfectly good reasons of my own.'

'Is that so? Miss Prune...'

'Yes, Constable?' Miss Prune appeared from behind the soap-flake pyramid looking rather flushed.

'Know anything about this young man here?'

'I've already told you all I know, Constable. He keeps sending odd telegrams to a Mr. Wilson in London.'

'What d'you mean – odd telegrams?'

'Er ... telegrams with odd names in them. Biblical allusions, as a metter of fect.'

'Arrr!'... said P. C. Root, seeing all in a flash. 'Never showed no signs of violence in the shop at no time, has he, Miss Prune?'

'Er ... no. He used haighly abusive language when he came into the shop helf an hour ago.'

'Such as might be used by a religious fanattick, as you might say, Miss Prune?'

'I really have no idea ... it was certainly not the kaind of language a normal person would use,

I'm sure...'

'Arrr!' said P. C. Root again, satisfied.

'Umum,' said P. C. Lightfoot, corroborating.

The anonymous P. C. contented himself with tapping his helmet with his forefinger in a way Derek did not at all approve of.

'We'll have to ask you to accompany us to the station, young man,' said P. C. Root.

'Anything you say may be used—' said P. C. Lightfoot.

'No need for violence,' said the anonymous arm of the law.

'Are you three birds trying to arrest me?' asked Derek.

'Come along, come along, now.'

'Of all the—'

''Ere, 'ere, 'ere, 'ere!...'

Mr. Wilson, junr., was led quietly but firmly to the door of the post office.

'Miss Prune!' he called out.

'Send this telegram, will you,

Your presence here essential on my way to local gaol arrested by nitwit policeman, Derek.

''Ere, 'ere,' said the idiot policeman.

'Same address as before,' said Derek.

'One-and-eightpence, sir,' said Miss Prune, just conscious enough to realize that business should never be refused even in the queerest of circumstances.

'There's half a crown,' said Derek. He was shuffled out, across the road, up the drive and into P. C. Root's cottage. He noticed for the first

174

time that there was a little illuminated sign tucked away in Virginia creeper above the door which remarked, 'Police Station'.

Well, there was all the excitement. Miss Prune dithered for a good while about the telegram. Should she send it? Or hadn't she better ask P. C. Root about it? But after all, she'd received the thing and been paid for the thing, and so off the thing went to London. With the result that in rather less than two hours Detective Inspector Wilson of Scotland Yard landed in person in the village of Craile in an Austin-seven several sizes too small for him.

'Police-station,' said Mr. Wilson, senr., brusquely.

'Beg pardon, sir?' said Miss Prune.

'The police-station, woman. Where is it?'

'Just across the road, sir. Thet house with the creeper, sir.'

'No, no – you don't understand. It's the police-station I want.'

'Thet's it, sir. Straight across.'

'My God!' said Mr. Wilson, senr., and went straight across.

At which point Miss Prune staggered back against her counter and called weakly for smelling-salts and her younger sister. And, there, as it happened, ended her brief, but exciting, connection with the affair. Not that she allowed the matter to drop then and there, of course; there was all the fuss in the papers to come yet, and for quite six months afterwards it was Miss Prune's main source of conversation. But her actual contact with the case dried up abruptly at the moment when Mr. Wilson, senr., bounded out of her shop and across the road. There were no more visits from the strange young man, no odd telegrams informing the gentleman in London that Nebuchadnezzar's wife had turned out to be Belshazzar's sister Salome – or whatever it was. From that moment on Miss Prune had to give up actual participation in the business, and drift back into her old rôle of *proprietrix du bureau de change*. Ten to ten – Miss Twigg, cucumber and *Home Chat*, and was there anything fresh about the Murder this morning? Ten past – the vicar's sister, notepaper and photographic paste, and had she read in the paper the queer way in which the Murder had ended up? And so on…

Mr. Wilson, senr., in the meantime, was well inside Craile Police Station (*née* Laburnum Cottage), and was throwing his weight about to fairly good effect. Constables Root, Lightfoot and Anon. appeared to be in a distrustful mood this morning, and it was only after a heavy argument and the display of a few indisputable credentials that Mr. Wilson was able to convince them that he was Inspector Wilson of the C.I.D. Once convinced, Constables Root, Lightfoot and Anon. grovelled, mumbled sheepish apologies, removed their helmets in the Presence, and were apparently struck dumb.

'Well?' said Mr. Wilson, sent. 'Come on – speak, one of you. Is my son here?'

'There's a young gentleman here, sir–' said Constable Root guardedly.

'Under arrest?' barked Mr. Wilson.

'No, sir,' said Constable Lightfoot, shocked.

'We just thought as how it would be better, in view of the somewhat suspicious-like conduct of the gent, to–'

'Oaf!' said Mr. Wilson. 'Produce him.'

Oaf Lightfoot disappeared into the bowels of the police-station and produced Mr. Wilson, junr.

'Good morning,' said Derek. 'Nice to see you. How's Martha's sister's neuritis?'

'Damn Martha's sister's neuritis,' said Mr. Wilson, senr. 'What the blazes are you doing here?'

'Ask the Prides of the Force,' said Derek. 'They seem to think I'm mixed up in something.'

'And what's happened? What's the "absolute sensation" you burbled about in your telegrams?'

'Gwen Astle was found murdered last night in the woods just outside the village.'

'Good God!'

'She's in there, if you want to look at her. Shot through the abdomen. Watcyns took her away from the hotel a bit after ten last night – said she was going back to London and he was driving her to the station. He came back alone about eleven. I went out afterwards and saw his car standing empty at the entrance to the woods. She was found round about midnight by Exhibit B here, who was studying bird-life at eventide with one of the lasses of the village.'

'Dangerous way of keeping her mouth shut, wasn't it?' said Mr. Wilson, senr.

'What d'you mean?'

'It looks to me as though Gwen Astle knew the real truth about Brandon Baker's death. She rings me up, and is removed to this nice quiet spot before I can get to her. And once here she

177

still refuses to keep her mouth shut – and has the job done for her. Doesn't it strike you that way?'

'Yes, I suppose that's it.'

'Ivor Watcyns still in the hotel?'

'Yes. At least, he was this morning. That's where I got into trouble with these flat-feet here – I did my level best to persuade them that I had a fairly good idea who had done the murder, and that our only chance of getting hold of him was to lie low and not let the news of the murder all over the village. I could have got in touch with him then – he's no idea who I am, you see. Thinks I'm merely a depressing example of the hiking genius. Unfortunately these birds wouldn't listen. They took one look at my zip-fastened shirt and put me down as N. B. G. right away. And then the Prune female in the post office started gibbering about the telegrams I'd been sending, and that I'd always acted peculiar-laike in her presence, and that settled it. I wasn't exactly put behind bars, but I was locked in Mrs. Root's back kitchen, which is the equivalent of a prison cell in Craile.'

'I see,' said Mr. Wilson, senr.

'I'm sure we're sorry, sir,' said P. C. Root, finding his tongue and making somewhat shaky use of it.

'We were only doing our duty, in a manner of speaking, sir,' said P. C. Lightfoot.

'You couldn't blame us, sir,' said P. C. Anon.

'That's all right,' said Mr. Wilson. 'I think we'll look up friend Watcyns at the hotel, Derek. You two – you'd better come along. I may have someone worth looking up for you this time. You'd better stay here and look after that girl's body. I'll

178

telephone to headquarters to send down some men.'

'Yes, sir.'

'Come on, then.'

The two centenarians on the bench outside the 'Craile Arms' stopped their debate on the state of the crops in pre-War England in mid-sentence as Mr. Wilson, senr., Mr. Wilson, junr., P. C. Root and P. C. Lightfoot stepped carefully inside the hotel. Centenarian A then ventured the opinion that there was Something Mighty Queer Up and No Mistake. Centenarian B concurred, adding that he had never liked the Look of that young gent in them there pants of his. Inside the hotel, the Wilsons and the guardians of the law punched all available bells and knocked on several windows and doors. The more intelligent maid appeared at last, carrying a bundle of bedclothes.

'Could I see the proprietress?' asked Derek.

'Sorry, sir. She's away, sir.'

'Away?'

'Yes, sir. She's gone off for a few days' holiday, sir. Left by the first train this morning. She's been feeling a bit run down like, sir, and she was going to take a few days off while we were slack-like, sir.'

'I see,' said Derek. 'Is Mr. Wright in the hotel just now?'

'Him that was in Number eight, you mean, sir?'

'That's the chap.'

'No, sir. He's gorn, sir.'

'Gone!'

'Yes, sir. He went away this morning. Just after breakfast. He'd meant to stay the whole week, I

179

think, sir, but he told me he got a letter calling him back to London and he'd have to go right away. He had his car brought round at ten and paid his bill – paid it right up for the whole week, sir – and off he went, sir.'

'Damn!' said Derek. 'Right, thanks very much. That's all.'

'Wright?' queried Mr. Wilson. 'What's Wright got to do with it?'

'Watcyns and Gwen Astle were registered here as Mr. and Mrs. Wright. Double bedroom. Two pairs of shoes outside the door. Breakfast in bed. All mod. cons.'

'I see,' said Mr. Wilson. 'Well, the bird's flown, damn him.'

'Anything up, sir?' inquired P. C. Lightfoot from a distance.

'Nothing – except that the man who murdered the woman you found last night has done a bunk,' said Mr. Wilson. 'Not that he'll get very far, though. Derek – where's the telephone?'

'In there – through that door.'

'Right. Put a call through to Scotland Yard. I'll speak when you get them. Now then, you two – I want as little publicity made about this matter as possible, understand? The fact that a woman was murdered here last night – that'll get into the papers, of course, but there's no need for anything more to get in, see? No "police expect to make an arrest immediately", or "Scotland Yard are already on the scene of the crime" stuff, get me? You'll have reporters swarming down here, but you've got to keep your months shut, understand? The man who stayed here as Mr. Wright

180

murdered the woman you found dead last night. We've no actual proof yet, but it's a thousand to one that he did. But what I'm trying to get at is something that happened before that, see?

'I'm not so interested in this killing, but I'm exceedingly interested in another – and the same fellow's going to answer for both. As it happened, my son was quite right when he tried to get you to hush it up – this man Wright hadn't any idea that there was someone down here watching him; what we want him to think is that he's got away with it without anyone being any the wiser. So – you understand – keep your mouths shut and I'll see you're thanked in the proper way, understand?'

P. C. Root and P. C. Lightfoot had nodded their heads vigorously at each of Mr. Wilson's 'understands', with the result that their helmets were now seriously impeding their vision.

'Call's through, dad,' said Derek, appearing out of the hotel office.

'Right,' said Mr. Wilson. 'I'll come and have a look over the place where you found the body, Lightfoot, if you'll hang about outside until I'm ready. Where's this 'phone?... Good God, I thought this type went out with crinolines... Hullo, Scotland Yard?... Inspector Wilson speaking ... put me through to Mr. Herries, will you?... Yes... Herries?... Wilson speaking from Craile... Craile ... C-r-a – oh, it doesn't matter – Wilson speaking from Llandudno... Listen, John ... Gwen Astle, the musical-comedy wench, was murdered down here last night... Yes ... and I know who murdered her, that's more important ... Ivor Watcyns... Yes, the writer-bloke... Listen –

181

remember I told you there was more in that Brandon Baker murder than met the eye?... Right... Well, I'll lay a thousand quid to my winter flannels that Ivor Watcyns killed Brandon Baker, and planted it on the other fellow – Foster, that's his name... How? – it's too long and too clever to tell you now, but I'm perfectly certain Watcyns has two stiff bodies to answer for... Yes... Listen, then... He's cleared out ... he was staying at the hotel down here, and he did a bunk a bit after ten... He'd come to London, sure, first of all... I want you to get every man you can on to him ... get round to his flat right away – three-eighteen Cluny Terrace, N... There's a chance he might go to Gwen Astle's flat, too, if there was anything he didn't want to be looked into ... three-eighteen Chalmers Street, I think it is ... you'll find it in the directory... But I want you to make sure he doesn't get out of the country ... watch the boat trains this afternoon ... send someone down to Southampton and Tilbury... and get in touch with Croydon right away – if he's moving he'll probably move by air ... there's a 'plane for Berlin in half an hour, I know – see he's not on that... Right ... I'm sticking down here just now to have a look round, but I'll be back in town to-night... Yes, I'll come along and see you then... Oh, ring me up here if you get hold of him... Yes – arrest him on the spot... What? For the murder of Brandon Baker and Gwen Astle, of course. Sure? ... I'm as sure as a hen that's laid a double-yolked egg... Righto... Thanks very much... Good-bye.'

'Surely and swiftly, the police net is closing in

in all directions,' said Derek, who had listened to the recitation.

'Yes ... he won't get out of the country if we can help it.'

'I shouldn't think he'll try to' said Derek.

'Why not?'

'It's about the stupidest thing a murderer could do. It's the first thing the police think of – watching the ports and the aerodromes. Much safer to go and book a room at the Strand Palace, in my opinion.'

'For a man who knows he's being chased, yes. But Watcyns doesn't know. That's our advantage. The woman who was found dead last night hasn't been identified as the woman who was staying with him here at the hotel. And won't be. "Another Unsolved Murder Mystery", the *Daily Record* will say. All to the good. Ivor Watcyns hasn't the least grounds for thinking that anyone is connecting him with the murder of Gwen Astle – let alone with the murder of Brandon Baker. And in those circumstances I'll be very much surprised if he doesn't slip quietly away from England's green and pleasant land some time to-day.'

'Well, he won't get very far,' said Derek; 'unless he's already aboard the lugger.'

'Hope not ... I wonder – what about ringing up Douglas B. Douglas? He might know something about him, mightn't he?'

'He might. I'll get him for you.'

'Right.'

Derek disentangled the various parts of the obsolete telephone and asked for Mr. Douglas B. Douglas's London office. Was Mr. Douglas in?

No, he wasn't. Oh any idea where one could find Mr. Douglas at this time of the day? Yes, Mr. Douglas was at the Grosvenor Theatre, supervising rehearsals for the reopening of *Blue Music*. Thank you very much ... Grosvenor Theatre? Oh – was Mr. Douglas B. Douglas in the theatre? Yes, he was. Could one speak to him, then, please? Sorry, but Mr. Douglas gave strict orders he was not to be interrupted during the rehearsal. Perhaps one could take a message, could one? Well ... it was really rather important – a personal message. Inspector Wilson of Scotland Yard speaking. Scotland Yard? Yes, Scotland Yard. Oh, well, I'll get Mr. Douglas right away in that case. Hold the line, please. Just a minute, sir.

'Here – you'd better speak,' said Derek, handing the receiver to Mr. Wilson senr., 'I said it was you. Sounds better.'

'Right ... what time is it now?' said Mr. Wilson while waiting with the receiver to his ear.

'Two-fifteen. And I've had no lunch.'

'Watcyns cleared out at ten. That's four hours. Damn – he may be anywhere by now. If only we'd got the Yard people on the job sooner.'

'Douglas may know the likely place he'd make for.'

'Yes, but– Hullo?... That you, Douglas?... Wilson speaking. Yes – sorry to interrupt the show... You don't happen to know anything about Ivor Watcyns, do you?'

'Yes,' said Mr. Douglas B. Douglas's deep baritone voice, 'I do. He's one of the most brilliant writers of the younger school. He's done a great deal of work for me, and I hope he'll do some more. Only he's getting a bit high-hat in matters of payment these days, and what with the depression and the weather hitting the theatre business the way it's doing, I very much doubt if–'

'No, no,' interrupted Mr. Wilson. 'I don't want a biography, thank you. I mean – I'm rather anxious to get hold of him right away. You don't know where I'd have any chance of finding him, do you? I've an idea he might have ... gone abroad, or into the country, or something like that. I suppose you couldn't...'

'Just a minute,' said Mr. Douglas's voice.

'What's he say?' asked Derek.

'He hasn't said anything important yet. Except, "Just a minute." I expect he's gone to find out from some of his damned secretaries or something – two-fifteen I'm afraid we've missed the boat, Derek. He could be in Paris by this time. 'There's a 'plane leaves at– Hullo?'

'Yes?'

'Who's that, please?' said Mr. Wilson, senr., preparatory to a few remarks on the subject of idiot operators who cut you off in the middle of a conversation.

'This is Ivor Watcyns speaking,' said Watcyns' smooth and pleasant voice in Mr. Wilson's right ear. 'I'm very busy with a rehearsal just now. What d'you want, please?'

Mr. Wilson, senr., put back the antique receiver on its prehistoric hook.

CHAPTER ELEVEN

Away back about the Genesis of this business wasn't it remarked that Douglas B. Douglas was a master of publicity? If there were any who doubted the truth of that statement at the time (and it is almost certain that there were not), they had the thing settled quite definitely by the way Mr. Douglas handled the reopening of his show *Blue Music*. From the moment when that heavy red curtain swept down and along and over the still body of Brandon Baker, Mr. Douglas realized that he was in on a Good Thing. There were temporary disadvantages, of course – the withdrawal of the show, the waste of the previous bout of publicity, the returning of a certain amount of good hard cash, the finding of another actor to take Brandon Baker's place, the rehearsals and the job of working up the public once more into a state of coma in which they would pay five guineas for seats at the first night and not think they were doing anything out of the ordinary in paying that sum.

There were those disadvantages, granted. But apart from them the thing (to use Mr. Douglas's own expression) was a Wow of Wows. After all, it wasn't every theatrical manager that got a perfectly high-class murder presented to him in the way of free publicity. It was an opportunity that came seldom to publicity-mongers, and Douglas

B. Douglas took hold of it with two capable fists.

Mr. Douglas B. Douglas (said the *Daily Record*) was negotiating with a world-famed American stage and screen star to take the leading part in his musical comedy *Blue Music,* vacated in such unhappy circumstances by the death of Brandon Baker. Mr. Douglas B. Douglas (remarked the *Daily Echo*) had left Croydon by air for Berlin, where he was hoping to fix up a contract with a famous Continental actor to play the leading part in *Blue Music* when the show reopened on the thirteenth. The famous theatrical manager Mr. Douglas B. Douglas (remarked the *News-Courier*) had left Berlin for Budapest, where he hoped to arrange for the appearance of a well-known European cabaret star in the late Brandon Baker's part in the show *Blue Music*. And so on. Actually, Mr. Douglas B. Douglas got hold of a young English actor whom he found shaking an elegant leg among the ladies of the Folies Bergère in Paris, and whom he persuaded to take over the part at a salary which was approximately one-twentieth of that which he had paid the late Mr. Baker, on condition that he went into rehearsal at once, and that he played the part with a pronounced foreign accent.

The young leg-shaker agreed, changed his name from Milton to Miltonne, went to seven Maurice Chevalier films to get the local colour Mr. Douglas demanded, crossed the Channel to his native shores and was billed as the 'Rage of Paris.'

That little job settled, Mr. Douglas fixed up an English actress who had been 'resting' for the past eight months (this time at a salary one-thirtieth of that recently received by Gwen Astle), announced the lady as coming 'Direct from Her American Triumphs', and put the show once again into rehearsal. There was a nice large theatre vacant in Glasgow, and the *Blue Music* company went North – lock, stock, barrel, and revolving stage – and played to audiences of rather more than fifteen hundred pounds per week while the two newcomers to the show were being instructed in their parts. And that, in case you do not recognize it as such, is Big Business.

There was also the murder side of it. A lot could be made of that. A lot was made of it. In an exclusive interview to the *Evening Herald* theatre correspondent, Mr. Douglas said that bad luck had dogged the show ever since it had gone into rehearsal. It would be remembered that Miss Astle's priceless emerald bracelet had been stolen when the show was having its preliminary run in Manchester, following which there had been the sad deaths of Mr. Baker and Miss Astle herself. Mr. Douglas, however, was defying superstition and putting on the show for its reopening performance on Friday, the thirteenth.

It was probable that the public would stay away from the show as a result of this succession of misfortunes, but Mr. Douglas had always believed in putting on a show for the Sake of Art, and could never have been accused of Pandering to the Taste of the Public. (A neat touch, this, the queue when the bookings opened being a mile and a quarter long, six deep, and causing traffic blocks at three different corners.)

The electric-light signs which had previously

yelled at London that *Blue Music* was a Douglas B. Douglas production now screamed forth the news that *Blue Music* was a musical comedy with murders. The posters outside the Royalty Theatre had a neat edging of black around their gaudy colouring and gay printing – ostensibly out of respect for the late Baker-Astle combination, but really as an added publicity-magnet. The net result of which being that the gallery queue formed five days before the second first night (instead of only three days before, as had been the case at the first first night), the libraries put over deals in seats that constituted a record for any musical comedy ever produced in Great Britain, and before the curtain went up on the night of Friday the thirteenth the house had been sold out for the first seven weeks of the run.

On the back of the tickets, which disappeared considerably quicker than hot cakes, there was printed the inscription, 'This ticket is sold on the express understanding that no monies will be refunded in the event of the performance being stopped by any untoward circumstance, as in the case of the previous performance of *Blue Music*.' Which, of course, only made the seats go quicker than ever.

At six o'clock on the Night, Mr. Wilson, senr., was wrestling with a white bow-tie in front of his dressing-table mirror.

'Yes,' said Mr. Wilson senior, 'it was a bit awkward, I admit. I certainly hadn't expected to hear our murderer on the 'phone at that moment.'

'Yet, when you come to think of it,' said Wilson *fils*, in the throes of a white waistcoat, 'it was the

189

natural thing to do for a man in his position.'

'What was?' asked Mr. Wilson, sent.

'Bluff it out. I mean, a man who's as well-known as Ivor Watcyns couldn't have expected to make a getaway without some questions being asked. If he'd been a nobody, like you or I, he'd have stood a fair chance of being able to clear out of the country without anyone caring a damn. But a man like Ivor Watcyns – well, D.B.D. would start asking where he'd got to, and then the papers would start shouting or him, and people would generally start to wonder why?'

'That's so,' said Mr. Wilson, senr. 'Damn this tie!'

'Here – I'll fix it. You'll have it into mince in a minute. No, the best thing he could do was to carry on as though nothing had happened. In a way, I admire the man. It must take a bit of doing – sitting about looking unconcerned when everyone's talking about the Astle-Baker murders.'

'If a man's got the nerve to plan a murder like Brandon Baker's, he's got nerve for anything... Steady with my Pomans Adami, if you don't mind.'

'Your what?'

'Adam's apple. You're very nearly suffocating me.'

'Sorry. You're quite definite that Ivor Watcyns did that Brandon Baker business as well?'

'Positive. It's funny how a man who plans a murder as carefully as he did should forget one thing. And yet they always do. In this case it was the direction of the bullet. That settled the fact that the murderer had stood in the wings. There's a door not more than four feet away from where he stood, connecting into the auditorium via the boxes. If we'd detained all the people in the boxes that night, we might have saved ourselves a lot of trouble. Watcyns was in B, the left-hand stage-box. It would take him less than a minute to nip out, do his stuff at the exact moment when Foster had his revolver levelled at Brandon Baker down on the stage, and nip back through the door and into his box in the confusion that took place.'

'A hell of a risk, though.'

'A risk, certainly. Anybody who commits murder has to take a certain amount of risk. But not a hell of a risk, Derek. I don't know if you noticed that the curtain – the big stage-curtain I mean – goes quite a long way along inside the proscenium frame – almost as far as the door which connects up to the corridors leading to the boxes. Our friend could quite easily open the door, step quickly in behind the curtains – that is, between the curtains and the proscenium wall – and do what he wanted to do. Where's Martha put my waistcoat?'

'Over there. Still, he'd have to be damned quick on his pins not to be seen by someone. The wings are usually about as crowded as the Black Hole of Calcutta on Cup Final night.'

'As a matter of fact, at this particular time they weren't. You remember the big number at the beginning of the act had just finished? The whole company was off the stage altogether, changing their undies in the dressing-rooms. And I asked Herbert about the stage-hands and electricians and people – it seems they were all away at the back of the stage getting ready for the next big set.'

'But isn't there a control-switch or something down in that corner? Or the laddie at the spot-lights – wouldn't he see anyone standing down there beside the curtain?'

'No – I don't think so. The revolving stage-controls are in that corner – but no one would be near them at the time. The lighting controls are at the other side of the stage. The man operating the spotlight above where Ivor Watcyns stood couldn't see him, of course. The fellow who might have seen him was the man at the other spot – on the opposite wings. I got hold of him and asked him if he noticed anything, but he didn't. He'd be too busy fixing his beam on poor Brandon's pro-file, I suppose – and, in any case, our murderer could conceal himself pretty well in the folds of the curtain.'

'He must have – seeing the shot was fired through the curtain and not clear of it.'

'True, O King,' said Mr. Wilson, senr., inside his tails at last and surveying the finished article in the mirror of his wardrobe. 'How do I look?'

'A thing of beauty and a joy for ever,' said Derek, 'apart from the dab of cotton-wool where you misshaved.'

'Right,' said Mr. Wilson. 'On with the motley. Ring up the curtain. To-night we dare to beard the lion in his den, then Douglas in his hall.'

'I beg your pardon?'

'Sir Walter Scott,' explained Mr. Wilson. 'Mar-mion, to be more exact – somewhere about the middle of the sixth canto.'

'What's D. B. D. done to get bearded in his den?' asked Derek.

'Not our Mr. Douglas, nitwit. An earlier member of the clan. I just gave you the whole quotation to show I didn't only know the bit everyone knows. Substitute Watcyns for Douglas and stage-box for hall, or den, or whatever it was – and there you have the rough lay-out of the evening's performance.'

'Thanks. It's all just about as clear as the Manchester Ship Canal. D'you mind telling me exactly what you're going to do to-night?'

'I'm going to be very theatrical,' said Mr. Wilson, senr., putting a stray hair back into its fit and proper place. 'Since we've sunk so low as to get mixed up with the show business, let's carry the thing out in the proper tradition. When in Rome, do as Mussolini tells you. Ivor Watcyns will be at the show to-night – I've arranged with old man Douglas that he'll occupy the same box as he did on the night Brandon Baker was murdered.'

'So what?'

'So this. You, I'm afraid, won't see very much of the actual performance. Because you're going to sit tight in Box D – the one next door to Watcyns'. There was a loose panel in the wall separating the two boxes – we've made it a little looser specially for your convenience. I want you to keep an eagle eye on your neighbour. If he does anything peculiar – get in touch with me. If he tries to slip out silently in the middle of the show – stop him and ask him to show you to the lavatory.'

'Sounds a very delightful way of putting in an evening.'

193

'You needn't grumble. It's the only time you'll ever get a seat in a stage-box. And it's the only time you'll have the pleasure of being less than three feet away from a murderer – unless I get tired of you some day.'

'Well – and then what?' asked Derek.

'After the interval at the end of Act One, I'm having the lights extinguished in the corridor outside the boxes. In the applause – if any – after that dreadful song at the start of Act Two, I'm going to open the door of Ivor Watcyns' box and insinuate myself into his company with a light and airy tread–'

'Joke over,' said Derek. 'And then?'

'Then I'm going to charge him – quietly, politely, and with all the charm and tact I can muster for the occasion – with the murder of Brandon Baker and Gwen Astle. And as I'm going to do it the exact moment when the shot is fired on the stage and this new actor bloke falls with a dull thud up against the footlights, just as poor Brandon did that other night, I think it's bound to have some little effect on Mr. Watcyns. In fact, if it doesn't bring the said Mr. Watcyns down on his knees on the floor of the box with a full and free confession pouring forth from his lips, then I'm a Nazi.'

'It's too dramatic,' said Derek. 'It's the kind of thing that happens in the cinema.'

'In this case, it's happening in the theatre. What's the difference? And what's the time?'

'Ten to seven.'

'Right. Come on and eat. I want to be at the theatre before eight to fix up one or two little details.'

194

And the Wilsons gave a last tug at their white bow-ties, without in the least disarranging them, and hailed a taxi and a head waiter in that order, and sat down to some extremely sad caviar at a corner table in a West End restaurant. And all over London the same kind of thing was being done by the fortunate thousand or so ladies and gentlemen who managed to obtain seats for the first first night of Mr. Douglas's new musical comedy, and who consequently had had those seats transferred for the second performance. In the one sex, tugging of ties, brushing of hair, filling of cigarettes-cases, clean handkerchiefs pushed up sleeves and down breast-pockets. And donning of wraps, patting of hair, powdering of noses, and much smaller clean handkerchiefs pushed – well, concealed somewhere in the case of the opposite sex.

And are you sure you have those tickets, John? – from the one sex. And no, damn you, I saw you put them on the mantelpiece last Wednesday – from the other. And a whirring of taxis and private cars from various homes to various restaurants, and instructions to taxi-drivers and chauffeurs to be at the theatre at say eleven-forty-five, and tables at all sorts of places, from the Dorchester to a Corner House, rapidly filled up with parties of lucky people going on to *Blue Music*. And, 'No, you haven't time for tournedos, John – it starts at eight-thirty, and the Douglas shows are always prompt in starting.' And grumbles, and coffee, and liqueurs, and paying of bills, and tips, and a few more taxis, and at last into the squash at the stalls entrance of the Grosvenor Theatre.

And very few of the squash ever thought that this was going to be anything other than just another first night. One or two, it is true, said, 'I wonder if anything awful will happen to-night – like the last time, I mean,' and were told gruffly by their husbands not to be such damned fools, and did they expect a murder every time they went to a show? The theatre filled up...

Herbert, shirt-sleeved behind the scenes, didn't like it a bit. There was something in the wind, and he couldn't quite make out what. The way D.B.D. was fluffing around, for one thing; because usually D.B.D. was a model of serenity on a first night. When everyone else was suffering from hysteria and abnormal blood-pressure, D.B.D. was the kind of man who sailed in immaculate in full evening regalia and red-carnation buttonhole, and said, 'Everything all right? That's fine. No need to worry, now. Just go on and do your damnedest. Herbert, see that your front batten in Act Two, Scene Four is kept up all the time – it wasn't quite right at the dress rehearsal. And, girls, remember to stay absolutely still in the duel scene. That's fine. Now don't worry. Cheerio.' And disappeared, leaving behind him a chaos and confusion to come right somehow of its own accord and with the help of Herbert. Tonight D.B.D. had been hopping on and off the stage like a tomcat on the tiles. With that Scotland Yard bloke, and his son, too – the pair that had been called in over the Brandon Baker business. No – there was something up, and Herbert didn't like it.

In his dressing-room, M. Paul Miltonne, direct from the Folies Bergère (late Peter Milton direct from a repertory company touring the Number Three towns in Scotland), didn't like it either. To be plucked like that from the second back row of the chorus into the star part ... and all that publicity, too. M. Miltonne was unique in knowing that as an actor, as a singer, and as a dancer he was something fairly near a wash-out. Oh, hell, what's it matter, thought M. Miltonne, having another gin-and-ginger to help him. Wasn't Brandon Baker a wash-out too? Yes, but he had a profile, hadn't he? Well, hadn't he a profile every bit as good as the Baker profile? M. Miltonne surveyed his profile worriedly in his dressing-room mirror, and emptied the gin-and-ginger at a gulp. And this murder business. Dead man's shoes, that's what it was. Once that scene at the beginning of the second act was over, he would be okay. It was the way everyone had said, when they were playing up in Glasgow, 'Yes, this is the scene where he was shot dead' – it was that that gave M. Miltonne the jimjams. Once he got that bit over... But Act Two, Scene One was a hell of a way off. He might get the bird long before then. Anyway, it was the first time he had ever had a dressing-room to himself. M. Miltonne had another gin-and-ginger.

Deeper in the bowels of the theatre, in Number eighteen dressing-room to be exact, Miss Eve Turner was another member of the company who was feeling none too good. Miss Turner, it seemed, just couldn't go on, 'But you've got to go on,' said various others of the cast in the true *Singing Fool* manner. 'You've simply got to, dear.' 'It's all very well saying you've got to,' Miss Turner kept saying in a high-pitched wail. 'You didn't go through what I went through. I was right up next to him when it happened. He fell down, and the look on his face and the blood... It was all right up in Glasgow, but here in the theatre, where it actually *happened*...' Miss Turner, too, had another gin-and-ginger.

And on the other side of the curtain voices buzzed, programmes rustled, chocolates were unpacked from their cellulose coverings, feet were trampled on as part of the audience made their way through the other part to get to their seats. High in the gods, the members of the Brandon Baker Gallery Club (now under process of re-organization under the title of the Brandon Baker Circle of Remembrance) conversed with one another over several rows of seats, and came unanimously to the conclusion that, however good this bloke Miltonne might be, it could Never Be the Same without Brandon.

Well-known resting actresses registered delighted surprise or infuriated venom according to whether the gods recognized them as they came into the stalls. The Cabinet was back *en bloc*, not being the sort of men who would waste their tickets, and being more or less free from the cares of the nations – Second Reading of the Government's Unemployment Bill, it was, and that would get through all right without them. Mr. Ivor Watcyns, author and composer of the show, arrived alone as usual and smiled sadly to the reception accorded him. His programme, opera glasses, and large box of chocolates were arranged neatly on the front of his box, and then the great man disappeared from the public view behind the curtains at the side of the box. Opposite, Mr. Douglas B. Douglas and party arrived with a flourish, and exhibited a surprised amount of gold teeth when acknowledging the applause on their entry... Mr. Douglas, Mrs. Douglas, an American film magnate, and a tall, distinguished-looking man whom no one knew but whom everyone put down at once as being the new Belgian Ambassador. (It was, in fact, Mr. Wilson, senr.) The box next to Mr. Watcyns' was unoccupied – the only blot on an otherwise packed house. It was noised throughout the dress circle that a Royal Personage was Coming On from a function at the Guildhall, and no doubt the empty box would be for Him. (Mr. Wilson, junr., sat in the back corner of the empty box and chewed butterscotch vigorously.) Eight thirty-two...

M. René Gasnier's bald pate loomed suddenly over the rail of the orchestra pit. M. Gasnier smiled to his usual round of complete strangers in the stalls, pulled down his cuffs, opened his score, tapped his desk, advised the wind on no account to behave as they had behaved last Saturday night in Glasgow, and launched the orchestra forth on the Overture and Introduction to Act One.

Mr. Amethyst, the *Morning Herald's* dramatic critic, arrived late. The One Hundred and Ten Ladies and Gentlemen of the Chorus had traversed the globe, tap-danced in the Blue Music Café in Budapest, paraded in near-nudity around the Swimming Pool of the Whittaker's Country House in Florida, scoffed cold tea cocktails on the floor of the Palm Beach Lounge in the Grand

Hotel, London, donned flowing robes and executed various versions of the shimmy in A Street in Algiers, and finally appeared in tennis-shorts and white berets and worked themselves into a frenzy in the finale of Act One, before Mr. Amethyst arrived at the theatre.

The pearls of the plot had already changed hands thrice, and M. Miltonne had been wrongly accused of theft as the curtain fell on a rousing bit of uproar by the Entire Company. Mr. Amethyst was having a hard night of it; there was a rival first night at the Aldwych, and Mr. Amethyst's editor had suggested that he might very well cover both shows for the paper. After a slight wrangle about salaries, Mr. Amethyst had agreed. After all, he had seen the first act of *Blue Music* once already, and it was so painfully obvious what was going to happen in the Aldwych play after he left it that he had no qualms whatever in writing complete notices for two shows he had not completely seen. He timed his arrival neatly, getting his nose in front of the surge from the stalls at the end of *Blue Music's* first act, led the field to the bar, and ordered a double whisky from Ruth the barmaid. Mr. Duncan, his prototype on the *Daily Observer,* arrived just in time to pay for it.

'How's it going?' asked Mr. Amethyst. 'Anyone murdered yet?'

'Up to the time of going to press, no,' said Mr. Duncan.

'Pity. I wish that man Foster hadn't committed suicide. His presence was much needed at the Aldwych show this evening. What's the new French fellow like?'

200

'Pretty good,' said Mr. Duncan.

'Not if I can help it,' said Mr. Amethyst, accepting another of the same. 'I've a marvellous epigram about the Necessity for Increased Tariffs on Foreign Imports that I mean to work in on him in my notice.'

'Mildred's marvellous,' said Mr. Duncan, referring to the lady playing the late Miss Astle's part.

'Age cannot wither her,' said Mr. Amethyst. 'Nor custom stale her infinite variety. I remember saying that about her when *The Belle of New York* was put on for the first time, and it's just as true today. I see her grandson's got his blue at Cambridge.'

'There's the bell,' said Mr. Duncan. 'Mustn't miss this scene – it's the bit where they went all Chicago last time, remember. Come on – your Import's probably dead by now...'

The stalls crushed back to their seats. M. Gasnier reappeared and invoked his percussion. He was looking a little pale ... remembering very vividly at this moment the last time he had conducted the orchestra in the particular bit of the score when poor Mr. Baker had fallen in front of his eyes and that unpleasant dark mark had begun oozing towards him over the footlights. The audience, too, were remembering. There was little applause at the end of the Riff Ruffian Rag number, and the encore that was taken if not given merely served to make the atmosphere a little more tense.

'Oh, dear,' said the elderly lady on Mr. Amethyst's right, 'I can't help thinking something dreadful's going to happen again.'

201

'Don't worry, madame,' said Mr. Amethyst. 'I'm afraid there's no hope. Providence doesn't bestow its blessings quite as liberally as that.'

M. Miltonne launched into his number, 'Say Your Heart is in my Hands'.

M. Miltonne was shaky. He got no encore, but a good deal of careful assistance from the brass in the orchestra over his sustained notes. But it was over at last, and out of the corner of his eye M. Miltonne could see the fellow who had taken over the part of the Rebel Leader from the murderous Mr. Foster slowly climb up the ladder in the wings before launching forth on the mountain-tops. He had the revolver stuck in his girdle, and a particularly unpleasant expression on his face. All imagination, of course; it was that beard and his makeup that did it. All the same, M. Miltonne's throat went dry and his stomach gave a peculiar little somersault of its own accord, and he had to be prompted before he could remember his line at the end of the song.

And Miss Turner, nestling in his arms and emitting Arabian sex-appeal as fast as she could, was remembering very clearly the other first night. How she had shrieked she would never be able to shriek to-night, that was quite certain. Even though she'd told M. Miltonne to fall with his back to the audience and give her a wink to show her everything was all right ... no, she'd make a hopeless mess of the shriek, she knew that.

On the canvas crags, Phillipo the Rebel Leader drew his revolver and obliged with his big line of the evening, 'So ... you make love to my woman, eh?' Miss Turner attempted to shield her lover from the range of the Rebel Leader's revolver. M. Miltonne thrust her nobly aside and behind him, wondering all the time about that damned gun in Philippo's hand... The Rebel Leader fired. M. Miltonne sank gracefully to the ground with a slight groan. Miss Turner waited until she saw his wink, and shrieked magnificently for sheer relief and joy. M. Miltonne staggered to his feet, drew his own revolver and gave Philippo exactly what he deserved and in just the place he deserved it. Philippo fell and the curtain followed suit.

M. Gasnier dabbed his forehead thankfully with his handkerchief, and raised his baton for the short piece of music between Scenes One and Two. The house breathed an audible sigh of release from suspense. Mr. Amethyst sat back in his seat and said to the elderly lady next to him, 'There! What did I tell you? You can't expect justice every time, you know.' It was over. And nothing had happened.

Though, as a matter of fact, quite a lot had happened during that first scene of the second act. Quietly, efficiently, and according to plan. At the beginning of the act, the box which the dress circle had decided was to have the pleasure of housing a Royal Personage was filled instead with Mr. Wilson, senr., Mr. Douglas B. Douglas, and two plain-clothes policemen. They were screened from the view of the audience by the curtains of the box, though several of the One Hundred and Ten Ladies and Gentlemen of the Chorus looked up at Box B in the middle of their Riff Ruffian Rag gyrations, and asked one another out of the corner of their mouths what the hell all that

203

bunch were doing up in that box. Mr. Wilson, junr., was putting in much useful work through the leaky panelling between the two boxes.

'He's getting a bit het up,' said the running commentary. 'He's been the last word in self-composure all night up till now, but he's looking a bit wonky now. He's leaning forward – got his head buried in his hands ... I believe your theatrical idea's going to come off, dad.'

Mr. Wilson, senr., did not answer. Instead, he stepped out of Box B into the darkened passage outside. The two plain-clothes men followed him. Mr. Wilson put his finger round the handle of the door of Box C, opened it inch by inch and stepped inside. Mr. Watcyns was directly in front of him and his back to the door, leaning forward in his seat and silhouetted by the glare from the stage. Down on the stage, M. Miltonne's song had finished and the line or two of dialogue before the shot was taking place. Mr. Wilson laid a hand on Mr. Watcyns' shoulder at the precise moment when the shot rang out, and whispered, 'This was when you killed him, wasn't it?'

Mr. Watcyns' head shot round. He stared at Mr. Wilson – a panic-stricken, horrible stare. On the stage, the second shot rang out and the curtain fell in a round of applause.

'What d'you mean?' said Mr. Watcyns slowly.

'I charge you with the murder of Brandon Baker and Gwen Astle,' said Mr. Wilson, still with his hand on Ivor Watcyns' shoulder. 'Will you come outside – as quietly as possible?'

Mr. Watcyns appeared to recover some of his composure. He smiled. Yes, actually smiled.

'Damn him!' thought Mr. Wilson.

'How very extraordinary!' said Mr. Watcyns quietly. 'Yes, of course, I'll come.'

And Mr. Watcyns rose slowly from his seat, gathered his programme, his opera glasses, and his large box of expensive chocolates, took a last look at the goings-on on the stage, and turned towards the door of the box. Still smiling.

'Out this way, please,' said Mr. Wilson.

'This will make a marvellous story for the newspapers, won't it?' said Mr. Watcyns softly. And selected a chocolate from his box and put it to his mouth with what seemed to Mr. Wilson an unnecessarily quick movement.

Mr. Wilson had the chocolate knocked out of his hand in a flash. Not quite quick enough, though. It was only half a chocolate – and a squashed and squelchy half at that – which landed on the carpet of the box as the result of Mr. Wilson's action. Mr. Watcyns munched the other half, smiling. Then he flopped quietly on to the floor of the box.

'Come in here,' said Mr. Wilson to the two men outside the door. 'Take him along to the station right away. I think he's poisoned himself. Go on – get a move on. I'll follow you there in a minute.'

Mr. Watcyns' limp body was carted away. Mr. Wilson picked up the large and expensive box of chocolates which he had left behind. Made by a well-known firm. Soft centres. All wrapped in silver paper except one row – the row from which Mr. Watcyns had just made a selection. He picked up the specimen from the floor which Mr. Watcyns had half eaten. Smelt it. A tinge of almonds … cyanide, of potassium maybe. Soon find that out, though.

On the stage, the low comedian made a joke about Yorkshire-pudding in front of a drop curtain showing the Grand Canal at Venice.

CHAPTER TWELVE

Not the least of the attractions of a Douglas B. Douglas first night was the party which took place on the stage after the final curtain had fallen. Grand shows, those parties, and Mr. Amethyst (who was always invited, in case he went over the mark in his paper next day) often thought it would be a good thing if Mr. Douglas would hold the party in public and keep the actual production *in camera*. Speeches were made, most of them inaudible. Everyone kissed everyone. Champagne flowed like water, and occasionally bore a marked similarity in taste to this latter fluid. Leading ladies gave their bouquets to members of the chorus with a display of generosity and sisterly love which proved definitely, if such proof were needed, that they were hopelessly, magnificently tight.

Excerpts from the show were given in slightly thick voices, and were received by the other members of the company as rapturously as though they were being heard for the first time, and had not been drummed into their ears for the past five weeks at rehearsals.

The gentleman from Yorkshire who had

financed the production left at 1 a.m. with one of the ballet dancers, and his name appeared some months later in an undefended suit in the Divorce Courts. At midnight, the debris, human and otherwise, was swept into a corner of the stage and M. Gasnier and his merry men staggered back to the orchestra pit and played dance music until four. At seven, the cleaners came in and expressed their opinions of Suchlike Goings-on in a few well-chosen phrases. The result of which being that the company gave an unbelievably bad performance at the matinée the following afternoon, and the poor provincials who had paid three-and-six for an upper circle seat went home and wondered why in heaven's name the papers had made all that fuss about the show.

Consequently it came as a bit of a bombshell when the last curtain-call had been taken and the final speech had been made and Mr. Douglas B. Douglas turned to his company and said, rather shortly, 'Thank you all very much. You have been splendid. Herbert has an announcement to make on my behalf. Good night,' and exited smartly between two flats of the Blue Music Café ballroom scenery. And another bombshell when Herbert, still in shirt-sleeves, announced that Mr. Douglas regretted that there would not be the usual first-night party to-night, but hoped to have a celebration of some sort on the occasion of the show's fiftieth performance. And started to dismantle the Café Ballroom as though tonight were the three hundred and fifteenth performance of *Blue Music* instead of the first.

'No party?' wailed the One Hundred and Ten

207

Ladies and Gentlemen of the Chorus. 'But why?' shrieked the Twenty-four Ballet Whos. To which Herbert, who knew nothing himself and was wondering what the hell was the matter with the boss, was a tower of mystery and contented himself – but not the others – by saying 'Aha!' several times, and suggesting that no doubt they would learn All About It Later On.

And so, instead of that customary first-night whoopee, there took place a series of smaller and slightly less noisy gatherings at a number of restaurants, hotels, boarding houses, night clubs and private homes. And the wildest rumours circulated over and around repeat orders of whisky, gin-and-gingers, port, Benedictine, Worthington, and – in one case – Ovaltine. The backer had gone smash and D.B.D. was in the soup, even if the show was a success. The new French bloke was walking out at the end of the week. That Scotland Yard man with the attractive smile had arrested D.B.D. on a charge of complicity in the murder of Brandon Baker. And so forth.

The most important of these gatherings took place in M. Miltonne's dressing-room in the theatre itself. Present, M. Miltonne (now feeling very well, and greatly anxious to sing three French songs which had been banned from his last Folies review); Mr. Douglas B. Douglas with half a dozen bottles of champagne; Mr. Amethyst of the *Morning Herald* as a privileged guest – privileged in the sense that he would have nosed in anyway, and it was much better for him to have the whole truth given him than have him get hold of it in a roundabout way; Mr. Wilson, senr., and

Mr. Wilson, junr.

'Now then,' said Mr. Douglas, pouring out champagne until the company had been made comfortable. 'Get going, Wilson. Oh, I should explain to you two that Inspector Wilson has been looking into the affairs of my show ever since the death of Brandon Baker. Aided and abetted by his son here. A bigger pair of blethers I've never met in all my life. Though I must confess they've done rather more than blether in this case.'

'For those kind words,' said Derek, 'much thanks. Damned good champagne, anyway.'

'But the Brandon Baker business—' said M. Miltonne. 'Surely there was no mystery about that? I mean – didn't the fellow who killed him commit suicide after he'd done it?'

'That's just it,' said Mr. Douglas. 'Come on, Wilson, put in a new needle and start off the record.'

'Well,' said Mr. Wilson, settling himself comfortably on the dressing-room settee and swaying the glass of champagne in his hand in a contented manner, 'well ... this is all rather like the last chapter of a mystery novel, isn't it? You know ... chaps. one to twenty-seven – utter and complete bafflement (if there's such a word), and then chap. twenty-eight ... along comes the brilliant detective and reveals in a few well-chosen sentences that the person who did the dirty deed was none other than the deceased man's Great-aunt Pauline, and that the whole thing was perfectly obvious from the time the string of pearls was found secreted in the wing of the butler's parrot at Margate.'

'Cut the cackle,' said Derek, 'and get on with it.'

'Right,' said Mr. Wilson. 'We'll start by squashing the obvious solution – the one you just referred to, M. Miltonne. Brandon Baker was not killed by the man Foster. He was killed by Ivor Watcyns. And I'll tell you how right away. Watcyns was sitting in Box C on the first night. Just before Riff Ruffian whatever-it's-called number finished, he got out of the box, slipped down the stairs which lead from the corridors outside the boxes, opened that little door which leads backstage, and hid in the folds of the curtain in the wings.'

'Objection number one,' said Mr. Douglas. 'How the blazes did he get out of the box without being noticed? I've sat in those boxes a score of times, and whenever anyone opens the door in one of the boxes opposite there's a glare of light comes and hits you bang in the eye. He'd be bound to be noticed by the people in the boxes opposite. I'd have noticed him myself, I'm perfectly certain.'

'You wouldn't,' said Mr. Wilson, 'because he got one of your attendants to switch off the lights in the corridor outside the boxes as soon as each act began. Said he was leaving the door open, because the ventilation of the theatre dated from the time of the early Holy Roman Empire. So that he'd be perfectly able to clear out of his box when he wished without the people opposite noticing anything. Objection overruled.'

'Objection number two, then,' said Mr. Amethyst. 'How d'you mean – he hid himself behind the curtain once he got through to the stage?

210

He'd be bound to be noticed coming through the door and going to the curtain, wouldn't he?'

'No,' said Mr. Wilson, 'I don't think he would. If you go and have a look at the curtains, you'll find that when they're drawn back they nearly overlap inside the proscenium a good bit. In fact, they very nearly come right to the door. And you've got to remember that the wings would be pretty well empty at the moment he arrived. All the chorus had just cleared off the stage and were in their dressing-rooms, changing for the next scene. Herbert and the rest of the scene-shifting gang were away backstage getting ready the next set. He might have been noticed, of course ... but he wasn't. Objection again overruled.'

'Isn't he marvellous?' said Derek. 'Another five minutes and he'll be sucking a briar and telling us that the whole thing was elementary, my dear Amethyst – elementary.'

'Shut up' said Mr. Wilson pleasantly. 'Right – where was I? Oh yes ... I'd got friend Watcyns in behind the curtains, hadn't I? On the stage, Baker and Miss What's-her-name were doing their love stuff. Another couple of minutes and Foster appears on the mountains, levels his revolver at Baker and fires. At exactly the same moment Watcyns fired from behind the curtains ... *through* the curtain, as a matter of fact, and unfortunately from his point of view. Commotion on the stage and in the wings, during which our friend sneaks back through the door, hops upstairs to his box, and then comes out again in a few minutes and asks an attendant what's the matter on the stage. Elem – simple, wasn't it?'

'Crikey!' said M. Miltonne, crossing the Channel in an unguarded moment.

'But why? I mean – how d'you arrive at all this?' demanded Mr. Douglas.

'That's rather more complicated. First of all, there was the question – why did Foster kill Brandon Baker? There wasn't a shadow of a motive anywhere. From what I can gather poor Foster was just about the last man on earth to take hold of a revolver, let alone level it at a fellow human being and pull the trigger.'

'I bear you out there,' said Mr. Douglas. 'I've known Hilary Foster on and off for the last twenty years, and he's definitely no killer. The sort of man who goes home after a show and spends the rest of the night reading Lamb's *Essays* or making fretwork pipe-racks.'

'Exactly,' said Mr. Wilson. 'Well, then, the natural thing to think was that Foster had had the murder planted on him by someone else. As a matter of fact, I believe our friend Watcyns had a sort of secondary plot in case anything went wrong with his first one. Don't you always send a message round at the end of your dress rehearsals if there's anything you want altered, Mr. Douglas?'

'That's right.'

'Yes ... well, the bold Herbert changed Foster's revolver just before the first performance started. Acting on instructions from you.'

'But–'

'Exactly – you never gave such instructions. I shouldn't be surprised if Watcyns intercepted one of your notes on its way round backstage and

212

added the bit about changing the gun. It might have made things look very black for poor Herb, especially as he destroys all these notes you send to him. He would swear that you told him to swap revolvers, and you and your secretary who writes the notes would swear that you said nothing of the sort. A very useful little bit of business to fall back on.'

'He doesn't seem to have overlooked anything, does he?' said Mr. Amethyst.

'One thing only. The hole in the curtain. My dear Watson here came across that in one of his rare moments of consciousness. It wasn't much to go on, but it was something. It told us that someone at some time or another had fired a bullet through the curtain either on to the stage or from the stage out into the auditorium. And that set us off looking for bullets.'

'And did we look for bullets!' put in Derek. 'Old man Wilson had his only son hopping all over the blessed stage firing imaginary bullets at imaginary leading men.'

'You see – if Brandon Baker had actually been shot dead by Foster, the bullet would have ended up at the very bottom of the proscenium wall. Either that, or it would have missed the proscenium altogether and finished inside the bassoon in the orchestra. Or even inside one of the front-row stall occupants. But it didn't. We found the bullet buried in the proscenium wall – about four and a half feet up. Exactly the position it would have adopted if it had been fired by someone standing in the wings opposite.'

'You're certain it was the type of bullet that

213

would be used in Watcyns' revolver?' asked M. Miltonne.

'Not knowing what type of revolver he used on the night, I'm not at all certain. It *is* the type of bullet that would be used in the revolver we found when we searched Ivor Watcyns's flat earlier this evening. But the actual revolver used by Foster seems to have completely disappeared.'

'And I'll tell you when it did disappear,' said Derek. 'That time we were in here reconstructing the crime – the morning after the night before, remember? When someone did a quick exit from the theatre. I'm willing to swear that was friend Watcyns, back to collect evidence that might be incriminating – in the shape of the revolver Foster used in the show.'

'Maybe. I don't see how it could be very incriminating, though. After all, I should think Watcyns took pretty good care to equip himself with a gun the same type as the one he'd planted on to Foster. But it's possible ... perfectly possible.'

'More champagne?' asked Mr. Douglas. 'And then what happened?'

'Thank you,' said Mr. Wilson, handing up his glass. 'Well, it's supposed to be bad policy for a detective ever to assume anything. Sometimes it's rather helpful, though, and in this case Derek and I assumed that we were on the right track with the synchronized-murder-from-behind-the-curtain idea. The next thing was to find out someone who, unlike Mr. Foster, *had* a motive for putting Brandon Baker out of the way. And Mr. Baker himself was a great help in putting us on the right track. Speak no ill of the dead, I know but Mr.

Baker hadn't exactly been leading a very ... er ... virtuous life for some years. Cutting out the details, we found that he was living with Gwen Astle at the time of his death. Cutting out some more details, we found that Gwen Astle and Ivor Watcyns had been exceedingly friendly – if that's the word – for about a year previous to this.'

'We found that out later,' said Derek. 'You're off the rails chronologically.'

'So we did – sorry. But in any case it proved the old, old story of the eternal triangle. And whenever you get an eternal triangle you get a possible motive for a possible murder. That's in Euclid somewhere, but I forget what proposition.'

'Women!' said Mr. Douglas vehemently, and poured out a further supply of champagne as though to drown the entire sex. 'Women! Why they don't shoot the entire sex right away without bothering about shooting the other men in the case, I don't know. Save a hell of a lot of trouble.'

'I got a summons from Miss Astle a day or two after the murder. Would I come round and see her right away, as she had something very important to tell me about Brandon Baker's death? I went – right away, but not right away enough, apparently. Miss Astle had disappeared, and from the look of her flat she'd been removed with a certain amount of force. And the only clue to her whereabouts was the word 'Craile' written on a chunk of wallpaper in one of her rooms.'

'Craile?' said Mr. Amethyst. 'What is it – a beef extract?

'No. It's a village in Buckinghamshire. It didn't take me very long to find that out.'

'Liar,' said Derek.

'Perfectly right,' admitted Mr. Wilson. 'You see, Gwen Astle had started to get suspicious about the Brandon Baker business. I don't think she suspected Watcyns of killing him on his own, but I do think she suspected him of planting the murder on to Foster. She threatened to throw up her part in the show; Watcyns had to keep her in it and keep her mouth shut.'

'Now that you mention it,' said Mr. Douglas, 'Watcyns was round in my office in a hell of a state because Gwen Astle was thinking of walking out of the show.'

'And from there he went to her flat. Upset the flat considerably, too. You don't think he would go to all that exertion simply for the sake of keeping his leading lady, do you?'

'He might,' said D.B.D. 'He was sweet on her, you know. But it's unlikely.'

'Very unlikely,' said Mr. Wilson. 'No, he had other business to transact than just that. And so he packed her off to a one-eyed hotel in a one-horse village in an attempt to bring her round to his way of thinking. From which point in the narrative, the heir to the Wilson millions had better take over the microphone. Because I sent him down to Craile on his own to look into things down there.'

'Disguised as a hiker,' said Derek. 'And on a push-bike. The things I do for England!... Well, I soon found Watcyns and the fair Gwendoline. They were living in the one and only pub in the place – as Mr. and Mrs. Wright. Funny name to choose, but there it is. And the rum part about it

was that the proprietress of the pub was a wife –
genuine, not synthetic – of Brandon Baker.'

'Good God!' said Mr. Douglas. 'Which one?
He had a couple that I knew of.'

'I know. Dad met one at the funeral, and I
bumped into Number Two at the inquest, funnily
enough. I don't know which this one was – short,
thin woman, rather tired look about her, nice fair
hair.'

'I've got you. He met her at a concert party.
Gwen Astle upset that little romance as well ...
little bisom!'

'I know. It was a pretty awkward situation down
there. If ever this proprietress female got to know
that the woman staying in her pub was the same
woman who'd wrecked her life and been responsible for the death of her husband, there'd have
been hell to pay. She wouldn't have stopped at...
I say!...'

'What's up?' asked Mr. Wilson.

'I suppose it isn't possible that she *did* get to
know? And–'

'Don't ramble. We know who killed Gwen
Astle. Get on with the broadcast.'

'Okay. Well, nothing much happened until the
night after I arrived. Gwen had had a shot at
getting back to the town during the day, but Ivor
Watcyns put amen to that. At night, he announced that his wife – Mrs. Wright – was leaving
for town by the last train, and he was driving her
to the station. He made such a fuss about it in the
bar that I might have known there was something
hooey about the business.'

'When my son says "hooey" he means peculiar,'

said Mr. Wilson.

'Quite. Well, Watcyns drove Gwen away in the car. Not to the station, though – we found that out from the booking-office when we'd brought them to life – he took her into the woods about a mile or so from the village, bumped her off, and left her in a ditch.'

'Mon Dieu!' said M. Miltonne, remembering his nationality.

'That was Gwen silenced for good and all. Then he came back to the hotel and went to bed. Another goodly fuss he made about it, too – coming into the bar for a drink, telling all the maids he wanted waking in the morning, and planking his boots outside his door with a clatter that would have roused the dead. All this, of course, as part of an alibi. I believe he paid you a visit late that night, Mr. Douglas?'

'He did,' said D.B.D. 'He came to me at the Rialto. I have a cabaret running there just now. I'd asked him to come back to town at the earliest opportunity to discuss some changes in the show that were necessary because M. Miltonne couldn't – because M. Miltonne here has a different style of acting to Brandon Baker.'

'But it wasn't essential that he should pay you a visit on that particular night?'

'No, of course not. I was damned surprised to see him as a matter of fact. Said he'd just got a new idea for the opening of Act Three, and come round from his flat to see me about it.'

'Exactly. You see, he established an alibi that worked two ways. He left his car ready and waiting for him at Craile. Went to bed. Slinked out of the hotel when the place was quiet. Hopped into the car and came off to London. Saw you at the Rialto. And got back to the pub in the early hours of the morning. Result – Mr. Wright who was living at the pub down in Craile couldn't be mixed up with the crime, since he'd been safe and sound in bed all night. And Mr. Watcyns most certainly couldn't be mixed up in it, since he'd been in London that night and talking to you, Mr. Douglas.'

'But they were bound to identify the body sooner or later,' said Mr. Amethyst.

'As Gwen Astle, yes. But as Mrs. Wright, who had left Craile earlier in the evening? No fear. Besides, I don't suppose half a dozen people had seen Gwen Astle since she arrived at Craile. She was kept under lock and key all the time. Right ... any more questions? ... no ... carry on, Dad.'

'There's not much more really,' said Mr. Wilson. 'No thanks, Douglas, not another drop. I could have arrested the man straight away. As a matter of fact, he left Craile early the next morning. Naturally I thought he'd clear out for good and all – I was a bit surprised to find him working at the theatre with you, Douglas, as though nothing had happened. He meant to bluff the thing out, evidently. And there's only one way to catch a bluffer – get him at the psychological moment. The psychological moment seemed to me to be the exact time the first murder was reenacted on the stage at tonight's performance. With Mr. Douglas's help, we got him installed in the box he'd occupied on the night of Brandon Baker's death. He wasn't keen on turning up at the show tonight, but I suppose he was afraid it would look suspicious if he backed out. So here he came, and I laid a strong right arm on his shoulder just when you, M. Miltonne, were being shot at by the new Rebel Leader from the mountain heights. He got the biggest shock I've ever seen any man get. But he recovered pretty quickly – quick enough to have a shot at taking poison, anyway.'

'Poison?' said Mr. Amethyst, who was wondering by this time how all this was possibly going to be included in a single issue of his paper.

'I don't know what kind for sure yet. Cyanide of potassium, I think. He had a hefty box of chocolates with him ... just in case. He got a bite of an innocent-looking specimen before I could stop him – and then flopped. I've got him along at the doctor's now – I'll get a report in the morning. It's all right. He won't die ... yet.'

'Well, gentlemen,' said Mr. Douglas, 'there we have it. Just about the neatest bit of work I've ever come across. You could tell that man had brain from the stuff he wrote – yes, I know, *Blue Music* was an exception, but I told him I wanted a box-office hit, and he gave me one – but I never reckoned on him having the brains to carry a thing like this through.'

'It's so – so watertight,' said Mr. Amethyst admiringly. 'I mean the idea of synchronizing that shot with the shot fired by the fellow on the stage. It was a thousand to one against him being found – especially after Foster committed suicide.'

'Yes,' said Mr. Wilson. 'As I say, there was one snag only – the direction of the bullet. Funny that a man who must have thought the whole thing out so carefully should forget a simple thing like that.'

'Well – if that's the only snag you can see, I'll make you a present of another, said Derek. 'It's been worrying me ever since the inquest. The expert chappie who did the post-mortem examination – what was his name? Bone or something – didn't he give evidence that the bullet had entered Brandon Baker's body in such a way that, from the position in which he was found lying, the bullet could *only have been fired at the back of the stage?*'

'God!' said Mr. Amethyst. 'So he did. I remember reading that in the report. The coroner asked him if there was any chance of the shot being fired from any other position, and he said no – only from the part of the stage where Hilary Foster stood.'

'Which squashes the whole ruddy argument,' said M. Miltonne, again lapsing from the Latin tongue.

'Not a bit of it,' said Mr. Wilson. 'You two don't know your own theatre. What's at the side of the stage, just at the point where Watcyns stood to fire his shot?'

'The switchboard up above. And the revolving-stage controls below.'

'Exactly. The revolving-stage controls. If you shoot a man, and wish it to appear that he had been shot by another man standing at an angle of forty-five degrees from you, wouldn't you have a shot at moving the position of the body to suit the circumstances? That's what Ivor Watcyns did. And since he couldn't go on to the stage and rearrange

221

the body just as it suited him, he pulled the revolving-stage controls and brought the whole affair round just the few necessary inches. There were only two people on the revolving part of the stage at the time – one of them dead. The other one – Miss Turner – says she *thought* she felt the stage move round after the shot had been fired, but she wasn't feeling so good at the time, and put it down to her own dizziness. The other man who was in a position to see was Gasnier, the conductor of the orchestra. He says he *thought* he saw the stage move round slightly, but put it down to his imagination. He wasn't feeling up to the mark either. Sounds fantastic, I know – but remember that stage moves round as smoothly as water running over a billiard-ball. Sometimes you hardly know it's on the go. I've been on it and tried. We've no proof that that happened, of course, but I'm willing to stake my worldly possessions that it did.'

'Have a drink,' said Mr. Douglas. 'You deserve it.'

Mr. Wilson, junr., retrieved his hat from amongst M. Miltonne's make-up.

'If the party's over, I think my paper might be interested in some of to-night's revelations,' he said. 'And remember, Inspector Wilson, you promised me on your oath that this was exclusive to the *Gazette*. Mr. Amethyst heard all this as a strictly ordinary human being – not as a newspaper man. Okay?'

'Okay,' said Mr. Wilson, showing that something attempted, something done, can make a man forget himself in the matter of choosing his words. 'Don't wake me up when you come home.'

Mr. Douglas B. Douglas poured the last of the last bottle of champagne into his glass and scoffed it with a single and exceedingly noisy gulp.

'Oh, boy!' said Mr. Douglas happily. 'The publicity of it I couldn't have thought of anything better myself!...'

CHAPTER THIRTEEN

There were four letters in the Wilson post at the last delivery on the following evening. The strange thing about them was that after reading each of the four Mr. Wilson, senr., said, 'My God!'

Letter to Mr. Wilson, senr., from the proprietress of the Craile Arms Hotel, bearing a London postmark of the same date,

Dear Inspector Wilson,

I see in the papers this morning that you've arrested Ivor Watcyns on a charge of murdering Brandon Baker and Gwen Astle. I don't know anything about the death of Brandon Baker – maybe he did do it, I shouldn't be surprised – but I can tell you something about the other. And that is that Ivor Watcyns didn't kill that woman.

Brandon, as you know, was my husband. He left me for Gwen Astle years ago. I hadn't seen her for ten years, and when she and Ivor Watcyns came to my hotel last week I didn't recognize either of them. I never knew Watcyns, and somehow I never suspected the woman with him of being Gwen Astle. If I had, I don't suppose I'd have let them inside the hotel, and then a lot of trouble might have been saved all round. I've wanted to meet that woman for years. She took my man away from me, and right from the beginning she's been responsible for the kind of life he led. She was rotten – and she made poor Brandon just about as rotten as herself, I'm afraid. At first I used to try to get him back – I don't mean just back to me, but back to a decent kind of life – and every time I thought I'd done it that woman came along and upset it all.

I killed her that night in Craile Woods. I began to suspect who she was when a young journalist started asking questions one day in the hotel. I made a few enquiries and I found out that it was Gwen Astle all right. I couldn't believe at first that she was living under my own roof I think the idea of her living down here and enjoying life in her own rotten way while I was slaving away running a third-rate hotel – I think that sent me sort of mad. I couldn't help thinking that if it hadn't been for her Brandon would still have been alive and still with me – she was mixed up in his death, I'm sure of that – and I killed her. I'm glad I did, too.

Watcyns drove her to the station that night to catch the last train to London. The train was late – he didn't wait. I think they'd had a row. I don't know what made her change her mind, but she didn't board the train when it came in. Maybe she planned to go back and have another night with her man. She came out of the station and started to walk slowly back to the village. She went by the long way – through the edge of Craile Woods. I made up on her just as she was going into the Woods. I told her who I was – we had a row. I shot her. I got an automatic two years ago, when I was

224

scared living down here by myself in the winter. I'm sorry that you can't see it and get some evidence that way, but I'm using it again.

As I say, I'm glad I killed her. If ever anyone deserved to die, it was Gwen Astle. She caused nothing but trouble and unhappiness all her life, and she didn't care a damn for it all. I've told you all this because I don't want Watcyns to suffer for something he didn't do. I shouldn't bother about looking for me – it's not worth it, really. Don't look in Craile Woods, anyway – I'm choosing somewhere a bit less public to finish this business.

Muriel Baker.

'My God!' said Mr. Wilson once again.

'But the car – why the blazes did Watcyns come into town that night?' asked Derek. 'Why all the damned alibi?'

'Don't ask me,' said Mr. Wilson. 'You said it was an alibi that worked two ways. He had to see Douglas about the show, hadn't he? Seems it wasn't an alibi at all...'

'And it's in the papers,' said Derek. 'That's the damnable part of it. It'll mean dropping the second charge against him.'

'It might mean dropping both charges,' said Mr. Wilson seriously.

'What d'you mean?'

'You'd better read that. Another long screed. It's from that Millicent Davis woman – the wench who came and visited us after Brandon Baker's murder ... wife, official or otherwise, of Hilary Foster...'

Letter to Mr. Wilson, senr., from Miss Millicent

Davis, latterly engaged in the part of matron to Abdul Achmallah's Harem in the show *Blue Music:*

Dear Sir,
I've read the reports in the newspapers this morning about the arrest of Ivor Watcyns. I only wish there could be some real grounds for thinking that he did kill Brandon Baker. My life hasn't been exactly rosy since Hilary committed suicide and everyone – except yourself it seems – assumed that he'd killed Baker.

I came and told you after the inquest that I didn't believe Hilary had killed Brandon Baker. That was the truth – then. Since then I've found something that changes the whole thing. I couldn't believe it when I found it, and I didn't see the necessity for making the thing public, seeing that nothing could be done with Hilary dead. But now you've arrested an innocent man for killing Brandon Baker and I've got to tell you what I now know about the whole rotten business.

Hilary left a letter in which he confesses to having killed Brandon Baker. I only found it this week – I've been away since it happened and I've only just started to go through Hilary's things. They'd worked together – Hilary and Brandon – for years, Brandon getting more and more successful and Hilary just the opposite. I never realized how dreadfully jealous Hilary was of Brandon's success – the more so because he'd helped him over and over again at the start of his career, and if it hadn't been for that help I don't suppose Brandon would ever have got where he did. Hilary was terribly worried about money matters at the time – he was ill, he had to have an operation, he was in debt, everything seemed to be going wrong. He tried to get a loan from Brandon as a sort of last resource, and Brandon refused. It was lousy of him, for I know Hilary loaned him money over and over again in the old days without ever getting a penny back. I want you to understand I didn't know anything about this at the time – it's all in the letter he left, that's the first I knew of it. I guess his mind must just have cracked up under the strain of it all. He says in this letter, 'They're giving me a revolver in this part to shoot Brandon with … I think that's overdoing temptation…'

I'd like you to see this letter. If you'll send someone for it, or come personally, I'll hand it over to you. If you can manage to keep my name out of any proceedings that may have to take place, I'd be very grateful. We weren't really married, and I've had all the publicity I want out of this affair.

Yours sincerely,
Millicent Davis.

Mr. Wilson got up slowly and walked across to the window. It was raining. It would be raining.

'But the bullet – all our pet theories about the direction of the bullet?' said Derek.

'You'd better read Herbert's letter while you're busy,' said Mr. Wilson. 'It'll save you asking all the questions you're going to ask. Taken all round, it's quite the lousiest post I've ever opened.'

Letter from Herbert Jenkinson to Inspector Wilson, Esquire, post-marked that morning. Scrawly handwriting, erratic punctuation, and the last half-dozen lines tapering off at an angle of forty-five degrees to the rest of the epistle,

227

Mr. Wilson, Dear Sir,

I see in the papers this morning as how it says you have arested Mr. Watcyns for killing Mr. Baker and I must say it fair took my breath away when I read it. I see as how it says in the paper that you first got suspiceous when you found that bulet hole in the curtain and then the place in the prosenium where the bullet had landed. Now, Sir, here is something what I have to tell you in connection with this, as it is only right and if I had known you were working on that idea about the bulet I would have let you know right away before this. When we were getting the theatre ready for the opening last night, sir, one of the cleeners came across something beried in the outside bit of the stage-box A. Well, Sir, when we got it out it was a bulet, and not knowing that you were working on this theiry (this last word crossed viciously out and 'notion' substituted) not knowing you were working on this notion I thought it must be the bulet what killed Mr. Baker. I kept it, Sir, and have it here in the theatre at your convenience. If it had been fired from where Mr. Foster was standing up on the mountains that night it must have missed the stage altogether and beried itself in the front of the box where we found it.

Now, Sir, with regard to the hole in the curtain what you found and also the bulet in the prosenium four feet up, in the show before 'Blue Music' there was a scene where a shot had to be fired from the wings right across the front of the stage. It had to knock a glass cleen out of the hand of one of the actors and was a tricky thing to do, Sir, but as the man what did the shooting was a crack shot everything went over all right except for one performance. There was a big screen put up in the oposite wings for to stop the bulet each night and this

228

night the bloke what did the shooting was a bit tight and we were all a bit scared. Well, Sir, he hit the glass all right only the bulet wasn't fired straight with him lerching in the wings and it went into the prosenium wall just where it say you found it in the newspapers. Mr. Douglas can tell you this is all right for he was wild about it at the time and had the scene changed after that. I don't know if this has anything to do with what has happened, Sir, but thought it only right for to let you know about same. If you want any more information you can get me any time at the theatre.

Yrs. faithfully, Sir,
Herbert Jenkinson.

'Well, I'm damned!' said Derek.

'The best-laid schemes of mice and men...' said Mr. Wilson, lighting his pipe. 'Moral – never be clever in the police business. The constable with a head of solid mahogany has far more chance of getting his man than your brilliant detective who's throbbing with theories and cluttered up with clues. Depressing, but true.'

'What's the other letter in the bunch?' asked Derek. 'Say it's a bill – even a bill would be welcomed in the present circumstances.'

'It's not a bill,' said Mr. Wilson. 'In some ways, it's the unkindest cut of all. It's a report from Anstruther about those chocolates that Watcyns had with him last night at the theatre. He's spent the whole morning diagnosing the filling of the one Watcyns had a bite of before I interrupted him and he fainted.'

'Fainted?'

'Fainted. Unfortunately, yes. Inconsiderate of

him, I know, leading us on like that – but you really can't blame the fellow. I mean, if someone came up to you and arrested you for the murder of two human beings bang in the middle of an enjoyable musical comedy, it would be a bit of a shock to the system, wouldn't it?'

'What does Anstruther say, then?'

'The sweets in the box were all perfectly normal. Well-known make, very expensive variety. Anstruther spent the whole morning trying to find out what was inside the one Watcyns nibbled. Then he realized that it was ordinary almond filling … extra strong flavour. You can read his note … he's quite sarcastic about it.'

'There's one thing to be thankful for, anyway,' said Derek.

'I fail to see it,' said Mr. Wilson.

'The filling wasn't raspberry. That would have been much more appropriate, but I don't think I could have stood it. What are we doing this evening, by the way?'

'I suggest a cruise round the world,' said Mr. Wilcox gravely. 'Two or three times round, in fact. Unless you've got anything better to suggest?'

'There is a first night at the Adelphi...' said Derek.

Mr. Wilson, senr., threw a cushion.

We do hope that you have enjoyed reading this large print book.

Did you know that all of our titles are available for purchase?

We publish a wide range of high quality large print books including:
Romances, Mysteries, Classics
General Fiction
Non Fiction and Westerns

Special interest titles available in large print are:
The Little Oxford Dictionary
Music Book
Song Book
Hymn Book
Service Book

Also available from us courtesy of Oxford University Press:
Young Readers' Dictionary
(large print edition)
Young Readers' Thesaurus
(large print edition)

For further information or a free brochure, please contact us at:
Ulverscroft Large Print Books Ltd.,
The Green, Bradgate Road, Anstey,
Leicester, LE7 7FU, England.
Tel: (00 44) 0116 236 4325
Fax: (00 44) 0116 234 0205

Other titles published by Ulverscroft:

DEATH OF ANTON

Alan Melville

Seven Bengal tigers are the star attraction of Carey's Circus. Their trainer is the fearless Anton, whose work demands absolute fitness and the steadiest of nerves — especially when dealing with Peter, the oldest, largest, and most dangerous animal. When Anton is found lying dead in the tigers' cage, it seems that Peter has finally won the long struggle for dominance and mauled his master — but Detective-Inspector Minto is not convinced. His investigations lead him deep into the circus world of tents and caravans, clowns and acrobats, performers human and animal, where nobody is above suspicion as the mystery deepens.